That's Where You'll Find Her

Also by this Author

THE WITCHES OF MARSTON DORNIE SERIES

A Far Cry from Summer
An Echo of Autumn
The Light from Winter Dark
The Spring Child's Whisper
Daughters of the Sunrise

That's Where You'll Find Her

Gary Warner

Copyright © 2020 Gary Warner

All rights reserved, including the right to reproduce this book, or portions thereof in any form. No part of this text may be reproduced, transmitted, downloaded, decompiled, reverse engineered, or stored, in any form or introduced into any information storage and retrieval system, in any form or by any means, whether electronic or mechanical without the express written permission of the author.

This is a work of fiction. Names and characters are the product of the author's imagination and any resemblance to actual persons, living or dead, is entirely coincidental.

The views expressed in this work are solely those of the author and do not necessarily reflect the views of the publisher, and the publisher hereby disclaims any responsibility for them.

ISBN: 9798651424788

PublishNation
www.publishnation.co.uk

For Jenny

Thank you Elsbeth

Visit the Author's Website at
www.garywarner.co.uk

Chapter 1

The raindrops on the rose petals sparkled in the early morning sun. Tiny diamonds against the deep red. Mattie had heard the rain on her bedroom window the previous night and had hoped that it might stop before morning. Her wish had been granted. The dawn was slowly giving way to a cloudless, bright blue sky.

She looked at the small bunch of roses that she had laid on the grave just the day before. Mattie decided she would replace them with fresh blooms on her next visit. She knelt and removed a weed that had begun to grow up through the grass near the grey, weather worn headstone with its now unreadable inscription. With loving care, she picked away until order had been restored.

Mattie looked up and saw an elderly man in the distance, on the furthest side of the cemetery. He was standing where he always stood, occasionally lifting his gaze from the headstone to glance briefly in her direction. Although he had seen her several times he had never attempted to talk to her as he walked past on his way to the main gates.

She would have spoken to him, had he wanted her to, because she felt she knew him. She would have asked him about the loved one whose grave he visited, and it wouldn't have been merely polite conversation. She felt a genuine interest to know something of the person that called him, early every morning, to their final resting place. She had speculated that it must be his wife and could have probably confirmed this by going to look at the headstone's inscription after he had left. But Mattie never had and never would. It would have felt to her like an uninvited intrusion, almost a betrayal of some kind of trust. Of course, she knew that thought would be considered by most people to be ridiculous. He wouldn't know she'd looked, would he? What would it matter? And yet, to her, somehow it did. And maybe, after all, it was best she hadn't engaged the old man in conversation because he would, inevitably, have asked her about the person whose grave she visited each day but, being a hopeless liar, she would have had to tell him the truth, and she knew she could never do that.

On returning to her car, she sat behind the wheel for some minutes before starting the engine, taking a few moments to prepare for the normality of the day ahead. She would never try to push away those precious thoughts, but just gently put them in their daytime place where they would remain until she could embrace them again. It was a daily ritual Mattie was now used to and, in a perverse kind of way, welcomed. As she drove out of her parking space and back towards town she took a quick glance out of the side window. She saw the old man turn away and begin to walk back along the path that led to the road on the far side of the cemetery.

Chapter 2

The neon strips flickered into life as Mattie pressed the switch. One of the tubes took several seconds longer than the others to fully light and she made a mental note to sort out a replacement. Not that it mattered. Customers never came into this room. It was her space in the daytime, such as it was. She pulled up the office chair and sat down behind the desk. Reaching down to her right, she removed the laptop from its bag and carefully placed it in front of her before opening the screen and switching it on.

While waiting for it to boot up she looked through the half open door that led to the shop. She could just see the high street from where she sat. The school bus had pulled up at the stop on the opposite side of the road and several children were getting on, Monday morning written all over their faces. Mattie recalled those first days at secondary school when it had been her climbing aboard, always claiming her seat on the lower deck and sitting as near to the driver as she could. She would never have ventured onto the top deck, into that world of shouting. swearing, name calling and bullying.

Before her memories could take her to some dark, scary places she returned her attention to the laptop. Logging into her shop's admin site she was pleased to see that she had had yet another good weekend of online orders and enquiries.

Having left college with a modest qualification in business studies, Mattie had been lucky enough to have a mother who, as well as having the desire to help her daughter achieve her dream, also had the bank balance to make it a reality. Not only did Mattie live rent free in a town apartment owned by her mother, she had also bought her daughter the freehold of a perfectly located property on the town's high street and given her enough to buy a good stock to fill her window and the safe, which was situated in a corner of the room where she now sat.

And so, three years ago 'Sparkle!' had appeared in the town centre, with its bright, attractive twenty-two-year-old owner whose enthusiasm had lit up and, some even said, reinvigorated a rather tired row of nondescript shops. Others around her had felt they needed to raise their game, the local newspaper had been eager to interview the bright young thing called Mattie Hayes, and all the buzz and publicity surrounding her new business had been enough to give it the kick start it had needed.

Of course most modern day enterprises, if they wish to turn any kind of meaningful profit, need an online presence, but that proved no problem for Mattie, being reasonably capable in the use of social media, although purely for business purposes. The college course she had taken had been invaluable as it had equipped her with the skills necessary for running her virtual shop alongside the physical one.

So what was 'Sparkle!' offering the public that they just couldn't do without? It had begun with an exclusive range of handmade jewellery. Unique pieces that offered something very special to the wearer, with a separate range that didn't require a second mortgage for their purchase. But it was Mattie's eye for an opportunity that had pushed her business on to even greater heights.

She had seen couples come into her shop and, on many occasions, also seen the look of polite boredom on the face of one of the pair, usually the man, while he waited for the love of his life (or possibly not) to select her new necklace, bracelet or earrings. So, it was with a desire to engage every one of her visitors, that she came up with the solution. Wristwatches. Not exactly a revolutionary idea for a jeweller, except her watches wouldn't be the normal, high street models but, like her jewellery, unique, limited edition, hard-to-find pieces. A service for collectors and aficionados. It had been a risk, given that anyone with a mobile phone now had accurate time all of the time. But, it transpired, there was an appetite for wrist wear that offered something that little bit special.

And so, with the name of her business now slightly amended to 'Time to Sparkle!', here was Mattie, about to open her shop on a sunny Monday morning with a beautiful day ahead. But if anyone could have looked into her heart at that moment they would have seen only a desire for the evening to come so that she might not be alone any longer. Because, even now, it was when she was alone that she still feared the darkness might return once more and drag her back into those shadows that, deep down, she knew still existed.

Chapter 3

It was a little over a month earlier when, for Mattie, everything had changed. There had been no warning, no gentle premonition of what was to come. Looking back now, did she still feel thankful that she had found her, even after everything that had happened? It was a question to which she now knew the answer.

It had been a good day at the shop. After being contacted some weeks earlier by a customer looking for a particularly rare wristwatch, she had been able to phone and tell him that she'd not only tracked one down but now had it in her possession. That afternoon he had called, paid for the watch and, before leaving, promised to recommend her to other collectors. She had to remind herself that it wouldn't be like this every day, but she would allow herself to bask in the glory for a short while.

After setting the alarm and locking up for the day, Mattie had chosen to take a walk by the river before heading for the car park. She could recall every detail of that walk in the late afternoon. The warmth of the early summer sun, the sounds of the children in the park, and the ducks calling to every passer-by in the hope of receiving some scrap of food.

As she finally made her way home, she felt a contentment and joy growing inside her because she had something to look forward to that evening. Her best and only true friend, Lucy, was travelling down from London to see her. It was a get-together that was always eagerly anticipated by them both. The fact that it didn't happen more often was purely down to Lucy's hectic and unpredictable lifestyle. Mattie didn't pretend to fully understand exactly what it was that she did, and Lucy seemed happy to keep explanations sufficiently vague. She mentioned words like commerce and corporate finance, and the fact that she often had to travel abroad at a moment's notice. But that was about the limit of any forthcoming information. Lucy always seemed keen to emphasise how boring her job was and, from that, Mattie took the lightly disguised hint that she, for reasons of her own, didn't want to discuss it in any more detail. But, reading between the lines, it seemed to Mattie that her friend may have access to information that might prove very valuable to business rivals and she couldn't risk a word out of place, even to her closest friend.

As soon as she arrived back at her apartment, Mattie had set about some superficial housework. Her place could never have been described as untidy, so it was just a case of straightening a cushion or running the vacuum over the living room carpet. The local Chinese restaurant would be providing the food and so there was little more to do except wait for Lucy to arrive.

She flicked the television on in time for the six o'clock evening news, but soon decided she'd seen enough and so turned to her phone's playlist and Clean Bandit. Dropping back onto the sofa, she allowed her eyes to close as the music played. Maybe just a short nap wouldn't hurt….it had been a long day….and there was time before….

Had that been the first time? She now believed that it had. For just a moment she had seen that place. Nothing more than a flicker of an image, a ghost that was there and then gone. And it had meant nothing. Not then. Perhaps eventually it might have, if the sound of the doorbell hadn't wrenched her back to consciousness. Mattie leapt to her feet, glancing in the mirror as she passed it on her way to the door.

"Lucy!"

They embraced in the doorway before she pulled her friend into her apartment, kicking the door shut behind them. Mattie gripped her shoulders and held her at arms' length.

"You look fantastic!"

It was true. But then she had never known Lucy to look anything but 'fantastic'. Not a strand of her honey blonde hair was out of place, her clothes nothing but designer labels, the shoes of equal exclusivity and her makeup, always a triumph of understatement, and confirmation that 'less is more'. Anyone would have forgiven Mattie for feeling just a hint of jealousy. For as long as she had known her, Lucy had always been the one who didn't have to try. The one for whom everything always turned to gold no matter what. And yet Mattie felt nothing but unbridled joy to be with her friend again.

"Thought we could work our way through these after our meal!"

Lucy produced from her shoulder bag a rather impressive looking box of chocolates, its Harrods label clearly on display in one corner.

"Oh, you so should have!...."

She took them with a broad smile.

"....and still slumming it, I see."

Mattie nodded towards the box as she put it on the coffee table.

"Only the best for us!"

Lucy kicked off her shoes and sat down in one of the two massive armchairs that were placed opposite the sofa. With due ceremony she carefully removed the Ray Bans that had been perched to millimetre perfection on the top of her head, placing them next to the chocolates.

"So...."

As she spoke Lucy swung her legs around so that they hung over the side of the chair.

"....how's my little shopkeeper?"

Mattie smiled as she sat back on the sofa. Ever since she'd acquired 'Time to Sparkle!' Lucy had referred to her as 'her little shopkeeper'. If anyone else had used that phrase she might have taken it as some kind of thinly veiled put-down. But different rules applied in this friendship, which had its foundations set firmly in a deep affection and mutual, unshakeable respect.

"Had a good sale today. Watch collector. Think he might prove to be quite a useful contact."

"Well done you!...."

And she meant it. There was no edge, no hint of sarcasm.

"....although I don't really get the whole watch thing. Who needs them these days?"

Mattie raised her eyebrows as she looked pointedly at Lucy's left wrist.

"A Vacheron Constantin, if I'm not mistaken? You didn't get that in Poundland."

Lucy glanced at it with a look of disdain.

"Oh, that little thing. It was a gift from a grateful client. You can have it if you want."

Mattie eyes widened.

"You're serious, aren't you?!"

In answer, Lucy began to undo the clasp.

"No! Stop! You can't just give it away!"

"Why not? I could say I'd lost it. He'd probably just give me another one."

"He…?"

Mattie leant forward.

"….Is there something you haven't told me?"

"Down girl! Nothing to tell. As I said, he's a client, that's all. I have female clients too."

"But none of them have given you a Vacheron Constantin, have they? Have they?!"

Lucy shrugged.

"Maybe not that exactly, but I've had some nice stuff."

"Such as?"

"Oh, just stuff. Are we ordering food?"

Classic Lucy. She'd never say 'I don't want to talk about it', and she knew Mattie would always take the hint and let it go. In answer to the question Lucy was handed the takeaway menu, and so the next few minutes were spent discussing what they might order. Actually, it was more a set ritual than an exploration of the menu's many choices because they usually ended up ordering much the same as they did the last time.

While Mattie was on her phone placing their order, Lucy was discreetly removing her mobile from her bag and quickly checking it for messages, but she had replaced it before Mattie had finished her call.

"Be about twenty minutes. And I don't mind."

Lucy looked puzzled.

"Don't mind what?"

"If you have your phone out. It's ok. I guess you must have people wanting to contact you all the time."

Lucy pushed herself up from the chair and picked up her bag, carried it over to the furthest corner of the room and dropped it down on the floor.

"This is our time, Matts, and the only person I'll allow to interrupt it is the guy who brings our takeaway. So tell me about the shop. I am interested. Genuinely."

And so, until their food arrived, Mattie gave her all the news of 'Time to Sparkle!' since they had last met, watching closely for Lucy's eyes to glaze over or the look to become fixed as she tuned out. But it didn't happen. Every so often she would ask a relevant question or make an encouraging comment, but there were no polite, disinterested smiles that might hide an underlying boredom. And, in those minutes, Mattie was reminded all over again why Lucy, and their friendship, meant so much to her.

In fact, the bond between them had been forged from Mattie's first term at secondary school. It was a time that she often thought about. Those days, far from being the best days of her life, had been filled with an introverted apprehension that was occasionally replaced by downright fear. And, of course, like pack animals, some other older pupils had sensed the vulnerability that shone like a neon sign above her head.

She still remembered their faces as they had surrounded her, their silence more threatening and more frightening than the shouted taunts and insults. But, just when Mattie had thought she couldn't take anymore, along came Lucy.

Even then, she had had that 'something'. A rare presence and confidence that was unmistakeable and impossible to ignore. Being a Year Nine student and therefore two years older than Mattie, their paths hadn't crossed before, at least not in any meaningful way. The odd exchanged glance in the corridor at break times or between classes had been the sum total of their interaction.

It had been pure chance that had put Lucy in the right place at the right time for Mattie. When, yet again, her life was about to be made even more of a misery by this small group of Year Ten bullies, a voice, quiet and calm, had cut through that awful silence.

"If I see any of you go near her again, or even look at her, I'll...."

One of the girls, obviously in no mood to back down, decided to round on the unwanted good Samaritan.

"You'll what?"

Lucy, far from being daunted by this, took a step forward as Mattie, eyes wide with a mixture of fear and astonishment, watched her. Could she see the hint of a smile touch her lips? Lucy was now standing directly in front of the girl who had now revealed herself to be the ringleader.

Even after all these years Mattie could still run the scene through her mind in the minutest of detail. She could recall the colour of the walls, that one of the light bulbs that hung from the ceiling was broken, and that the Year Ten girl was, for some strange reason, now lying on the floor clutching her stomach. Lucy stepped over her but, before any further confrontation could occur, the other girls had scattered in all directions.

"You ok?"

Mattie remembered those kind eyes and the voice that had now lost all of its edge.

"Yes. Thank you. But you'll get into big trouble for that."

Lucy flicked a disdainful glance in the direction of the girl she'd just hit.

"No I won't. She'd be finished if it got round she'd been put down by a Year Nine. She'll keep quiet and, if she doesn't, I'll hit her harder next time."

Lucy aimed the last words in the direction of the girl, who had now got to her feet and was making her unsteady way back along the corridor.

"Why did you help me?"

Mattie had asked when, at lunchtime, they had sat together in the refectory. Thinking about it now, she was sure that Lucy had sat with her that day to make a point. The geeky little Year Seven girl now had a friend, and don't any of you dare forget it.

"Why? Because bullies make me angry. Ok. That's not the main reason. Thing is, I've been wanting to hit that girl for a long time. Thanks for giving me an excuse!"

Mattie smiled. It had been a while since she had smiled.

Chapter 4

Mattie knelt by the dishwasher, putting the last of the cutlery into the plastic basket before closing the door. By the time she returned to the living room Lucy was already opening another bottle of chilled white.

"Are you intending to drink most of that, because I'm not sure I can put away much more?"

Mattie flopped onto the sofa next to her.

"We'll see how far we get, shall we?"

Both glasses were now refilled and one was slid across to Mattie.

"I have to open my shop in the morning!"

"So open it with a hangover! No one'll complain, and if they do just refer them to me!"

Mattie picked up her glass and lifted it in a toast.

"To my beautiful friend, the wonderful, successful, disgustingly rich Lucy, who still has my back after all these years!"

"Of course I do. I promised. Remember?"

And yes, Mattie did remember. After the bullying had stopped, after her school days had returned to something that might pass for normality in Mattie's world, she had sat with Lucy by the netball courts watching the first team practice. It was after school and there were only a few spectators sitting on the grass verges that surrounded the courts.

"They think we stand a chance of winning the Croft this year."

Lucy was referring to the inter-school netball trophy, a prize that their school had never won in the competition's twenty-three-year history. Mattie didn't seem convinced.

"I expect they say that every year, don't they?"

Lucy laughed.

"Maybe they do, but nothing wrong with a bit of optimism, is there?"

But to Mattie, in those days, optimism was something forever kept at bay by the shadows that were always at her shoulder. If anyone had known about them and asked her to describe her demons she couldn't have given them a name. Not that she would ever have discussed them with anyone. Not even Lucy. All she knew was that they served only one purpose. To make her life as difficult as they could, and to suck away the potential pleasure of any situation before she could experience it. Had Lucy sensed them? Looking back now Mattie thought that perhaps she had.

"I haven't seen them since. Those girls."

Lucy hadn't intended to ask the question, thinking that she wouldn't want to talk about it.

"Good. Told you they wouldn't bother you anymore. You didn't believe me, did you?"

Mattie didn't want to say it in so many words but, no, she hadn't believed her.

"Thank you, for what you did for me."

Mattie turned away as she spoke, wanting to look anywhere but at Lucy.

"You don't need to keep saying that, Matts…."

It had been the first time she had called her that.

"….I'll always keep an eye out for you, on one condition."

"What's that?"

Lucy smiled.

"That you stop thanking me!"

Mattie laughed. Mattie had actually laughed.

"Promise. Lucy?"

"Mmm?"

There was a pause, as if she was finding it difficult to say what she so wanted to say.

"I've never had a friend before."

It was Lucy's turn to look away as she felt tears well in her eyes.

"Well, you've got one now."

She took her hand and held it, a simple gesture that had the effect of making her words tangible and genuine. Thinking back, as she so often did, she saw that moment as some kind of turning point. It was no longer her alone against the world, fighting each day's battles knowing that she would, inevitably lose. She now had a chance. But the concept of having a friend was so alien to her that she had had no idea how that should work. And, once again, it had been to Lucy's eternal credit that she had known how to respond to someone like Mattie.

Her tactic, which had gone unnoticed by Mattie at the time, had been to hold back. To be around but not to overwhelm. Lucy had, by and large, let Mattie come to her when she felt she needed to talk, or just to have some company. There had never been an occasion, that Mattie could recall, when she hadn't been there when she had needed her.

The strategy, she could see now, had been a successful one because slowly but surely Mattie had begun to gather around her a small, select group of acquaintances. Not friends. That would have been far too strong a word. But she was no longer the little girl lost. There was now something resembling confidence about her and she was able to function sufficiently to become a part of the whole, to pass exams and begin to get something back from those daily battles. They hadn't gone away, not by any means, but now it was a far more equal fight. Thanks to Lucy.

Chapter 5

"The spare room's all made up. Why don't you stay?"

Lucy looked at the empty wine bottles and the two glasses next to them.

"It's tempting, Matts, but I haven't bought anything for an overnight."

"I've got stuff you could use. Wouldn't be a problem, unless you need to be in Dubai or New York or wherever by dawn."

Lucy looked at her watch.

"Bit late for that even if I do….which I don't."

"So?"

"Ok. I'll stay. Thanks."

"Excellent! Our first sleepover!"

Mattie couldn't hide her delight, especially as she had expected her to have to leave long before this moment. Even though they were truly best friends, they had struggled to find opportunities for quality time together, and so this evening was even more precious to them both. Lucy's work had always come first and, now being in business herself, Mattie had completely understood and had never given Lucy a hard time about that.

"This is fun!"

They both sat on the sofa, each nursing a steaming mug of coffee. Mattie, after promising Lucy that she had all she would need for 'an overnight', realised that what she had to offer by way of nightwear might not be what her friend was used to. There wasn't a designer label among any of her collection of pyjamas, all of which owed everything to comfort and practicality, and almost nothing to style.

"Oh yes! And I love this!"

Lucy tugged at the cotton top she was wearing. It was adorned with images of baby elephants. More Disney than Dior.

"Really?"

"It takes me back. Haven't worn anything like this since I was in primary school!"

Mattie was still unconvinced. "Is that a good thing? Being taken back, I mean."

It had been a simple, throwaway question, but Lucy's mood suddenly changed. The carefree, warm smiles were suddenly replaced by a faraway expression, as if she was no longer with Mattie in that room. She remained silent for some seconds before replying, and when she did her voice had become soft and quiet, almost inaudible.

"Yes. It is a good thing. I'd give anything to be back there now. Matts? Can I stay here with you for a few days?"

Where had that come from?

"I....er...."

"If it's too much trouble, or not convenient...."

Mattie shook her head. "No. No, not at all. Of course you can stay as long as you want. You took me by surprise, that's all."

"I could maybe give you a hand in the shop?"

"Do you want to tell me what's wrong?"

Mattie felt she owed her that. If she didn't want to talk about it, fine, but she had to let her know that she was ready to listen.

"I just need a bit of downtime, that's all. No big deal, Matts. Honestly."

She knew Lucy well enough to get the subtext of that. 'I want to tell you, but not right now.'

"Ok." Mattie judged that to be the best, and safest, response.

"Let's find a really scary film!"

Lucy grabbed the remote and began to search through the all the movies on offer before settling on The Horror Channel.

"Susperia! The 1977 original! Haven't seen this in years! It's a Dario Argento classic! Best Italian horror film ever made!"

It may well be, Mattie thought, but watching it might not be conducive to a peaceful night's sleep afterwards. However, tomorrow was already going to be a challenge thanks to the wine, so why not? And, being swept up by Lucy's obvious enthusiasm, Mattie settled back to 'enjoy' the 'Argento classic'.

Chapter 6

The film had finished at one in the morning. Lucy had helpfully explained, during the commercial breaks, the finer points of Argento's direction and had almost succeeded in converting Mattie to seventies Italian horror. Almost.

After she'd made sure Lucy had everything she needed, Mattie fetched herself a glass of water from the kitchen and made her way to her own bedroom. She'd need to be at the shop by nine thirty at the latest with, it seemed, Lucy. She was still trying to work that one out as she climbed into bed and closed her eyes.

Just before Mattie fell asleep she found herself worrying about her friend. When she had, out of the blue, asked if she could prolong her stay, there had been something in her that Mattie hadn't seen before. There had been, for a fleeting moment, a vulnerability. It was almost as if it had taken Lucy by surprise too. She had shown something close to embarrassment that she should have allowed those feelings to break through, and had certainly not been slow to change the subject. And so, with a confusion of thoughts and concerns about Lucy, sleep finally claimed a worried Mattie.

The jolt from sleep to consciousness was instant. In a moment Mattie's eyes were wide open. She saw a clear blue sky and felt the warmth of the sun on her skin. She looked around her, turning full circle as she took in her surroundings.

She was standing in a clearing near the edge of a wood. To her right there were trees as far as she could see, and she heard their leaves rustling in the gentle breeze. Away to her left there was a meadow that sloped down to where a river meandered its way along a shallow valley. Mattie walked a short way into the meadow, kneeling down in the long grass and running her hands through its soft, warm blades. In amongst them there were wild flowers, their delicate pastel blooms reaching above the grass, small bursts of colour against the rich green.

She looked down to the river and saw two horses grazing on the lush pasture. One of them lifted its head lazily to look briefly in her direction before returning its attention to the grass. There was only one other sound above the rustle of the leaves. The birdsong. It was coming from all directions, in the meadow itself, from the trees, and the sky.

As Mattie stood she picked one of the flowers beside her. It was a beautiful bright pink with a centre as golden as the sun. She carried it with her on her way down to the river, walking slowly so as not to startle the two horses, who were now paying no attention to her at all. She sat down and let her bare feet swing into the cool water, feeling the slow current push against her legs. And, as Mattie rested there, she felt nothing but peace, contentment, and an overwhelming sense of belonging. She lay back onto the warm ground and closed her eyes, knowing that this place wanted her. It had always wanted her.

Chapter 7

"Scrambled egg? Think I've even got some smoked salmon in the fridge if you fancy it."

Mattie was quietly impressed that Lucy was not only up but fully dressed and seated at the kitchen table. She had expected to creep out of the apartment, leaving her to spend most of the morning in bed. But this wasn't the first time her friend had surprised her this visit, was it?

"No, cereal's fine, thanks."

Mattie walked over to one of the eye-level cupboards and removed an assortment of muesli, cornflakes and porridge oats. She poured some milk into a jug and placed it on the table next to the boxes.

"Orange juice?"

Lucy nodded.

"Thought when we go into town I might buy a few clothes and some other bits and pieces. I'll need some stuff if I'm going to be around for a while. That is, if you're still happy for me to stay?"

Mattie sat down opposite her and filled her own bowl with some muesli.

"Of course, I said so last night."

"Might've been the wine talking."

"Well it wasn't. The offer's still good. But I feel I should point out that you're not going to find the sort of clothes you're used to wearing in any of the shops here."

Lucy took a sip of juice.

"I don't only shop in Harrods, Matts."

"Even so…."

"Don't worry! I'll find something. Anyway, I may not want all that sort of stuff anymore."

Should she respond to that? Mattie decided that it would be best to wait and allow Lucy the space to tell it in her own time. The more pressing question was, if she was coming to the shop with her, what could she give her to do? Lucy was used to all that high powered commerce, or whatever it was she did. Sitting in a little town's jewellers with, in all probability, only a handful of customers might not prove to be the most challenging time Lucy had ever experienced. Mattie felt she should mention the chance that more than a small amount of boredom might set in before the day was out.

"And what makes you think I won't be happy being bored?" was the immediate response.

"I just....er...."

She held up a hand to stop Mattie from struggling on.

"I'm so looking forward to seeing your lovely shop and just spending some time with you. I won't get in the way, and I'll be fine. Look, if you really would like me to be gainfully employed I can maybe check out your website? I did a short course on web design a few years ago, I might be able to suggest a few improvements if you'd like me to take a look?"

"That'd be wonderful! Thank you!"

Mattie wasn't completely sure that her website was in need of improvement but at least the immediate problem was solved.

"And, of course, I'll only go shopping during my lunch hour!"

They laughed and for a moment everything was as it had always been. Back in her bedroom, Mattie set about applying the finishing touches to her makeup, taking her lead from Lucy's minimalist approach. She flicked through her modest selection of outfits, nothing spectacular but all perfectly serviceable for the shop. She still had some concerns about Lucy finding anything in town that she would deem acceptable but, having pointed that out, she couldn't do any more.

One last check in the mirror and Mattie was happy with the result of her efforts. Had she felt the need to 'up her game' because Lucy was coming with her? She immediately told herself not. Well, maybe not. She had always had a problem with her own looks. Perhaps having a stunningly attractive best friend didn't help, but Lucy never ever made reference, oblique or otherwise, to her own beauty. In fact, she had always made a point of telling Mattie how pretty *she* looked. Pretty. Yes, ok, Mattie could live with 'pretty'. And, anyway, the image thing was probably just another insidious little demon, lining itself up with all the others to make her life as difficult as it could.

It was as she turned away from the mirror that she caught a glimpse of something on her pillow. Something that she didn't recall being there earlier. She picked it up. It was a small, bright pink flower with a golden centre. Mattie caught a hint of its delicate scent as she held it. Where had it come from? She couldn't recall having seen one like it, and yet....

As she laid the flower down on her bedside table her mind was struggling to pull something from her memory. It was there and then gone. Perhaps it would come back to her later. Still, no matter. But it was a beautiful little flower.

"You can put all of these in the window display."

Mattie handed Lucy a tray of bracelets that she'd just removed from the safe in the back room.

"Do you do this every day?"

Mattie nodded.

"I leave the less valuable stuff in the window overnight, just so the place looks loved, but I don't want it to attract the wrong sort of attention."

Lucy set about arranging the various pieces of jewellery so that, she considered, each was shown off to its best advantage. When she had finished she fully expected Mattie to move everything to where she had wanted it all along but, no, she went outside, took one glance in the window and gave her the thumbs up.

"You never have to try, do you?"

Lucy looked puzzled.

"I don't follow."

Mattie smiled.

"Are you good at everything you do?"

Lucy leant back against the glass counter.

"It's all an illusion, Matts. All bluff."

She smiled as she spoke, attempting, but failing, to add humour to her words and Mattie, again, saw a look in her eyes that she hadn't seen before.

"Do you remember at school when you used to help me with my exam revision?"

Lucy did recall those long summer days, sitting under one of the trees that grew around the edge of the playing fields. Mattie had been struggling with one subject in particular. Physics, wasn't it?

"You sat with me for hours, going through my notes, testing me, trying to convince me I could do it."

"I seem to remember you got a good pass, didn't you?"

Mattie nodded.

"Thanks to you."

"You took the exam, not me. Anyway, remind me, why are we discussing this?"

"Because I once asked you how long you spent revising. I think I was trying, in my clumsy Year Seven way, to see if I could help you in return for what you'd done for me. Do you recall what your answer was?"

Lucy shook her head.

"I don't even recall you asking the question!"

"You said that you didn't really bother with revision much. That you could usually remember all the stuff you needed to. I really admired that. I still do."

"I think you should find someone more worthy of your admiration, Matts…."

Lucy glanced at her watch.

"….and shouldn't we open up? It's just gone nine thirty."

Mattie smiled, thinking that even if Lucy was right, there was one aspect of her that was worth admiring. Her ability to always find some way of changing the subject.

It had been an interesting morning. Mattie, by lunchtime, had made a mental note to add 'saleswoman' to Lucy's financial and IT abilities. Their first customer had been a young woman whose eye had been caught by a delicate silver necklace she had seen in the window the day before. Mattie noticed, while she was assisting her customer, Lucy studying the window display intently. It had been as the lady removed her credit card from her bag that Lucy had seized her moment. Producing a pair of earrings that she had, seconds before, removed from the display, she held them next to the necklace.

"They go beautifully, don't you think?"

It couldn't be said that Mattie wasn't tuned in to sales opportunities when they arose, but she had always been careful never to come across as 'pushy' for fear of losing future custom. But, as Lucy proceeded to work her magic, she found herself looking on in approval as the young woman listened to all the reasons why she couldn't possibly buy the necklace without having the earrings too. It took only seconds to double the amount of the purchase, and one very happy customer left 'Time to Sparkle!' vowing to return with a friend in a few days' time.

"Hope you didn't mind."

Lucy seemed genuinely concerned that she might have overstepped the mark with her sales technique, but Mattie was quick to put her mind at rest.

"On the contrary, I'm impressed."

Lucy's relief was almost palpable.

"But that's me. Always think I've got it right. Too sure of myself."

"I see that as one of your best assets. Saved me all those years ago, didn't it?"

Mattie found herself, once more, attempting to boost the confidence of someone who saw themselves as over-confident. It was an enigma that Mattie was rapidly becoming drawn into, and one that she desperately wanted to solve because, of course, she cared. Lucy, her wonderful friend, whether present (not that often) or in contact by phone or email, had been a positive influence in her life for so many years. Perhaps it was time to give her something back, if only she could discover exactly what that 'something' should be.

In fact, the earrings weren't Lucy's only triumph that morning. An hour or so after her first sale, a middle aged man had come in looking for a watch. Mattie gave her the nod and, with no further encouragement needed, Lucy homed in on the gentleman, who couldn't have known at that moment that he didn't stand a chance of walking out of the shop without making a purchase.

Mattie watched with some amusement as Lucy, using a blend of charm and overt flirtation, steered the gentleman in the direction of watches that had the highest price tags. Actually, she quickly came to realise that her friend had more wrist wear knowledge than she had previously let on and that, combined with the flirting, meant another lucrative sale.

"Ok. I think you've earned your lunchbreak...."

Mattie handed Lucy her jacket.

"....but don't forget I warned you about the clothes shops around here! Couldn't you go back to your place and get your things?"

She took her jacket and picked up her bag.

"I don't want to, Matts. Not right now. Maybe not ever."

She left, quickly closing the door behind her before Mattie could reply.

Chapter 8

"I did warn you."

"What do you mean? These are great!"

Lucy held up the blouse before placing it back on the sofa with the other five, together with the assortment of trousers, skirts, underwear and several pairs of shoes.

"Say it often enough and you might even begin to believe it yourself. I bet that store couldn't believe its luck!"

Lucy sat down beside her new wardrobe.

"It's all good quality, and very reasonably priced."

And now Mattie knew there was something Lucy wasn't telling her. Up until that last sentence she might have been convinced that she was imagining things.

"Reasonably priced!? You're talking a foreign language! Your shoulder bag is Ferragamo, your shoes are Gucci. Since when has 'reasonably priced' ever entered into it?"

Lucy looked towards the TV, briefly avoiding eye contact. Was this a precursor to another deft change of subject? Mattie was preparing for it but unsure what she should do. Go with it and, once more, wait in the hope that Lucy would eventually tell her, or challenge the evasion and risk upsetting the one person who meant more to her than anything? And then....

"I no longer want it, Matts. Simple as that."

"No longer want what?"

She turned back to her, now looking directly into her eyes.

"My way of life. I want what you've got."

To say Mattie was unsure how she should respond to that would have been an understatement.

"And what's that?" was all she could think of.

Lucy smiled.

"I guess you don't even know, do you? Why should you?"

Mattie remained silent, wanting to allow her to say it in her own time.

"You're content. Aren't you?"

Mattie nodded.

"I hadn't really thought about it but, yes, I suppose I'm content."

'On my better days' she could have added.

"Good. It helps me to know that."

Was Lucy implying that she *wasn't* content, whatever that might mean? The answer wasn't long in coming.

"I feel I'm losing control of everything, and I just want it all to end."

Lucy seemed on the verge of tears as Mattie sat beside her on the sofa and put a comforting arm around her shoulder, that simple gesture representing a complete role reversal in their fourteen-year relationship.

"But you're successful. Look at what you have, the life you lead. I've always looked up to you, admired your drive, admired what you do...."

"You don't know what I do."

And, the truth of it was, no she didn't. Mattie had read between the lines and tried to fill in the gaps. Designer clothes, expensive jewellery, exclusive London apartment. All of that *sounded* as if it added up to Success with a capital S, didn't it?

"Not exactly, no."

There was little point in pretending.

"Actually, Matts, you don't know at all."

"Do you want to tell me?"

It was a question she had no choice but to ask. There was a pause as Lucy tried to decide how she should answer. She took a deep breath.

"After I left uni I joined a very prestigious company. London based but international representation. Good salary and the work they said they were offering was well within my skill set. The interview was pretty much a formality and I was presented with a contract there and then. Now I regret ever taking their fucking job. I regret the day I walked through their door."

Mattie was thrown by that, unsure what she should say.

"You don't have to go back. I told you, you can stay here as long as you want."

Those words, Mattie judged, would be what Lucy needed to hear at that moment. There was no point in questioning what she had just said, not right then. Maybe later. But what Mattie hadn't expected was the effect of her words. As Mattie held her she felt a gentle shuddering as Lucy gave up the fight against the tears that had been wanting to come for some time.

Nothing more was said for several minutes. They sat together, Mattie keeping her arm around Lucy and holding her head close to hers. In the background the radio quietly played on, barely loud enough to hear. Eventually, when Mattie was happy that Lucy was calm enough, she stood up.

"Drink?"

Lucy nodded, prompting Mattie to make her way over to the modest drinks cabinet in the corner of the room. Moments later she handed her a small brandy which was downed in one. As Mattie sat beside her once more, so Lucy reached for her hand, holding it tightly as she spoke.

"I'm sorry. I overreacted. Not like me to be a drama queen, is it?"

She tried to laugh, but failed to convince not only Mattie but herself.

"I know you, don't forget, and I doubt you've ever overreacted to anything in your life. Whatever's got to you, we can deal with it, ok? All those times you've been there for me…."

Lucy shook her head.

"Please don't. I don't want to lose it again."

Mattie had no desire to add to her friend's distress.

"If you want to tell me the rest, I'll listen. If you don't right now, that's fine too. Your call."

She could see in Lucy's eyes, still moist with tears, the conflict between wanting to tell it all, to unburden herself completely, and being almost too scared to talk. Or had Mattie got that wrong? She had never known Lucy to fear anything, ever.

"Could we go out for dinner tonight? Anywhere you like. On me."

And so that couldn't be clearer. The conversation was over for now. Lucy needed to walk away for a while, and a meal out was as good an excuse as any. There was a very pleasant tapas bar just a few streets away that they had visited in the past, and a quick phone call found that, yes indeed, they did have a table for two free in half an hour.

They were met by a waiter who said he remembered them, although Mattie wasn't convinced of that. As was usual whenever they ventured out together, eyes invariably turned in Lucy's direction which, far from feeling any pangs of jealously, Mattie had always been grateful for. She had never craved that kind of attention and, even when she had opened her shop, the short-lived ensuing local media interest had been something to be endured rather than embraced.

Even with her concerns, whatever they might be, Lucy still exuded that aura of confidence and positivity that had always seemed to surround her and draw others in. She even wore her department store clothes with the same self-assurance that she had when wearing Givenchy or Balmain. It wasn't the money, or 'the look' that made Lucy special. Whatever it was came from within.

They sat opposite each other, with an impressive assortment of small dishes set out in front of them. All around, the buzz of conversation from the other diners provided a comforting backdrop, allowing them to talk without any concern of being overheard. There were three couples on nearby tables and a larger group, celebrating a birthday judging by the array of cards, presents and balloons, on the long table that ran almost the full length of, thankfully, the furthest part of the restaurant.

"Do you think we may have over-ordered?"

Mattie looked at the array of food with what might have been described as a degree of doubt, but Lucy was too busy helping herself to a delicious looking prawn dish to reply. At least whatever it was that was troubling her didn't seem to be affecting her appetite. However, as if by some kind of twisted telepathy, when, after she had despatched her fourth prawn, Lucy did finally speak it was to say

"These are sooo good! I haven't been eating so well lately, but since I've been staying with you...."

Another prawn met its fate.

"....I've really started to enjoy stuff again. The food, the shop, the new clothes!"

Mattie smiled, although she was still unable to fully appreciate how she could be giving her friend such a feeling of comfort and security, but clearly she did and that, in the end, was all that mattered, wasn't it?

"Did you mean what you said about looking at my website?"

She had been intending to ask Lucy, and now seemed the right time. It was a safe subject, one that Mattie had been holding in reserve for when the conversation needed something other than Lucy's concerns about her job.

"Of course. I'll do it tomorrow. Might be able to suggest a few tweaks."

"I'd appreciate that. Tell me about your...."

Lucy's raised hand stopped Mattie before she could finish her sentence.

"No more about me this evening. Let's talk about you, Matts. Not your shop, lovely though it is, but you."

She saw the look on Mattie's face but decided to press on.

"I know 'you' isn't your favourite subject. Never has been, has it? But let's give it a go, shall we?"

Mattie took a large mouthful of something Lucy had ordered, salmon and cream cheese? Yes. It was not only very pleasant but had the added bonus of preventing her from replying for several seconds. Lucy saw the ploy and sat back smiling, her expression saying 'I can wait.' However, as soon as the small plate was empty she took her chance.

"How're those demons? You seem more in control these days. More confident being you."

Mattie reached for another plate, this time something with green and red peppers, but didn't begin to eat immediately, knowing that tactic couldn't be played again.

"Maybe, or maybe I've just become more adept at covering up."

"Is that what you think? No point in trying to blag it Matts because, firstly, I'll see straight through it and, secondly, it won't help you. If you lie to everyone else, if that's what gets you through, ok, but don't lie to yourself."

Mattie went to speak but found her mouth had suddenly become very dry. She took a sip from her glass of wine.

"Truthfully, I'm not that far from the frightened little Year Seven you rescued all those years ago. I think I've come to accept that I never will be."

Lucy reached across the table and gave her hand a quick squeeze. She knew enough not to try and give some vacuous 'Oh, I'm sure you will' little speech, and Mattie wouldn't expect her to.

"Just concentrate on what you've achieved. I've seen enough to know you've got something really good going with your business, your beautiful apartment….be anything you want, but don't be frightened Matts. You don't have to be that anymore."

In that moment, words didn't seem to want to come for Mattie and so she just gave the slightest of nods and the weakest of smiles. But she knew that would be enough for Lucy, because it always was. She understood. Even though she clearly had her own problems which were eating away at her, she understood. And Mattie realised that, maybe for the first time, they now needed each other.

Chapter 9

Much against Mattie's better judgement, after they had left the restaurant, Lucy had insisted they moved on to a wine bar which, fortunately or unfortunately, was situated only a few doors away.

"Shall we have champagne?"

Lucy's question was plainly meant to be rhetorical because before Mattie could reply she had already ordered a bottle. She then grabbed her arm and led her to an empty table.

"What are we celebrating?"

Lucy thought about that for a moment.

"How about 'us'? That'll do, won't it?"

Mattie agreed that it would and, although at first quite unenthusiastic, she found herself being slowly drawn in by the lively, feel-good atmosphere and, quite possibly, the champagne. She looked around her. There didn't seem to be anyone older than thirty in the room.

"Bet you've never been in here before."

After they had finished their meal in the restaurant Lucy had had the idea of the wine bar, although she knew it would be taking Mattie well out of her comfort zone. It was a carefully calculated decision, and part of Lucy's ongoing attempt to gently nudge her friend in the direction of the big bad world, while at the same time understanding and respecting Mattie's right to see things differently. With that in mind, Lucy decided to say nothing until they had left the tapas bar because she knew Mattie would only sit and worry herself into deciding she couldn't possibly go.

"I've been in here once actually. Thought I'd have a look one day after I'd closed the shop."

Lucy waited for her to continue but it seemed that was the beginning and end of the story.

"Not impressed, then?"

She shrugged.

"It was ok, but....you know."

Lucy smiled.

"Yes, Matts. I know."

She picked up the half empty bottle and topped up Mattie's glass, despite her protests.

"Enjoy it! I won't be buying us champagne every day!"

"I didn't think you drank anything else. I imagine on your salary...."

A shadow seemed to pass over Lucy, but was gone as quickly as it came.

"You only get the salary if you have the job...."

Mattie was about to ask her what she meant by that when they became aware of two young men who had suddenly appeared by their table. Both women tried to avoid eye contact but it soon became apparent that their uninvited visitors were not about to disappear just because they were being ignored.

"Champagne. Expensive taste. I like that."

It was the taller of the two men who spoke, and both Lucy and Mattie now felt they couldn't keep up their blanking tactics any longer. Lucy, with a weary resignation, slowly turned in their direction and regarded them with what might be described as a degree of disdain.

"Good evening, gentlemen. Can we help you?"

The men exchanged glances before the one who'd spoken pulled up a chair from a nearby table and sat down next to Lucy.

"There's a nightclub not far from here. We can be there in ten minutes. Bring your champagne. We might even let you bring your friend."

Lucy looked from one to the other while considering how to respond to that, while Mattie just looked deeply uncomfortable with the whole situation. Up until *'even* your friend' Lucy had been trying to find a way of letting them down gently, but with that last sentence he had just kissed goodbye to anything approaching politeness from her. Lucy would tolerate and overlook many things, but insulting Mattie was not one of them.

As Lucy turned to the young man sitting next to her, Mattie looked away, images of a Year Ten girl lying poleaxed on the floor flashing through her mind. Quietly, Lucy leant forward, her mouth just inches from his ear. She whispered something that only he could hear while removing something from her bag and briefly holding it just inches in front of his face. She then sat back and watched as he stood up and returned to one of the tables on the far side of the room, his friend following a few paces behind.

"What did you say to him?" Mattie asked when she was sure they were safely out of earshot. Before answering, Lucy emptied her glass and refilled it.

"I just told him he needed to improve his chat-up technique."

Mattie was unconvinced.

"You said more than that."

Lucy sighed.

"I also told him that the management were concerned about young women receiving unwanted attention on these premises and we'd been brought in to identify any possible offenders. I then gave him a glimpse of my ID...."

"But...."

"It's my company's security pass, and 'glimpse' is the operative word."

"What if he'd wanted a closer look?"

Lucy leant forward, whispering confidentially.

"Then I'd have had to kill him."

Lucy sat back in her chair, her eyes fixed on Mattie, waiting for the reaction. A moment later it came in the form of a broad smile that succeeded in lifting her mood that had, with the brief attention of the two men, threatened to take a downturn. They might, after all, not have to leave just yet.

"How's your mum, Matts?"

Lucy was quite pleased with herself because that was not only a genuine enquiry but also served as a further distraction. She knew that Mattie's mother now lived in America with her latest acquisition (Mattie's description, not hers). When, previously, Mattie had told her of her mum's intended relocation across the Atlantic, there had been no bitterness or regret in her voice. It had been only a short time after the purchase of her daughter's shop that her mother informed her of the impending move, and Lucy had always wondered if the shop had been some kind of emotional payoff, although Mattie had never suggested that she had ever thought of it as such.

"She's good. Phoned last week to see how everything was."

Lucy, on the few occasions she had met Mattie's mother, had found her to be perfectly pleasant but quite controlling towards Mattie. It had seemed to Lucy that this attitude might have been born out of a desire to protect her daughter but, in her far-from-expert opinion, it had had the opposite effect. But, hey, she had bought her a shop and given her a rent free apartment, so that was ok, wasn't it?

"What did you tell her?"

Mattie thought for a moment.

"I said I was fine, the business was doing well, said you were coming to visit."

"Was she happy about that?"

"Oh yes! She likes you. Thinks you're 'good for me'."

"I'm flattered, seeing as your mum sets the bar pretty high."

"I know she still worries about me."

"So much so that she moved to America?"

As soon as she'd said it, Lucy regretted the way that had sounded.

"I can compete with most things where mum is concerned, but a man isn't one of them."

She said it in a matter-of-fact way, as if she had accepted that as a given a long time ago.

"Well, she does love you Matts, and that's what counts, isn't it? And it's a small world these days. Why don't you see if you could go and visit her? Might be fun."

Mattie was quick to shake her head.

"I couldn't leave the shop. I'd worry what effect closing it for any length of time might have on the goodwill I've built up. People want reliability and speed of delivery, especially online. I pride myself that I get orders out…."

"Who said anything about closing the shop?"

"But I'd need someone I could trust to…."

Lucy waited until the penny dropped.

"Oh, that's really kind of you but…."

"You don't trust me *that* much?"

Mattie seemed horrified that Lucy would think that.

"No! No, that's not it. Not at all. I'd trust you with anything. It's just I…."

Their years of close friendship told Lucy what was coming next.

"....I just don't think I could, that's all."

Of course, having her business gave Mattie the perfect excuse. It anchored her to her little world, her own sanctuary where she felt as safe as it was possible for her to feel. Had her mother known that when she had set her up? Lucy liked to think so.

The waiter removed the empty bottle from their table and politely enquired if they would like another. Lucy threw a questioning glance in Mattie's direction and received a clear answer.

"Thank you, no. But the champagne was excellent."

Lucy punctuated her reply with a generous tip which was gratefully received.

"Ok, Matts. Let's go. Unless, of course, you want to try the nightclub?"

The fact that she asked with a broad smile told Mattie no reply was required or expected and, as they made their way towards the door, the look of relief on her face was plain to see. As Mattie felt the cool night air surround her she realised how good it felt to be going home. She knew Lucy only ever had her best interests at heart, and she would always try her hardest to play the game. However, it never got easier and, Mattie now accepted, it probably never would. But, far from wanting Lucy to stop trying, to finally write her off as a hopeless case, her efforts to help her friend the best way she knew how never failed to warm Mattie's heart.

"Cup of coffee and maybe a late film?"

Lucy asked after they had put a reasonable distance between themselves and any possibility of further social interaction.

"That sounds perfect. Another scary one?"

"No. You can choose tonight."

"I fancy a comedy, or maybe a rom com?"

Lucy put an arm around her shoulder.

"Ok Matts, I think I can cope with that!"

They laughed together, as they had so many times in the past, and neither heard the two men as they appeared from the shadows behind them. Only when they were within a few paces did Mattie and Lucy hear their footsteps and turn to face them.

"Did you honestly believe I'd fall for that crap back there?"

Mattie recognised the man as the one who'd spoken to them in the wine bar. Lucy, in a moment, had placed herself between him and Mattie.

"Well, I certainly thought you looked stupid enough to."

This prompted the second man, who up until then hadn't spoken, to move forward.

"Give her what's coming to her, and her sad little friend."

He looked towards Mattie.

"Oh, how wonderful! It can speak!"

Whatever Lucy had planned to get them out of this, it was clear that diplomacy and conciliation weren't going to play a major part and Mattie wasn't sure if Lucy had noticed, but these two were not Year Ten girls.

"Should we run?"

Mattie whispered as the taller man began to move closer.

"I wouldn't give them the satisfaction" Lucy replied, making no effort to keep her voice down, and standing her ground. Mattie glanced around her, looking for any passers-by who she might call on for help, but the street was deserted. She moved forward to stand next to Lucy. However this was going to go, she wasn't going to allow her friend to face it alone. Lucy turned to her and in that moment Mattie saw something in her eyes that she hadn't seen before. Was it anger? Certainly something now seemed to be driving her towards this confrontation that, for her own reasons, she seemed determined to pursue. It was as if Lucy, regardless of her own and Mattie's wellbeing, wanted the fight. And that made no sense, because if there had been one constant theme running through their relationship over the years, it had been Lucy's love for her friend, and her overwhelming desire to protect her.

"What satisfaction *would* you give us?"

The taller man took another step forward, the distance between them little more than a few paces. The second man, now standing beside him, looked from Lucy to Mattie and was about to say something when the taller man suddenly clutched at his arm, before dropping to his knees and falling forward onto the ground. There was a sickening crack as his head hit the pavement and he lay, face down, unconscious. Mattie was the first to react, kneeling down beside him, gripping his shoulder and gently pulling him over onto his side.

"Call an ambulance!"

Lucy removed her phone from her jacket and quickly placed the call, she then knelt next to Mattie, who seemed to know what she was doing. The man's friend, who seemed in a state of shock, just stood rooted to the spot and looked on, saying nothing, his face white with fear.

It was only a short time before they heard the sound of the siren and seconds later, the paramedics, a man and a woman, had taken over from Mattie, who stood back as they worked on their patient. Lucy put an arm around Mattie and guided her away from the scene.

"You ok?"

"I think he's dead, Lucy."

When, eventually, she looked over her shoulder, she saw that the paramedics, who had spent minutes kneeling by the unconscious man, were now standing. The male paramedic returned to the ambulance, while the woman spoke to the man's friend. They exchanged a few words before she then made her way over to Lucy and Mattie.

"Are you friends of his?"

It was Lucy who replied.

"No. We…."

"We only met them a few minutes ago. They stopped us to ask the time."

Lucy turned to Mattie and was about to say something, but received the merest shake of the head from her friend.

"Ok. Well, the police will be here soon and I expect they'll want a quick word, if you could just wait here. It's only a matter of procedure, don't worry."

"Is he dead?"

She nodded.

"I'm afraid so."

She briefly rested a hand on Mattie's shoulder before returning to the man's body.

"Why did you say that, about asking the time? They were going to…."

Mattie held a finger to her lips, stopping Lucy before she could complete the sentence.

"It doesn't matter now, does it? Whatever was going to happen, it doesn't matter."

Lucy looked as if she felt it did but, as the police car drew up behind the ambulance, decided to back off, for now. The policewoman spent a short time talking to the paramedics and then to the young man who, every few seconds, looked over to Mattie and Lucy.

"He's worried about what we're going to tell her."

Lucy wanted to say something along the lines of 'he bloody well should be' but again resisted, for Mattie. Moments later the policewoman joined them.

"This must have been very distressing for you both, and I won't keep you long."

She spoke quietly, her voice calm and reassuring.

"May I take your names?"

"Lucy Foster."

"Mattie Hayes."

There then followed a short conversation in which she took further details and confirmed their version of events.

"So, I'm told that the two gentlemen stopped to ask you the time, is that correct?"

Mattie avoided looking in Lucy's direction as she nodded.

"The paramedics believe that the gentleman suffered a massive heart attack. They tell me there was nothing anyone could have done."

The policewoman again offered her reassurance and said they would be in touch should they need anything further. They turned and walked away, both wanting to put as much distance between them and the flashing blue lights as they could. Lucy threw a glance over her shoulder before she spoke.

"Why? Can you tell me now?"

Mattie stopped and took Lucy by the hand.

"Did you see his face, the other guy? The last thing he needed right then was some kind of harassment allegation."

"What he needed…!"

She could see Lucy fighting hard against her rising anger. Mattie squeezed her hand tighter.

"....they shouldn't get away with it. There's no excuse, Matts."

"Nothing actually happened though, did it?"

Lucy took a deep breath.

"But it would have! It was pure luck...."

"Luck?! That man died, Lucy! He died in front of us!"

Mattie seemed on the verge of tears. Lucy put her arms around her, holding her and saying nothing. She wasn't sorry for her words or the sentiment behind them, but she did bitterly regret having upset the person who meant more to her than anyone.

Chapter 10

"Thanks."

Lucy took the mug of coffee as Mattie sat down on the sofa next to her.

"You can tell me whenever you want, you know that don't you? Because what happened tonight, how you reacted, it wasn't just about what those men said to us was it?"

Lucy remained silent, and that silence told Mattie more than anything her friend could have said at that moment.

"I'm sorry Matts."

"You don't need to say that. You don't ever need to say that to me."

"I really do. After tonight you must think I have no heart at all, but there's stuff you don't know. Stuff that makes me...."

She struggled for the right word.

"Angry?" Mattie offered.

"Yes. It's not who I am."

"I know that."

Lucy smiled a humourless, sad smile.

"But I still hate him. Him, and his friend. I'm trying not to, I'm trying to think the right things, say the right things. But I can't. I can't. I'm glad he's dead."

Mattie knew then that she had to help her. Perhaps she should have tried harder, sooner. But, at the time, she had thought it best to allow Lucy the freedom she felt she needed. Maybe that had been a mistake.

"I've checked the movie channels. Couldn't see anything I wanted to watch. So let's just talk, shall we?"

"It's late."

"We can do 'late' though, can't we? You and me?"

Lucy finished her coffee and placed the empty mug on the table.

"It won't change anything. Whether I tell you or not, nothing will change."

"One thing *will* change. You'll have shared whatever it is that's upsetting you so very much. You don't believe I can help and maybe I can't, but I can listen."

Lucy, right then, didn't seem able to respond to that.

"Where did you learn all that lifesaving stuff you tried?"

Ok, that's fine, they could talk about that.

"Mum had proper first aid training when she was younger. She taught me the basics. I managed to remember some of it. Wasn't enough to save him though, was it?"

"But you heard what they said, there was nothing that could've been done."

"No, I know."

Another short silence before

"I've made an error of judgement, Matts. I thought I was playing a game I could control."

She took another moment before continuing.

"I loved my work, I really did. Getting that job was just the best thing ever. All that hard work at uni was now showing in my bank balance. I had my own office, a shared secretary, a decent salary and a good company car. Not bad for a girl from a care home."

Mattie knew that Lucy had spent some of her younger days in care but it was a subject she had never spoken of in any detail, and Mattie had never felt she had the right to ask. However, she had often wondered if the toughness Lucy had shown both at school and since owed something to that part of her life and, the fact that she had chosen to mention it now, gave Mattie even more cause for concern.

"I could do the work they gave me with my eyes closed. Anyway, I put the hours in, took the money, drove the car and life was good."

"So what changed?"

Lucy gave a quiet laugh.

"Just about everything. One morning, shortly after I arrived in my office, I was given a message that I was required in one of the top floor boardrooms. The last time I'd been up there was the day I was offered the job."

"Were you worried?"

"God, yes. As I waited for the lift I was trying to think what I might have done wrong, and I couldn't come up with anything. Maybe they'd realised they'd made an error when they employed me, mistaken me for someone else or something. Just about every doomsday scenario ran through my mind before I was shown into the boardroom by a rather stony faced young woman...."

"Miss Foster! Thank you for coming up so promptly. I do place such a high value on punctuality."

Lucy took a few steps into the room. To her right, one whole wall was comprised of tinted, toughened glass from floor to ceiling. Beyond it, the London skyline looked grey and uninviting under the low cloud that had closed in overnight. If she had been shocked to see who was sitting behind the large oak desk, she made an excellent job of hiding it.

"Do take a seat, please."

The company's CEO, a middle aged man, high flyer, typical of the type, pointed to a large, padded leather chair in front of his desk. Lucy did as she was asked, settling back into the chair. As the seconds passed, so she began to relax, coming to the slow realisation that the atmosphere was definitely not that of an imminent dismissal.

The man turned to his laptop and began to type. He read from the screen as Lucy waited patiently, unsure whether she should look at him or out at the overcast scene beyond the window. She decided instead to focus her attention on the painting that hung on the wall behind him. It was an abstract, a series of circles and lines, all in various shades of red. Probably worth tens of thousands she considered as she continued to wait. Finally, he looked up from the screen.

"Sorry about that. Just checking one or two facts. I see from your profile you enjoy the finer things that life has to offer. A fair proportion of your salary goes on designer labels, good restaurants and the like. You're quite the 'material girl', it seems. Now, Miss Foster, I expect you're wondering what you're doing here."

"The thought had crossed my mind" she said, now fully on the defensive. How the hell did *he* know where she spent her money?

"Firstly, this meeting will only continue on the understanding that nothing I say will leave this room. Do you understand, Miss Foster?"

She nodded.

"I would like to *hear* you confirm your silence."

"Yes, I understand."

He gave her a warm, benevolent smile as Lucy began to wonder exactly where this was going.

"We recently had a visit from one of our wealthiest competitors. Although visiting under the pretence of sharing operational practices, I believe he was weighing up the possibility of a takeover. Whilst here we gave him a short tour of our offices. That was when he first saw you. He asked me who you were. I have to be honest, Miss Foster, I had no idea and had to make some hurried phone calls and do some enquiring."

He said it almost as if she owed him an apology for that.

"Anyway, I was soon able to inform him and he expressed a desire to meet you. That was when an idea occurred to me. I've arranged that you'll meet him this lunchtime at the Savoy Grill. Ensure you make an impression, get close to him, gain his trust, listen to his conversations, note anything of significance that might give our company an advantage in future dealings, especially any likelihood of a takeover bid. You have a head start because he's already shown an interest in you. His attraction to you is an opportunity we can't afford to let slip through our grasp. As soon as you commence your new 'duties' I'll personally increase your salary so you may indulge yourself even further at all those boutiques and restaurants. But make no mistake, Miss Foster, if you talk to anyone but me about this, you'll never find employment in the City again."

Lucy stayed in her seat although it was clear that, as far as he was concerned, the meeting was over and she was expected to leave.

"May I just get straight what you've just said?"

He had already returned his attention to his laptop and looked up with no small degree of irritation.

"I thought I'd made myself perfectly clear."

Lucy wasn't about to be brushed off like some insignificant little minion, CEO or no CEO.

"I'm being ordered to go and have lunch with a man I've never met, who is not requiring the pleasure of my company because of my stunning intellect. You want me to spy on him and report back to you. If I don't then, professionally, I'm dead. I'm guessing you expect me...."

"To be nice to him" the CEO offered, hoping to avoid Lucy's choice of a more forthright description.

"....to fuck him."

Forthright description not avoided, but he was still hoping that he'd read her right. Lucy allowed some seconds of silence to pass, wanting him to begin to worry as to which way this was going to go. In all probability he wasn't used to dealing with someone who would challenge and question. How badly had he misread her?

"I won't do it."

It was clear from the look on the CEO's face that those were words he wasn't used to hearing. But he prided himself on being able to read people. Body language, expression, eyes, and all his instincts were telling him that this wasn't over.

"Miss Foster, do not underestimate me. I am offering you what you crave most. Money. More money than you've ever seen in your life. And what do I expect in return? For you merely to listen, observe, ask some questions and report back to me. And don't tell me that the sex is an issue. My reports on you suggest you aren't a stranger to one night stands and your choice of partners seems comprised...."

He glanced back at his laptop.

"....of both male and female."

He saw a flash of anger in her eyes. Good. At least he still had her attention.

"Do you have such detail on all of your employees?"

He smiled.

"Information is power. That's why you're going to help me to get more of it."

He fixed her gaze, daring her to refuse again. Some seconds passed.

"Ok. I'll do it if you can tick every box on my fairly short and modest wish list."

"Go on."

"Two hundred per cent salary increase, one of those nice apartments in Mayfair your company owns, and the Ford will turn into a Porsche."

"Now, listen…."

But Lucy felt she'd done enough listening.

"The extra you'll have to pay me will be a drop in the ocean compared to any potential financial advantage my cooperation will bring. True or false?"

Minutes after Lucy had left the boardroom, the CEO remained staring at the door, slowly replaying over and again in his mind, his first encounter with Lucy Foster.

Chapter 11

"I know what you're thinking, Matts. How could I have agreed to it?"

Mattie had listened intently while Lucy had been telling her story.

"You seemed happy with the situation. What's changed?"

Asking that helped her to sidestep Lucy's question, as she had no intention of passing any kind of judgement on her friend's decisions.

"What's changed? I've changed. Everything's changed."

"Tell me" Mattie almost whispered.

Lucy took a moment.

"It moved on. What I thought of as some kind of game became something else. I agreed to the Competitor and I was his part time mistress for a while. He got what he wanted and I got to hear stuff, sensitive financial information, pillow talk, overheard telephone conversations, that I'd pass back to the CEO. Anyway, he wasn't unattractive and my bank balance was becoming a thing of beauty. When the CEO had got everything he needed from him, he found me new 'targets', for want of a better word. I told you my clients were male and female...."

"This may be a naïve question, but didn't this 'Competitor' ever suspect you? I mean, you were in the pay of one of his rivals."

"No, it's not naïve. It's a fair question, but there were several things that were working in my favour. For one, he made the first move. It wasn't as if I was a plant. He asked for, and wanted, me. Secondly, and you'll just have to believe me on this, when sex is involved any man will generally lose the capacity for any degree of rational thought. All he can think about is the next screw. And, of course, I knew exactly how to exploit that. Couple that with the fact that he'd want to keep his relationship with me as quiet as possible, and my pure brilliance in handling the situation, and I was never in any danger of being found out."

Lucy sounded very proud of her achievement, and Mattie, although not wanting to rain on her parade, had to ask.

"He wanted to keep it quiet because....?"

"Oh yes, he's married. Although I don't think his wife would have cared too much if she'd found out. He doesn't know but I understand she's screwing her personal trainer. It's the done thing these days, almost compulsory."

Mattie suddenly felt quite grateful that this wasn't a world she moved in.

"Did anyone else in your company know this was going on? Wasn't there someone you could have spoken to when you decided you wanted out?"

"And say what? I agreed to it in the first place. That's not going to elicit much sympathy. And, no, as far as I'm aware, only the CEO knew. That way there was no chance of someone letting something slip. I was doing good business for the company and was being well paid."

"You said you've changed."

"I don't know what it was. Maybe it was you, Matts."

"Me?"

"I saw the simple beauty of your life. You may not see it. Those living it rarely do. But I woke up one morning, alone in case you were wondering, and knew I wanted out. But it was never going to be that easy, and I don't think I expected it to be."

"What did you do?"

"Went to the CEO. Spoke to him. Told him. He came back with the usual bait that had always kept me onside. Money. When he could see that wasn't going to work anymore...."

"Did he threaten you?"

Mattie moved closer to her, sensing Lucy's growing anxiety.

"Not in so many words, no. But the insinuation was there. He's the head of one of the City's most reputable companies, makes a big thing of its ethics and adherence to the rules. If whispers of what he'd been employing me to do got out, its share price would drop like a stone. Good reputations are difficult to gain, easy to lose. There's a lot at stake, Matts. If I were to talk...."

"You're not going to, are you?"

"What I'm going to do is irrelevant. It's what he *thinks* I might do that matters."

Mattie was liking this less and less.

"Do you think he knows you're here?"

Lucy shook her head.

"Doubtful. I've never talked about you, and he'd have no reason to have me followed, but I can't say absolutely. Also, I don't think he'd risk involving others for the reasons I've mentioned."

"Then just lie low here. After a while he'll realise you're not going to blow the whistle."

Lucy smiled as she put an arm around Mattie.

"Sounds like a plan, if that's ok with you."

"Of course it is."

"Thank you….and now can we check out the movie channels again?"

In fact, Lucy, with her uncanny instinct for tracking down great horror films (all thoughts of a rom com long forgotten), had found Pascal Laugier's 'Incident in a Ghostland'. Although not Mattie's thing at all, she had to admit that the two female leads, Crystal Reed and Anastasia Phillips, were frighteningly convincing. However, as she lay in bed, Mattie once again questioned the wisdom of watching a scary film just before you want to have a calm night's sleep. It was as she tried to turn her thoughts in other directions that she suddenly remembered something about a flower. She recalled its colours. Pink and gold. Hadn't she found it on her bed that morning? Mattie flicked on her lamp so she could check the bedside table. She was sure now she'd left it there, and yet she couldn't see it. Maybe it had fallen on the floor. She'd look in the morning.

Mattie closed her eyes, wanting sleep to come, but she couldn't stop thinking about Lucy. An impartial observer might say her friend was the architect of her own misery, that she should have straightaway refused point blank to cooperate with the CEO. But it was clear he'd been clever. He'd seen a weakness in Lucy and seized a chance to exploit it. Mattie had never met the man, but how she hated him.

Five more horses had joined the two by the river. This time there was no reaction at all as Mattie approached them, the small herd seeming to accept her presence as if she belonged and they knew her. She reached out and touched the nearest horse, running her hand down its back as it grazed. Walking among them she somehow felt safe and protected. One of the younger ones began to nuzzle her, pushing its muzzle against her hand, demanding her attention. As she put both arms around its neck she closed her eyes, concentrating on the sounds that surrounded her. She could hear the young horse breathing, the sound of the river as it flowed over and around the small rocks, and the breeze as it gently blew through the long grass.

The evening was coming, the sun now low, just dipping below the tops of the taller trees as it began to set. She walked up through the meadow, towards the edge of the wood. She stopped once to look back to the horses and the river. She didn't want to leave them but she felt drawn to the trees and whatever lay in the wood beyond. Mattie glanced down at her bare feet and saw, growing taller than the lush grass, the small, bright pink flower. She knelt to look into its golden heart and became lost in its beauty.

It might have been minutes that passed before she stood up and continued on her way, into the wood's cool shadows. The moss-covered ground was damp and soft, and like walking on a plush, deep carpet. Shafts of sunlight shone through the almost unbroken canopy of leaves, creating sporadic patches of light that served to illuminate her path. Mattie reached out and pushed aside some low branches, forcing her way through the dense undergrowth that had briefly hindered her progress. But, as she moved on, so the way ahead opened out into a wider path of moss and grass. Ahead, she could see a clearing that was bathed in the evening sun. The sight of the glade, like a beacon in the shadows, stopped Mattie in her tracks. She stood, momentarily hypnotised by the scene. Did she know this place? Did she belong here? It was a question that had been running over and again in the back of her mind. She was sure she did, and yet....

But this wasn't somewhere to be questioned, it was somewhere to be accepted and embraced. She was wanted here, and that was a wonderful feeling. She began to walk forward towards the clearing and, as she got closer, the walk turned into a jog and then a run. It was calling to her, wanting her. There was no darkness for her in this place, no demons to fight. There was only freedom.

She slowed as she reached the glade, stopping in the centre of it. She turned full circle, taking in the sights and sounds. Everywhere there was life, lush, green and beautiful. In one of the trees, away to her left, a red squirrel ran along one of the higher branches before making its way down the trunk and disappearing into undergrowth. And there was still the birdsong, showing no sign of abating with the setting sun.

Mattie looked across to the farthest side of the clearing and saw the cottage, where she knew it would be. It was partially covered by a large climbing rose bush that had made its way up the front of the small building and onto the neatly thatched roof. The whole scene was saved from chocolate box perfection, however, by the peeling paint on the front door and the weather worn, stone walls that had clearly seen much better days. The garden that ran all the way around the cottage had an uncared-for charm, and looked as though nature was slowly reclaiming it.

Mattie made her way towards the door, pausing to look through the window next to it. There was no light coming from inside and she couldn't see anything except her own reflection. She now stood within reach of the door and, with only a moment's hesitation, she gave it a gentle knock. She waited but there was no sound from within. She knocked again, and this time the door swung in just an inch or so. She pushed it fully open.

"Hello?"

No reply. She stepped into the small living room and looked around her. There was little in the way of furnishings but it was clean and obviously loved. There was a table in one corner, and next to it a simple wooden chair. Opposite these was another, much smaller table with a vase of freshly cut flowers resting upon it, a rocking chair and a cupboard. The curtains at the window were made of white lace and pulled back as far as they would go.

"Hello?"

Mattie called out again as she walked over to the door near the rocking chair. It was already open and led from the living room through into a short passageway. Halfway along it was another window that provided enough light for her to see that there was a doorway at the end. Moments later and she was standing in an equally sparse bedroom. The bed, set against the far wall, was the size of a small double. Its construction owed more to practicality than elegance, and it was covered by several blankets. The top cover was embroidered with floral patterns and, on closer inspection, Mattie could see that it was in fact a very beautiful, intricate, skilled piece of work.

"I made that. Do you like it?"

Mattie spun round and saw the silhouette of a young woman in the doorway. She could tell little except that she wasn't much above five feet tall and slight of build. It was when she stepped forward into the room that she could see that she was wearing a simple, plain cotton dress. The sight of it prompted Mattie to glance down at her own clothes, something she hadn't given a thought to before, and she saw that she was wearing a similar garment, but that came as no surprise to her.

"I like it very much. You're very clever."

The girl smiled. It was a smile that seemed to brighten the room, and Mattie could see her features now. She had the kindest face Mattie thought she had ever seen. She guessed her age to be somewhere in the late teens, although her eyes spoke of a wisdom and experience beyond those years. Her jet black hair was shoulder length and shimmered where it caught the light.

"My mother taught me. She made some beautiful things."

There was an edge of sadness to her words.

"She taught you well. I'm Mattie."

"Yes. I know. Just as you know that I'm Sarah."

She walked forward and put her arms around Mattie, who responded by slowly bringing her own arms up to embrace her.

"Sarah, I…."

She put a finger up to Mattie's lips.

"Come with me."

Sarah took her by the hand and led her back along the passageway to the living room. She sat down on the floor and looked up at Mattie apologetically.

"It's either the rocking one or the uncomfortable one."

She indicated to the two chairs, smiling. Mattie considered the choice before deciding to join Sarah on the floor, folding her legs under her.

"I hoped you would come to me. I've wanted you to come for so long, but I knew I would have to wait."

"How long have you waited?"

She looked into her eyes and saw the answer.

"Now you're here it seems like no time at all."

Mattie allowed the lie to pass.

"But I have to know, Sarah. Why me?"

The young woman looked away, just for a moment, before turning back to her.

"Search your heart, Mattie. Your answer is there."

Outside, the setting sun disappeared below the horizon.

Chapter 12

The insistent 'beep beep' of her alarm clock dragged Mattie into consciousness. She reached out to silence the clock and slowly sat up. As she climbed from her bed images began to flash through her mind. Images of a place, and a young woman called….she tried to pull the name from her memory, but already everything was fading, and the more Mattie tried to grasp at the memories the further they moved away until, in just seconds, they had gone.

After her shower, she quickly dressed and made her way to the kitchen where Lucy was already standing over the hob giving some scrambled eggs her undivided attention.

"Thought we'd push the boat out this morning. Eggs ok?"

Mattie nodded as she sat down at the table.

"Perfect. Any reason for the MasterChef breakfast?"

Lucy removed two slices of toast from the grill and put them on plates before dividing the scrambled egg between them. As a final touch she tore several leaves of parsley from the small, fresh herb plants that grew in their pots on the windowsill, placing them with some ceremony on top of the eggs.

"Voila! Enjoy! And, no, no particular reason, just thought it was my turn to do breakfast. Sleep well?"

Mattie had to think about that for a moment.

"I believe so. You?"

"All things considered, yes, actually I did. You were right, Matts. I think our chat last night helped."

"Good, however, do I sense a 'but'?"

Lucy thought she'd hidden the 'but'. She should have known that her closest friend would see straight through to any undertone, however subtle.

"I've been thinking about what I said, about the CEO and whether he'd come looking for me. I'd rather not be wondering all the time if he was going to turn up, put pressure on, try to force me back."

Mattie put her toast down, sensing she needed to give Lucy her undivided attention.

"So what have you been thinking?"

"That I might go back and try to clear the air. Draw a line under it all, convince him he has nothing to fear from me."

"Well, you know him better than I do."

Mattie couldn't disguise her scepticism.

"It's just, I'm not sure I can cope with not knowing. I think I'd rather face it head on."

"Let me come with you!"

By the look on Mattie's face she clearly thought this was one of the most brilliant ideas she'd ever had. By the look on Lucy's face she clearly thought that it was the worst idea her friend had ever had.

"No. No way. I'm not dragging you into this. Believe me, Matts, you don't belong in that world. But I appreciate you wanting to help me, I really do."

"I don't think you should go."

Mattie had no intention of being anything but truthful, even at the risk of upsetting her.

"And I appreciate your concern. I really do. Hey, let's finish our breakfast shall we? I'm having some orange juice, would you like some, or a coffee maybe?"

And so conversation turned to safer ground. Lucy was keen to tell her about her ideas for the shop's website and, although Mattie couldn't pretend to understand all the finer details, it all sounded good. They agreed that Lucy would work her website magic at the shop, probably in between demonstrating her outstanding ability to sell anything to anyone. But Mattie was more than happy to encourage Lucy's involvement because she hoped that the shop might prove a distraction from thoughts of returning to the City.

After breakfast Lucy returned to her room to put the finishing touches to her already immaculate appearance, while Mattie cleared the table before going to her bedroom. It was while she was giving her hair a final brush that she suddenly remembered that she had meant to look for something. Last night, just before she had fallen asleep. What was it? The flower! She had seen it yesterday, hadn't she? Mattie knelt down to look under the bed and table, but there was no sign of it. Had she imagined it? She thought not, but then again....

She stood, took a quick mirror check and left to join Lucy who was ready and waiting by the front door, the Ray Bans, once more, perfectly positioned on the top of her head. Even her new department store clothes seemed to take on a designer air when Lucy wore them.

"Good to go?"

Mattie nodded as Lucy opened the front door, holding up her car key in front of her.

"Shall we take the Porsche today?"

"You've still got it?!"

Mattie's eyes were wide with disbelief. Lucy merely shrugged.

"Of course. How do you think I got down here?"

"But you can't keep the car if you want out. He'll demand it back, won't he? I mean, how much is it worth?"

"Oh, about fifty k, I think. Maybe a bit more. Let's go."

Lucy was already on her way to the lift leaving Mattie quite unsure how to solve a problem like Lucy Foster.

Mattie placed the last bracelet onto its display before walking outside to give the window display a final check. Happy with the result, she made her way through to the back room where Lucy was sitting in front of the laptop, her face a picture of concentration.

"How's it going?"

Lucy, without lifting her eyes from the screen, gave her a thumbs up.

"I think we should put a photo of you on the home page, Matts. Makes it a bit more personal if people can put a face to the name."

Mattie didn't feel overly enthusiastic with that idea but she could see the business sense in it.

"Don't know if I've got one I'd be happy with."

Lucy looked up as she considered this for a moment.

"We'll take one now! Come on!"

She picked up her phone and grabbed Mattie by the hand, pulling her out through the shop and into the street.

"Stand there, in front of the shop, that's it….and *try* to look as though having your photo taken wasn't the very worst thing in the world!"

About ten shots later and Lucy seemed happy that she had at least one that she might be able to use. They returned inside and Lucy went straight back to the laptop, eager to continue with her redesign of the 'Time to Sparkle!' website. Mattie, meanwhile, busied herself with ensuring the shop's interior was ready for any customers that might grace them with their company. She picked up a duster from a shelf behind her desk and proceeded to give every glass cabinet a quick wipe, although each was spotless before it received her attention. It was as Mattie finished the last one that she heard the shop door give its familiar ring as someone entered. She turned in time to see the policewoman walk in and close the door behind her. Mattie recognised her as the same officer who had spoken to her and Lucy the previous night, after the death of the man from the wine bar.

"Good morning."

"Morning Miss Hayes."

Her gaze shifted to over Mattie's left shoulder as Lucy appeared from the back room.

"Miss Foster."

"Hi."

Lucy gave her one of her winning smiles as she joined Mattie, standing by her side.

"How can we help you?" Mattie enquired with slight trepidation.

The policewoman tried to match Lucy in the 'winning smile' department, and almost succeeded.

"I just wanted to check up on you both before I go off duty. Last night must have been quite traumatic for you."

Mattie had wondered if they were to be asked again about why the men had approached them. The 'asking the time' response she had hurriedly given, she had hoped, might fit in with any CCTV that may or may not exist. It couldn't be denied that the men had spoken to them, but it was improbable it could be ascertained exactly what had been said, and the other man was unlikely to tell anyone. Lucy would have had no qualms about giving a verbatim account but to Mattie it hadn't, and still didn't, seem the right thing to do. After all, there was no argument for protecting other women. The man was dead, and Mattie felt sure that his friend was shaken to such an extent that he would be unlikely to repeat the performance anytime soon.

Except, of course, looking back on it and for all that she had said at the time, Mattie now knew that her motive for lying owed little to any sympathy she might have had for either man, and almost everything to her desire to take the shortest route to getting them both away from that situation as quickly as possible. Make the interaction between them seem as innocuous as possible, make it sound like something and nothing. Just draw the line and get out. Had Lucy realised that? Perhaps, after her initial anger and confusion, her understanding of Mattie had told her. And, if she were honest, Mattie now felt a little ashamed of herself for unconsciously hiding behind a false altruism.

"That's very kind, thank you."

"Yes, absolutely" Lucy added and offered another of her brightest smiles.

"And I just wanted to confirm what I told you last night. There was nothing anyone could have done. The medics have confirmed a massive and inevitably fatal heart attack."

"I'm sorry. Did he have a family?" Mattie asked as Lucy thought to herself 'I couldn't care less'.

"I'm afraid I don't have that information. All that's being dealt with by my colleague. I just wanted to check that you were both ok and that you didn't have anything more to add to what you told me last night."

Mattie and Lucy exchanged glances before both shaking their heads, Mattie a little more enthusiastically than Lucy.

"That's fine. I'll be on my way then. I'm Constable Traynor, by the way…."

She turned to Lucy.

"….Vicky Traynor. You can contact me at the local station should you need to. Goodbye Miss Hayes, Lucy."

Mattie opened the door for her and waited until she'd climbed into her police car and driven away before closing it.

"How come I get 'Miss Hayes' and you get 'Lucy'? I think she likes you."

Lucy shrugged.

"Everyone likes me, Matts. You should know that by now."

"No. I mean *'likes'* you."

She punctuated that with a raised eyebrow that the late Sir Roger Moore would have been proud of, and waited for the penny to drop. It only took a moment.

"Shut up! She does not!......Does she?"

Mattie seemed to be enjoying this.

"You did say you had male *and* female clients, didn't you?"

"But that was business."

"So?"

Lucy had no intention of providing Mattie with any further entertainment.

"I'll be out the back working on your site if you need me."

"What if Vicky needs you?"

"The second word's 'off'!" Lucy called over her shoulder, smiling as she returned to the laptop, leaving Mattie in the shop. She sat down beside one of the display cabinets, knowing that the day ahead was quite likely to be what might be termed as 'slow'. As soon as Lucy had finished with her site revamp she'd check her online orders, of which there were usually a healthy number. But as she sat, in the peace and quiet, before the town's shoppers got their act together, her thoughts began to drift, and Mattie let them drift, relinquishing any control she might have had over them.

She closed her eyes and she could see a beautiful place. And someone was there, waiting for her. A young woman, but she couldn't recall her face, and the more she tried the more the distance between them seemed to grow. She knew her name. She had told her, hadn't she? Perhaps if she concentrated. The image of a flower filled her imagination and she felt the warm breeze and heard the river. But *she* wasn't there. Where was she? Why didn't she want to be found? Her name. She knew her name, and if only she could remember it....

"Good morning."

Mattie's eyes flicked open and she quickly jumped to her feet as the well-dressed woman entered.

"Good morning."

She was welcomed with a warm smile.

"How may I help you?"

The woman looked around her and finally to the door behind Mattie.

"Is that delightful young lady I saw yesterday here? She sold me the most beautiful gold ring and suggested that I call back, when I had time, to discuss a matching necklace."

Should Mattie have felt the slightest irritation that Lucy now seemed to be the star of her show? Maybe she should but, actually, she thought quite the opposite. It was now coming as almost a relief to her that she was being given the chance to take a backseat.

"That would be Lucy. I'll fetch her."

Mattie walked through to the back office.

"You're on, Miss Foster."

Lucy looked up with a puzzled expression.

"The lady who bought the gold ring?"

"Oh. She's come back, has she? I didn't think she would."

Mattie wasn't completely sure she believed that, but what she believed was irrelevant. Lucy's presence was the best thing to have happened to her business since it opened and Mattie wondered, as she sat down in the chair that Lucy had just vacated, whether her wish that Lucy remain with her wasn't an entirely unselfish one.

Chapter 13

"Girls' night in?"

Lucy dropped down onto the sofa and kicked off her shoes.

"If you can cope with something simple like a salad. I haven't prepared anything" Mattie called through from the kitchen.

"Sounds perfect. I'll come and give you hand if you like."

"No. You're fine and anyway, I owe you."

This prompted Lucy to push herself up from the comfort of the sofa and walk through to join her.

"And why do you owe me?"

"Because...."

Mattie had her head in the fridge, gathering together whatever ingredients might go into the aforementioned salad.

"....at this rate my shop takings for this week alone will outstrip my opening month, which was pretty damn good. Do you realise...."

She turned, kicking the fridge door shut as she did so.

"....we're close to equalling the week's online sales? And that's never happened."

Lucy took a seat as she watched Mattie deposit various salad vegetables onto the kitchen table.

"It's your stock, Matts. People know quality when they see it. I just nudge them in the right direction, that's all."

"Don't be so modest."

"Me? Modest?"

Mattie smiled.

"Difficult to believe, I know."

She returned to the fridge and proceeded to instigate a detailed search, the result of which was....

"Not many options, I'm afraid. I'll drop into the supermarket tomorrow. But the smoked salmon does need finishing up."

"Sounds good. And we do have a bottle of that rather nice white."

Lucy walked over and took the Riesling from the shelf inside the fridge door.

"We're sorted then."

Mattie returned to the table to prepare the salad while Lucy concentrated all her efforts on finding wine glasses and a corkscrew.

"So, are you going to return the car?"

Mattie asked as she sliced some celery sticks.

"The Porsche? Thought you didn't want me to go back."

"That was before I knew you had something worth fifty thousand that, since you say you've resigned, strictly speaking, you shouldn't keep."

Lucy thought about that for a moment.

"But it could be argued that I've probably made the company enough money to pay for it a hundred times over and then some."

Wine glasses and corkscrew duly tracked down, Lucy returned to Mattie's side and was handed a small knife, a chopping board and several tomatoes.

"Yes, that could be argued...."

Although Mattie sounded that she, personally, wouldn't.

"....but, even if we gloss over the ethics, or lack of them...."

A sideways glance in Lucy's direction.

"....I still don't think you should keep the car."

Lucy continued dutifully slicing the tomatoes as she considered how she should respond, saying nothing until the last tomato had received her attention.

"Ok. Fine. I'll take it back. It's only metal and rubber after all."

That was much too easy and it took Mattie only a moment to see why.

"You look after the shop tomorrow, and I'll drive it back. I can get the train home. Would there be somewhere I could leave it without having to speak to anyone?"

Mattie wanted to do everything she could to discourage Lucy from returning to her employer. She hadn't said as much to her, but she had her own concerns about her friend's safety. She had never met this CEO, and didn't want to, but she knew enough to understand that these kind of people had the propensity for varying degrees of ruthlessness. Perhaps she was being overly dramatic, maybe seen too many TV dramas. And yet, she had a feeling, which had to be the most stupid thing ever. There was absolutely no reason at all to be overly concerned for Lucy's welfare. The CEO wouldn't be happy to lose such a profitable asset but, given the potential fallout, he'd more than likely want to brush it all quietly under the carpet. But how would he do that?

"I told you, Matts. It's not a place for you. It's my problem and I have to sort it."

But Mattie had no intention of giving up.

"Let me do this one thing for you, Lucy. I don't even have to see anyone. I can leave the car and make a phone call to say it's there."

"But that'll only be part of it. It won't draw the line."

"You said you spoke to him about ending it. So he knows your thinking on the matter."

"Knowing my thinking and accepting it are two very different things. I know he won't let it go until I've convinced him I'm serious."

Mattie wondered if it was only her that could see the very real danger of that.

"What if you can't convince him? I still think you should let me take the car while you continue to lie low. Do nothing and let time eventually close the issue."

As soon as she'd said it Mattie knew that 'doing nothing' would never be an option for Lucy and, thinking back to their school days, perhaps she should be grateful for that.

"I'll think about it, Matts. I promise I will."

Maybe that was the best she could have hoped for. In any event, Mattie decided that there was little point in pushing it further for now. She passed Lucy the avocado she'd been holding for no other reason than she disliked preparing them. And so together they organised their evening meal while making inroads into the Riesling, Lucy having decided to pull the cork as soon as she'd tracked down the glasses and corkscrew.

Ten mellow minutes later, and both women were sitting on the sofa with trays on their laps, their wine glasses on the coffee table in front of them. The bottle of Riesling was now little more than a quarter full and Lucy regarded it with some concern.

"Do you have another one of these? If we're staying in we'll need more than this."

Mattie gave her what could only be described as a very smug look.

"It just so happens that when you popped to the loo I raided my secret supply and put another in the fridge."

"I knew there was a reason I was your friend!"

Lucy proceeded to empty what was left in the bottle into their glasses, dividing it equally between them. They ate their meal without too much more conversation apart from the occasional comment about the news which was on in the background.

"Does your mum ever ask how the business is doing?" Lucy asked after she'd eaten the last mouthful of avocado.

"Well, she doesn't demand to see my accounts every week, if that's what you mean. But when we talk she'll sometimes make a polite enquiry. I don't think she cares too much, actually. I mean, she cares that I'm successful and making enough from it, which I clearly am, but as to actual details, I think her attitude is that it's my business to run how I please."

Lucy was quietly impressed by that. Maybe not so controlling after all.

"Good for her. I just wondered, as she bought it for you…."

Mattie shook her head.

"No. She's never played that card, and I don't think she ever will."

"Doubly good for her. See, Matts, even with all your demons, you have a great mum. I envy you that."

Was that an invitation to ask? Did she want to talk about her own parents? Mattie decided to go along with the veiled hint, knowing that if she'd misread the cue Lucy wouldn't hesitate to move the conversation on.

"I'm sorry that was something you never had."

Better than a question, that simple comment opened the door. It was now up to Lucy whether she wished to walk through.

"You don't need to be sorry. It was probably for the best. I grew up and toughened up pretty quickly. Those Year Ten girls weren't dealing with a Year Nine, they were dealing with an adult disguised as a schoolgirl."

Mattie could hear the emotion behind her words. She said nothing but waited for her to continue.

"It's not because I don't trust you, Matts. It's because I know you have enough to deal with in your own life. That's the reason I haven't told you much about my childhood. In some ways I've always thought of it as irrelevant. It's the past. Gone. Of no consequence."

"But that's not true, is it? Not for you."

Mattie said, softly.

"No. It's not true. There's not a day goes by when I don't think about what a normal childhood might have been like."

Mattie edged closer so that she could remove the tray from Lucy's lap. She placed it next to her own on the coffee table before gently putting an arm around her.

"I did have a family. Maybe that makes it worse. It was there, and then it wasn't and I was just about old enough to remember it falling apart around me."

"What happened?" Mattie whispered.

Lucy gave a sad smile that was etched through with heartache.

"I thought they loved each other. Now I'm not sure. But our home did seem a happy place to me."

"Seem?"

"To innocent young eyes, yes. How could a five year old girl know anything of depression? I couldn't see what my father saw every day. I couldn't see the toll my mum's depression was taking on him. It was slowly tearing him apart. Sometime later, when it was felt I was old enough to understand, it was decided I should know the truth, that they should tell me the whole story."

"They?"

"Social services. My social worker. Anyway, I was told how my dad had been unable to cope with my mum's mental state anymore. I can still recall the day he left…."

Mattie waited, not wanting to interrupt Lucy's most private thoughts.

"….he closed the door and walked down the path. I never saw him again."

"Why didn't he take you with him? If your mum was in such a poor state of mind...."

Lucy thought for a moment.

"They told me they believed he may have thought that taking me might have pushed mum over the edge. I don't know. Perhaps he thought the responsibility of a young daughter would be enough to bring my mum back from her dark places. Anyway, he was wrong. Not long after he left she killed herself."

"Oh, Lucy. I don't know what to say."

She rested her head against Lucy's, now bitterly regretting having invited her friend to return to those memories.

"No one needs to say anything. As I said, it's the past. It's gone. Nothing's going to bring her back, so what's the point?"

But it was painfully clear to her that it mattered to Lucy very much, and that her words seemingly making light of the tragedy were nothing more than that. Words to cover something so unbearably sad.

"What about your father? How could he not come back for you?"

Lucy picked up her glass of wine and took a sip before replacing it.

"I don't think he loved me or mum at all. I believe he took the first opportunity he had to bail out. I think what I've been told about him are just lies. Lies to keep the little girl happy and give everyone a quiet life."

"But you can't *know* that."

"Maybe, maybe not. Maybe it's easier to think the worst of him."

And suddenly Mattie understood. The pain that Lucy felt, the pain that she kept hidden, could only be managed if she believed that she had lost nothing when her father had abandoned her.

"I'll help you look for him, Lucy! I think you should try to find him. Find the truth. You never know, maybe it could be a whole new start for you both. But if you're proved to be right, then you're no worse off are you?"

Mattie had expected this to rally her friend, to perhaps bring some hope to what seemed a hopeless situation. What she hadn't expected was to see Lucy's resolve break down into uncontrolled sobbing, and all she could do was hold her for however long it took to regain her composure. When, finally, she was able to speak her voice was quiet and faltering.

"I found him, Matts. Three years ago. I was helped by a lady from Social Services who remembered me. We became quite close during my days in the care system, and she made some enquiries on my behalf. She's retired now so wasn't worried about treading on toes or falling foul of some by-the-book boss. Anyway, it didn't take long. I remember Catherine, the lady, called me and asked if I could come round to her house. She wouldn't tell me anything more on the phone. So I drove over, it wasn't far from where I was staying at the time. As soon as she opened the door I knew. I'd wanted her to give me his home address, phone number, email, something like that. But all she had for me was a copy of his death certificate."

"I'm so sorry."

"He didn't even have the decency to wait for me."

"How did he die?"

Lucy smiled weakly, the tears still filling her eyes.

"Cancer. His illness didn't last long, apparently. So there you go, Matts. I can think what I like about him, because there's no one who can tell me I'm wrong."

Mattie gave her one last squeeze before releasing her embrace.

"I can only try to imagine what it took to say what you've just said. I'm so grateful you chose to share it with me."

"I've got no one else, Matts. No one who would listen and understand, or care."

"Then would you permit me to offer an opinion? You can take it or leave it."

Lucy shrugged, which Mattie took as 'go ahead'.

"As you'll never know about your father, one way or the other, why not allow that possibly, just possibly, he may have loved you more than you could imagine. I think he did, and there's no one who can tell me *I'm* wrong. Now I'm going to get that other bottle of wine."

And before Lucy could reply, Mattie had disappeared into the kitchen.

Chapter 14

As Mattie lay in bed, some hours later, she could think of nothing but Lucy. Had it been worth it? It was generally accepted that a problem shared was a problem halved. Perhaps, she thought, that had now been well and truly disproved. How she wished that Lucy might be lying in her own bed and feeling some kind of release from her pain. But she doubted it. Like the shadows that continually haunted her, Mattie knew that Lucy's shadows, although taking a very different form, would be equally resolute, debilitating and, at times, almost unbearable.

But, at least, Mattie now felt she had some understanding of what had shaped Lucy, both when she first knew her as that feisty, confident Year Nine girl and now, as a woman who would go for something she wanted, no matter what the price or consequence. Except that Lucy no longer wanted that 'something'. It was with a growing anxiety about her friend, that Mattie eventually fell asleep.

Outside the cottage darkness had descended, and from somewhere in the heart of the wood the call of an owl reached out into the night. The full moon, that had been bright against the stars, was briefly covered by a small cloud, its edges now a bright silver against the deep black.

Inside, in the candlelight, Sarah stood and walked over to the cupboard. She knelt and opened one of its doors, removing two woollen shawls from a shelf before closing the door again. She draped one around her own shoulders and handed the other to Mattie.

"It can get a little chilly in here at night. I can fetch some wood from outside if you'd like me to light the fire."

Mattie gratefully took the brightly patterned shawl, immediately feeling its warmth envelope her. She had begun to feel the cold but hadn't wanted to say anything.

"No, no need for a fire, the shawl is perfect, thank you. Did you make these too?"

Sarah nodded.

"I enjoy creating beautiful things. I can teach you if you'd like."

Mattie smiled.

"Yes. I would like that. I'm afraid I'm hopeless at anything practical though. I may not be a very good pupil."

Sarah sat down next to her.

"And I may not be a very good teacher! We'll have to see, won't we?"

Her soft, gentle laughter filled the room.

"I've never known such peace, Sarah. I've never known a place like this. Am I truly safe here?"

"You're quite safe. The things that scare you, that darken your life in that other place, they can't touch you here. I won't let them. This is as much your sanctuary as it is mine, Mattie."

Sarah reached out and rested her hand on Mattie's, and for the first time Mattie felt the warmth of her, and how real and alive she was.

"I've never been free before. There's never been anywhere for me to go. I can't tell you how thankful I am…."

Sarah lifted her hand and, gently holding it under Mattie's chin, she slowly turned her head so that their eyes met. Mattie felt her reach into her soul and time seemed to stand still.

"I can sense your shadows, Mattie. I understand their power. But you must not allow them to define you. I will seek to protect you, everywhere and always."

Mattie turned to the window as the cloud drifted away and the wood was, once again, bathed in moonlight.

"You told me I should search my own heart, that I would find my answer there. But all I find is confusion. You give me a world where I can be safe, a haven that I've yearned for all my life, but why do I deserve this? Why would you do this for me?"

Sarah looked over to one of the candles that was beginning to flicker and die. She returned to the cupboard and found another.

She took it back and, using one of the other candles, lit it. Carefully she removed what was left of the dead candle from its brass holder and replaced it with the new one. When, at last, she had finished she returned to where Mattie was still sitting on the floor.

"There. That's better, isn't it? We can't sit here in darkness, can we?"

"No, I suppose not."

Sarah turned to her.

"You question why you belong here."

"I'm sorry, I don't mean to…."

"Ssh…."

Sarah held a finger to her lips.

"….you must never say sorry to me. But I will never stop saying sorry to you."

Sarah saw Mattie's look of confusion.

"I don't understand."

In response she said nothing but stood once more. As she did she reached out and took Mattie's hand, lifting her to her feet.

"Come with me."

As they passed the candles Sarah picked one up and handed it to Mattie before taking one for herself. Each now holding their own candle, Sarah led her along the passageway, past the bedroom, to the rear of the cottage. She pushed open a door and, the next moment, they were out into the moonlit garden. In fact, it was so light that it rendered the candles almost unnecessary.

"This way."

Sarah beckoned her on and they walked together, through the garden's flowers and dew soaked grass and towards the trees behind the cottage. It was just before they reached the first line of trees that Mattie saw the remains of the small stone chapel. Cautiously they picked their way through some of the larger stones that had fallen from what remained of the front wall.

"Be careful. Some of them have sharp edges."

Sarah lowered her candle so that they might better see their path through to what was left of the inside of the building. Mattie looked down and saw only earth and meadow grass beneath her feet. If it had ever had a proper floor it was long since gone.

"Here we are."

Sarah stopped and rested her candle on one of the larger stones that stood waist high in the middle of the old ruin. Mattie put her candle down next to Sarah's.

"What do you feel here, Mattie?"

She looked around her. The flickering candles were making their shadows dance on the ruined walls. What *did* she feel here? Was there something more, something other than the 'belonging' that she had initially sensed in this place? Surely Sarah wouldn't have brought her here if she didn't think there was.

"I….I'm not sure."

Sarah took her hand.

"I will help you. Close your eyes, and allow your memories to return."

For a moment there was nothing, but then, without warning, her mind was filled with images and her surroundings were transformed. The building was no longer a ruin. The walls were now intact and there was a roof above her. With her eyes still tightly shut, she suddenly became aware that she *did* know this place. She could hear laughter, the laughter of children. They seemed so happy, and their happiness made her smile.

"Keep your eyes closed" Sarah whispered, and Mattie felt her hold tighten around her hand. A warm breeze ruffled her hair and she sensed that she was now outside. It had recently rained and she could smell the grass and trees. In the distance she could hear lambs bleating and above her a crow cawed as it circled, looking for prey. It reminded her of her childhood. Except that it wasn't *her* childhood, was it? These memories didn't belong to her. She opened her eyes and was back in the ruined stone building. It was night once more and everything was as it had been. Except that she was now alone and the candles were gone.

Mattie tried to fight the growing panic that was threatening to overwhelm her. Fortunately, the moonlight was sufficient for her to see her way out of the ruin. Retracing her steps, she fought the desire to run fearing that, in the half-light, she might miss her footing and fall. Even at a slower pace, she hit her knee against part of the wall, crying out in pain as she left the derelict building.

As Mattie approached the cottage she thought she could see, through one of the windows, candles flickering. She pushed at the wooden door and made her way back along the passageway to the living room. As she reached the doorway she saw Sarah, who was now sitting in the rocking chair.

"It was so beautiful. Why did it all disappear?"

She fought hard against the tears that she knew were close to coming. Sarah stood and walked over to her. She put her arms around her and pulled her close. As she held her she spoke softly.

"You opened your eyes. What you saw, what you felt, they exist now only in your imagination and so could no longer be seen when you opened your eyes and returned to this reality."

"Exist now? Do you mean they were once real? The children? The laughter?"

Sarah nodded.

"Yes. Yes, they were once real."

She failed to disguise the sadness in her voice.

"Did you know them, the children?" Mattie asked.

"Oh my love. We both knew them. They were us."

Mattie pushed herself away from Sarah, so that she could look directly into her eyes.

"I don't understand. Were we friends?"

"My dear, darling Mattie. I am your sister."

Chapter 15

Mattie woke with a start and turned over to look at the alarm clock. There was still another twenty five minutes before it was set to go off. She reached out, cancelled the alarm, pushed herself up and pulled her pillow behind her back. She sat upright, allowing herself a few minutes to fully wake up. But it was when she swung her legs around and off the bed, and put her feet down on the carpet, that she felt the pain in her knee. She reached down to rub it. It wasn't too bad and would probably walk off. Strange though, she had no recollection of doing anything the previous day to cause it to hurt. She made her way to the bathroom, aware that as she'd woken up early, there was no need to hurry and she could take her time getting ready for another day.

It was as she stepped into the hot shower that she glanced down and saw the small bruise on her knee. It had almost gone out of her thoughts but, as is always the case, the sight of it suddenly brought the nagging little pain back. After her shower, Mattie rummaged in the medicine cabinet and, after a few seconds of searching, she found the small tube of arnica cream. She put a little on her finger and rubbed it into the bruise, smiling as she recalled how her mum had done this many times when she was a child. When she was a child. There was something in the back of her mind about childhood. No. She couldn't remember. But it was as she began to towel herself dry that the name suddenly came to her.

"Sarah!"

She said it out aloud. But, even as she spoke the name, she struggled to recall where she might have heard it. Where had it come from? As Mattie got dressed she searched her memory for anyone called Sarah. A customer? Further back than that? School maybe? But why should she suddenly remember her now? It was a question she was still thinking about when she walked through to the kitchen. Lucy wasn't there this morning. Mattie smiled. She'd beaten her to it today.

She opened the fridge and took out the jug of milk. If Lucy wanted anything other than cereal she would have more than enough time to sort that out once she made an appearance. Mattie flicked the kettle on and sat down at the table. A short time later, as she sipped her mug of coffee, her thoughts again turned to 'Sarah'. She repeated the name over and again to herself and, as she did, so other images flashed into her head. Each was there for a fleeting moment and then gone, but the feeling that accompanied them was one of an overpowering, devastating love. It was an emotion so powerful that she could think of nothing else until it slowly subsided.

Mattie looked up at the wall clock. Where had the last twenty minutes gone? She had no recollection. She lifted the mug to her lips. Her coffee was all but cold. She put it back on the table and looked over to the door. Still no Lucy. She pushed her chair back and walked along the hallway to Lucy's bedroom. Her door was slightly ajar.

"Lucy?"

There was no reply. Mattie pushed it fully open. There was no sign of her. Her bed was made and the pyjamas she had loaned her were folded neatly on the pillow. On top of those was a piece of paper with a short message written on it. Mattie picked it up and read Lucy's neat, perfectly formed handwriting.

> *Dear Matts. I've gone to hand in my resignation and finish it once and for all. I know you wanted to help but I have to sort this out myself. Oh, and I'm returning the car, you'll be pleased to hear! See you later. Love, Lucy.*

She dropped it back on the bed and ran from her apartment, down the stairwell and around the rear of the block to where she knew Lucy had parked the Porsche the evening before. The parking space was empty. As Mattie returned to the apartment all she could think about were her words of caution when Lucy had previously discussed such a course of action. God, how she hoped she was wrong.

Walking through to the living room, Mattie picked up her phone, selected Lucy from her extremely small list of contacts, and touched the 'call' icon. It went straight to voicemail. She had probably expected it to, but knew she needed to try. And so, there was nothing more she could do but look forward to a day thinking about little else but her friend and willing her to walk back through her door with those ridiculously expensive sunglasses perched on her head and a smile that said 'told you it would be ok'.

Of course, it would be, wouldn't it? Mattie was well aware that her mind was programmed to expect the worst possible outcome from any of life's scenarios. So, maybe, this was yet another in a long line of examples of Mattie worrying for no valid reason. She had lost count of the times she had put herself through hell agonising over things that had never happened, or were ever likely to happen.

Forgetting about her mug of cold coffee and breakfast, she decided she just wanted to get to the shop. Breakfast had always been a meal she could take or leave but had been making the effort for Lucy, who clearly placed some value on it. Except today.

As Mattie made her way to her own car she knew that the best form of defence against the shadows that relentlessly threatened to engulf her was distraction, and the shop would give her that. So would 'Sarah'. But, as she swung her car into its usual space, it was Lucy who was now occupying her thoughts. Sarah, whoever she might be, was slipping into the background, overshadowed by a greater concern.

Mattie wasted no time in switching on her laptop and immersing herself in the business of checking for overnight orders that had come through the website. She smiled as the shop's homepage appeared. Lucy had done an amazing job on something that Mattie hadn't thought could be significantly improved. Note to self, she thought, don't always think that you know best.

Fortunately, it had been another good night for orders, with particular interest shown in a limited edition wristwatch that Mattie had been able to source from Japan. It gave her quiet satisfaction that she'd guessed correctly that it would have sufficient appeal to collectors. She'd managed to obtain three and all three had sold overnight. Also, although not quite as popular, there were several profitable orders from her bespoke jewellery line. Enough to keep her occupied for the best part of the day. Of course, she didn't have her star saleswoman today but, hopefully, she would be busy enough not to have to dwell on that. Mattie had made the decision to have her mobile phone in the top pocket of her jacket. Normally it would have stayed in her desk drawer in the back room but, in the event that Lucy did try to contact her, she didn't want to miss her call.

The day, as it turned out, was busier than expected. There had been a steady flow of customers into the shop, and Mattie was very pleased with herself because she had made a sale, or taken a deposit for an order, from every one of those customers. She couldn't wait to tell Lucy. She *really* couldn't wait to tell Lucy.

After she had locked the door and turned the hanging sign to 'Closed', Mattie removed her phone from her pocket to check it for messages, although she knew there wouldn't be any because she'd checked it just five minutes ago. She tried calling Lucy's number only to hear the voicemail message again. Lucy had gone before she'd got up that morning and she had heard nothing from her all day. As Mattie left the shop she felt her shadows creeping in on her once more. Within these shadows she knew there was lying in wait something that couldn't be wished away, something that had the potential to get through all her defences and all her time-learnt coping strategies. And she felt alone and scared.

Chapter 16

Before she had gone to bed, Lucy had set the alarm on her phone, giving herself at least an hour before she knew Mattie's own alarm would go off. Having carefully laid out her clothes the previous night, she had chosen the designer labels she'd worn on the first evening of her visit. She had also sneaked a chocolate bar from the kitchen. It would have to do as a makeshift breakfast. As quietly as she could she visited the bathroom which, fortunately, was nearer her room than Mattie's. She dressed quickly and straightened her bed, placing the note she'd written on top of her pyjamas. She read it again, recalling how she'd thought long and hard as she had written it. The last thing she wanted was to add to Mattie's worries.

It was probably true to say that Lucy understood her friend better than anyone, better than maybe even Mattie herself. Therefore, she knew that she was condemning her to a day of concern, and perhaps worse, because Mattie's anxieties, of which there were many, could rapidly turn much darker. She just had to hope that she was making the right decision and that the end result would be worth the short term pain, for both of them.

It had taken over an hour for Lucy to fall asleep that night. It had been a difficult decision, and she had seriously considered Mattie's offer to return the car. But that, she had decided, would not have ended matters. She would have always been looking over her shoulder, waiting for the phone call or, much worse, the knock on Mattie's door.

Lucy was also, on reflection, regretting letting her defences down. She had never intended to burden Mattie with the truth about her parents, having taken so much care for so many years to protect her from that. Maybe she shouldn't have worried, maybe she should have given Mattie more credit for being able to deal with it. But then she recalled her reasoning. It had been her mother's depression, the darkness that had eventually destroyed her. She believed she had seen something like it in Mattie or, at least, traces of it, and hadn't wanted to risk being witness to another, similar tragedy.

Was that why Lucy had taken Mattie under her wing? A psychoanalyst would probably say she felt a sense of guilt that she had failed to save her mother even though, as a young child, she could have done nothing to prevent her suicide. But perhaps Lucy desperately needed some kind of atonement, although she would never admit to that even if, deep down, she knew it to be the truth.

As Lucy climbed behind the wheel of the Porsche she pulled the Ray Bans down from their usual resting place on the top of her head. Even though the early morning light and partially cloudy sky didn't require a pair of sunglasses, she felt them absolutely necessary to complete 'the look', which she wanted to perpetuate for just one more day.

Ten minutes later and she was guiding the car down off the slip road and onto the London bound side of the motorway. Seeing the speed camera on its central reservation gantry she pressed down on the accelerator pedal. She smiled to herself as she considered whether any speeding tickets would find their way to her, or have to be settled by the company. However, maybe it wasn't worth taking the chance. She lifted her foot and saw her speed, that had been slowly building, drop away, but it would have been fun to have given the Porsche just one last run off the leash.

As the miles counted down so Lucy's thoughts turned more and more to what might lay ahead. She realised that, until now, she had thought about this day only in the abstract. The idea of walking into that building, laying it on the line and leaving with her head held high, had gone unchallenged in her mind. Why wouldn't it happen just the way she envisaged it? She could now think of a thousand reasons.

Would the CEO agree to see her? Yes, she had decided, that was pretty much a given. He'd want to put further pressure on one of his most valuable assets. What form that pressure might take was something that Lucy, either consciously or unconsciously, had decided not to think about too deeply.

She swung the car into a side street, now just a few blocks from the company's building. A track from the Billie Eilish album 'When We All Fall Asleep, Where Do We Go?' was playing on the radio, and Lucy slowed the Porsche so that she could hear her song, 'All The Good Girls Go To Hell', through to the end before she arrived at the underground car park directly beneath the building. Another assumption she'd made had been that her security pass would still raise the red and white barriers that stretched across the entrance.

The car's bonnet dipped as it hit the ramp, and she entered the brief half-light that lay between the open air and the neon lit car park. She removed the security pass from her jacket's inside pocket, lowered the window and held it in front of the laser scanner just below the barriers. There was the softest whirr and click as the command was given for the barriers to lift.

Lucy pressed down on the accelerator, maybe a little too hard. The tyres squealed on the concrete and the Porsche shot forward between the large square pillars. In seconds she had travelled half the length of the car park but Lucy's reactions were fast. She rapidly slowed her car before guiding it expertly into an empty space. After putting on the handbrake she remained behind the wheel for some minutes, just giving herself time to gather her thoughts. She looked in her rear view mirror as another car, a silver Mercedes, drove past and into a parking space at the end of the row. Lucy waited until the driver, a young man in what looked to her like a Tom Ford suit, had made his way to the lift in the far corner of the car park. When she was as certain as she could be that there was no one else around, Lucy climbed from the Porsche and, turning to lock the car, she walked over to the lift, its indicator showing it was parked at the ground floor. She reached out and pressed the 'Call' button.

It took only seconds for the cabin to arrive. The doors swished open and Lucy stepped inside. She pushed the button marked 'G'. Her gaze fixed on the Porsche as it disappeared from view behind the closing doors and she felt a pang of regret that, in all probability, she would be leaving without it. But Matts, of course, was right. She couldn't keep it. There was no way she could keep it....

She walked into the spacious reception area and looked around her, surrounded once more by the symphony of steel and glass. The company's employees were beginning to drift in from the street, heading for the myriad of identical offices, filled with computer screens and neglected pot plants.

Had she made the right choice coming here? Matts hadn't wanted her to. But there was no backing out now. On the journey up she'd gone through this moment over and again in her mind, trying to decide how she should play it. Be soft and apologetic? Attempt to appeal to his better nature? No. He didn't have one. He would only respect one approach. Forthright. Bordering on the aggressive. Lucy took a deep breath and strode purposefully towards the smartly dressed young lady sitting at the main reception desk who immediately went into regulation welcome mode.

"Good morning. How may I help you?"

"Good morning. My name is...."

"Lucy Foster?"

Lucy spun round to see who had spoken her name. She was confronted by one of the female security guards, who was standing just a little too close for comfort. Her name badge declared her to be Tanya.

"Yes."

She felt the lightest of touches on her arm.

"Would you like to come with me please?"

"I assume your question is rhetorical?" Lucy enquired.

Tanya's response was to gently steer her away from the desk and back towards the lifts. Although she had no intention of arguing with the redoubtable Tanya, Lucy quickly got the impression that, had she shown any form of reluctance to comply, the young security officer had the capacity to become quite persuasive. They reached the furthest of the lifts, which was already at the ground floor, doors open and waiting. Tanya ushered her inside but before Lucy could say anything the doors had closed, leaving her alone and travelling in a fast ascent, up through the centre of the building.

She watched the floor indicator counting up. It continued past the last floor of offices and boardrooms and carried on for another few seconds before slowing and coming to a gentle halt.

The doors opened. Lucy didn't step out immediately, waiting to see if anyone would appear to meet her, but there was no welcoming committee.

As she took a few paces into the room the lift doors swished shut behind her. She now stood in the CEO's private office. There was the designer furniture, impressive desk and comfortable padded leather chairs for visitors although, Lucy noted, the chair behind the desk was unquestionably superior. One main difference though was the massive tinted window, which comprised one whole wall of the room. Whereas in the past she had been able to look out of it, across the City skyline, that was now impossible because it was completely opaque.

"Welcome once more, Miss Foster. I could say I've been expecting you, but I think we want to keep the melodrama to a minimum, don't we? Please take a seat."

The CEO, who had seemed to appear from nowhere, walked over to his chair and sat down.

"I hope I didn't startle you. I have my own private lift to this room."

He indicated over his right shoulder to another set of sliding doors, recessed in an alcove and out of sight from the main lift that had delivered Lucy seconds earlier.

"I'm impressed at how quickly you knew I was here."

He laughed.

"I knew as soon as you used your pass to open the car park barriers."

Lucy shrugged.

"I'm still impressed."

"I also noted from the CCTV that you seem to be continuing to enjoy your Porsche. Hardly a typical arrival."

Lucy forced a smile which she hoped looked unforced.

"I like to make an entrance."

She knew where this was going but would continue to feign ignorance. Perhaps she still harboured some distant hope of keeping the car.

"However, I'm forgetting my manners. Would you care for some coffee? Something to eat, maybe?"

Although she would have very much liked both, she decided that accepting any form of hospitality would put her on the defensive and, of course, he knew that. She shook her head.

"Thank you, but no. Nice trick with the window, by the way."

He leant back into the soft embrace of his chair, regarding her for some seconds before responding.

"Isn't it? I don't pretend to understand how it all works. Something to do with liquid crystals and polymer, I believe, but I leave all that to the more practically minded. Now, shall we 'get down to business', as it were? I assume you're here because you've had time to reconsider what you said at our last meeting?"

Lucy had the feeling that he knew full well that wasn't why she was here, but there was no way he was going to make this easy for her. In some kind of show of defiance, she reached into her pocket and removed the Porsche's key, placing it on his desk. There was no acknowledgement of the gesture and it was Lucy who was the next to speak.

"I've done a lot of thinking since we last met. And you're right about me. You always have been. My love of money, and all the nice things it buys. I bet you couldn't believe your luck when that man showed an interest in me. But then I don't suppose you get to be a CEO by not spotting an opportunity when it presents itself, do you?"

He said nothing but indicated she should continue, seemingly wanting her to get whatever it was out of her system before launching a counter attack. He obviously already knew the direction of Lucy's thinking and her assertion that, suddenly, money no longer mattered to her. He doubted that very much but, in the event that she would continue to insist upon it, he did have at his disposal other means of, what would be the phrase, 'keeping her onside'?

"I'll miss it, of course I will. The salary, the car, all of it. But I came to ask myself what did I actually want from my life? What's really important? Did I want to be doing this? It isn't right and we both know it."

He gave a heavy sigh which was accompanied by a pained expression.

"Oh dear. Lucy Foster has suddenly discovered morality. How tiresome, for both of us. You ask what's really important.

Shall I tell you? It's being the best. It's being unrivalled in your field. It's being feared by your competition. I've rewarded you exceptionally well for your services to this company, Miss Foster."

"I've never said you haven't."

"Together we've made this work for the benefit of all of us. We've used *your* best asset to *our* best advantage. I think many would applaud that."

Lucy gave a wry smile.

"I doubt your competitors would."

"Is that a threat, Miss Foster?"

She realised it might have sounded like one and shook her head.

"No. Merely an observation."

She tried to sound nonchalant, as if she hadn't even given the remark a second thought. Did he believe her? She would soon find out.

"The information you've acquired for us, for me, has proved invaluable. You are unquestionably good at what you do, Lucy."

Ah, it was 'Lucy' now. A change of tactic? Be careful. He'll be at his most dangerous when he's being, or pretending to be, friendly.

"But what is it, exactly, that I do? For the first time, I asked myself that. I put aside the bling, the fast car, designer clothes, and expensive restaurants. They were blinding me to what I'd become. When it comes down to it I'm nothing more than a prostitute for your company."

"I think you'll find the accepted term now is 'sex worker', and you're so much more than that. Your abilities go far beyond just giving a performance and taking the money. You have to display a degree of judgement, of tact. You've learnt how to extract the most valuable information and disregard that which is of no importance. You're an exceptional young lady with an exceptional skill set and talent. An irreplaceable talent."

He spoke the last three words with a barely disguised insinuation however Lucy, although understanding the implication, chose to disregard it.

"Earlier, you accused me of discovering morality. I know you intended it as an insult, but I don't see it like that."

"Then how, exactly, do you see it, my dear?"

She felt a rising anger, but fought to keep it under control. She knew he was sneering at her and the 'my dear' had been calculated to provoke. But she knew that, if she took the bait, he would have the upper hand.

"I've found a better way."

She'd only just thought of that and was quite pleased with herself. Sufficiently vague, suitably bland. He, on the other hand, didn't seem quite so impressed.

"Someone's offered you more money?"

She should have seen that response coming. Of course he would think of that. To him, there was only money. It was the beginning and the end and everything in between. Lucy shook her head wearily.

"No. But if that had been the case, please credit me with some loyalty."

The use of the last word had been a conscious choice. Perhaps it might strike a chord in the mind of a businessman. Because, she thought, it wouldn't hurt to remind him that she had shown him nothing but loyalty over her time at his company. He stared at her for some seconds, saying nothing, until finally

"Oh God, you're not *in love*, are you?"

He said the words with something bordering on revulsion.

"No!"

The 'love' accusation had momentarily caught her off guard. Had it touched something deep within her, something of which even she had been unaware?

"Then, Miss Foster, just what, exactly, is your 'better way'?"

What happened to 'Lucy'? Obviously the charm offensive, such as it had been, was over.

"All I know is, it doesn't involve London, this company or any other company, and a ridiculously high salary. It doesn't involve using peoples' weaknesses against them, and exploiting their desires. I'm going to enjoy a simpler life and be able to live with myself again."

Another mocking look.

"Ah, I see. And might this simpler life also involve a certain little friend who lives in a pathetic little town and runs an inconsequential little jewellery shop?"

Lucy tried to hide her shock.

"You've had me followed."

It was a statement, not a question.

"Of course I've had you followed. Oh, don't worry, it was only some two-bit private investigator, very good at his job though, you wouldn't have spotted him. I wasn't angry with you, just curious to see where one of my finest assets had chosen to run."

You might not be angry, Lucy thought, but I am. How dare he involve Matts!

"This has nothing to do with Mattie....Miss Hayes. You'll keep her out of this."

As soon as she'd uttered the words she knew she'd just handed him the advantage, and he was well aware of it. He'd found the chink in her armour, just as he had with so many who had sat in that chair over the years.

"I can appreciate how you would wish that. I really can. But life is never that simple, is it?"

Don't rise to it again. Don't give him the satisfaction. But, deep down, she now realised the weakness of her position. What could he do to Mattie? Maybe nothing. Maybe it was just a bluff. But could she risk her friend's safety and wellbeing on a 'maybe'? She had spent so long trying to help Mattie deal with the shadows that haunted her, so long building a special relationship that had been so hard won. Lucy knew she couldn't possibly take the risk. She remained silent. Let him do the work, put his cards on the table. Don't give him anything more. She watched him as he opened a drawer down to his left and removed a small brown folder. He carefully placed it on the desk next to the Porsche's key.

"This is your next target. We will, obviously, obtain a fuller picture in due course and before you deploy, but this will give you a preliminary sketch. She is the wife of a company director. Her husband is, as we speak, attempting to organise a hostile takeover of one of our rivals. At least, that is the rumour. I need you to perform your usual services and find out the truth. You know the drill."

Be compliant. Play along. At least for now.

"All right. You win."

"Of course. I always do. Now, do you wish to ask me anything regarding the target?"

"Yes. Why am I going after the wife and not him?"

He smiled. His most valuable asset was back within the fold and a potential crisis had been averted.

"Legitimate question. Using his wife will put you in under the radar. She won't wish to share with anyone the fact that she's having a relationship with you, and you can use that. But I don't need to tell you anything about your business, do I? You're the expert."

"Are you sure she's....?"

"She's bisexual and I'm certain will be open to your charms. All the confirmatory background work's been done, although no one knows the reason for their investigations. As usual, it's only you and I who will have the complete picture. So, Miss Foster, I want you to take another couple of days, return to your friend while I make final preparations. Events are not imminent as far as I am aware, but don't be far from your phone. And please don't forget, should your doubts return...."

"You don't need to remind me. I'll do what you ask, but I'm warning you, if you or any of your paid morons go anywhere near Mattie, I will bring your company down. That's not a threat, it's a promise."

If her warning had meant anything to him, he showed no outward reaction. His only response was to lean forward and push the Porsche's key back towards her. After just a moment's hesitation, Lucy reached out and took it, quickly forcing it into her pocket as if the very action of hiding it might somehow mitigate accepting its return.

She picked up the folder and proceeded to look through it, scanning each page, out sorting anything she felt relevant and committing it to memory. Several minutes passed in complete silence until, finally, Lucy closed the folder and pushed it back across the desk. Without another word she stood and turned away, walking back to the lift. Although the floor indicator showed that it was still at that floor, its doors remained closed. She waited in front of them, determined that she wouldn't turn back to him to request they be opened. Some seconds passed before, with a soft swish, the lift doors parted. Lucy stepped inside and pressed the ground floor button.

Once alone, the CEO pushed himself up from the luxury of his plush leather chair and walked over to the vast opaque window. He reached around one of the steel support frames that ran from floor to ceiling and lightly touched the hidden pressure pad. In a moment the window transformed into clear glass and he looked out over the London skyline, his thoughts now focussed upon the future. Or, to be precise, Lucy Foster's future.

Although he would never acknowledge the fact to her, she was correct. Lucy had the capability to, if not bring the company down, then to cause it considerable damage. He had, of course, factored this in when he had begun the whole project and was aware that it was always going to be a delicate balancing act. It could be legitimately argued that he had given her too much power over him and his company, but he had gambled on her love of the salary and the expensive lifestyle. However, now it seemed that the time was fast approaching, as he had always known it eventually would, when he would have to ensure that Miss Lucy Foster's silence was guaranteed. Just one last throw of the dice, one more target to exploit and then, regrettably, it would be time to draw the line.

Chapter 17

Lucy sat in the Porsche, staring through the windscreen at the concrete wall. As she climbed behind the wheel she had already decided that she wouldn't return to Mattie straightaway. She needed somewhere to think, to clear her mind and to try and find a way forward.

She was angry with herself for not giving enough consideration to the possibility that he might find out about Mattie. And, of course, once he had, it was obvious that he would use her love for her friend against her. She began to question the wisdom of her outburst. It had been stating the obvious. He knew that her knowledge posed a very real threat to him, and yet he'd chosen to keep the game going. Did that mean that her value to him still outweighed the risk? She had to hope so. It was with that thought that she started the Porsche's engine, reversed out of the parking space and headed up the ramp and out onto the London street.

Lucy took the decision to return to the Mayfair apartment that she rented at a nominal rate from the company. It had been offered to her as part of the 'enhanced' package that had come with her new role. It went with the salary and the Porsche. And oh how she now wanted them all (except maybe the Porsche) to be consigned to the past. But that, in the short term at least, seemed a distant dream.

She wasn't looking forward to telling Mattie that she was going back to work. Somehow she regarded it as a personal failure that she found herself in this position. But she had no intention of telling her about the CEO's thinly veiled threats. Firstly, because she wasn't sure those threats weren't just empty rhetoric, a shot across her bows to remind her where the true power lies. The more Lucy thought about this, the more she managed to convince herself that for him to make, or instigate, any kind of move against Mattie would potentially pose as much of a threat to him and his company as Lucy making a call to a national newspaper. The overriding concern, of course, had to be for Mattie's welfare and nothing could be allowed to jeopardise her safe, enclosed little world. She needed stability and certainty. They were her shield against an uncertain, scary outside world.

Ten minutes after leaving the company building, Lucy rolled the Porsche to a stop in one of the residents' reserved parking places at the rear of the luxury apartment block. She entered the foyer, a place so familiar with its large vases of fresh flowers. For some time after she had first moved in Lucy had thought they were artificial. But perhaps that belief had been more a reflection of her life at that time. Blinkered, focussed, to the exclusion of all else. It hadn't been until she had returned from work one day earlier than usual, and had found the florist working her magic, that she then began to appreciate those fresh, beautiful blooms.

She caught the merest hint of the flowers' delicate scent as she walked past on her way to the stairwell, not wanting to take the lift to her second floor apartment. She pushed the swing door open and climbed the two flights of stairs, removing her key from its small, zipped compartment in her shoulder bag as she made her way along the short corridor to her door.

Once inside the bright, modern living area, Lucy dropped her bag onto a nearby chair and walked through to the kitchen. She opened the fridge, looking for something cold and thirst quenching. She smiled as she saw the bottle of champagne, a particularly good Krug, sitting on one of the shelves inside the door. If she hadn't intended to drive back to Mattie's later in the day, it might have proved much more of a temptation but, as it was, she decided an unopened carton of long-life orange juice would have to suffice.

After she had poured the juice into a tall glass and added several ice cubes, Lucy returned to the lounge and sat down, her thoughts now exclusively about Mattie. Obviously she knew she'd be anxious and, as soon as she felt able, she'd get back to her and attempt to set her mind at rest. However, Lucy knew that wasn't going to be easy because, as far as she could see, the only way to allay any fears Mattie might have would be to lie to her. Could she do that? She could try, but their relationship over many years had been based upon a deep, unshakeable trust. If Lucy were now, even with the best intentions, to break that trust there was a real possibility she could lose Mattie, and if that happened she knew she would never forgive herself.

No. She would tell her the partial truth. She would tell her that she'd failed to break the CEO's hold over her and that she was going to continue to work for him. Mattie didn't need to know anything of the threats from the CEO. Such knowledge would merely serve to add fuel to her bonfire of fears and insecurities.

Lucy desperately wanted some alcohol, but again resisted and instead emptied her large glass of orange juice. After placing the glass down on a nearby table, she lay back in her chair and closed her eyes, trying to work the problem and come up with a way through, some kind of compromise that would hurt neither Mattie or their friendship.

But, sometime later, with her thoughts on a seemingly endless road to nowhere, and with no definitive solution in sight, Lucy got up and made her way through to her bedroom, knelt down and pulled out one of the large drawers from under the bed. Pushing aside an assortment of underwear and tops, she removed a small folder that she kept well-hidden to the back of the drawer. Holding it close to her, she returned to her chair in the living room. She carefully put it down on the table and opened it to the first page.

Lucy stared at the photograph. It showed a young couple sitting on a picnic blanket. They were looking at each other and laughing. And it always made her smile. That image was so precious to her because it told her that, at least for a short while, her parents had once been happy. Whatever darkness had been waiting for them, biding its time just out of sight, there had been moments in the sun. But, as is usually the case, neither had known just how precious those moments were.

She turned the page to reveal another photo. It was a second image of her parents, this time her mother was holding a baby and there was love in her eyes. Lucy's smile disappeared from her lips and the tears welled in her eyes, as they always did. She closed the folder. There was nothing more to see, as it held only those two photographs.

Lucy rested a hand on the folder's cover. Of all her possessions, the luxury watches, the designer clothes, even the Porsche, all of it, there was nothing that meant as much to her. The photographs were all she had of a time when there had been the smallest chance of happiness. When everything might have been ok. That's all she ever would have wanted. For everything to be just 'ok'.

She stood and returned to her bedroom with the folder, placing it back in its hiding place. Many times in the past, she had sought refuge in the memories that it conjured for her, somehow taking comfort from the sadness as well as the joy. But maybe the memories were not the most important thing. Maybe it was simply seeing her mother and father together that gave her that safe place. There had been more photographs, so she had been told, but her mother had destroyed them, only missing the ones she now owned because they had fallen down the back of a drawer. Sometimes she tried to imagine what those lost images might have shown, but liked to believe that the two that had survived her mother's depression were the best of them all.

Maybe it had been the early start, or perhaps the stress of her meeting with the CEO but, whichever it was, Lucy was suddenly overwhelmed with a desire to sleep. She lay down on her bed and closed her eyes. If nothing else could deliver her from her worries, then possibly there was, after all, a haven, however transient, within her reach.

She became aware of the sound of the traffic outside her apartment and slowly opened her eyes. The first thing to come into focus was her bedside clock and it took some moments to realise what it was telling her. She pushed herself up into a sitting position and shook her head in a vain attempt to try and clear it, feeling an almost unbearable fatigue weighing heavily upon her whole body.

Seven hours? Had she really been asleep for that long? Lucy swung her legs over the side of the bed and, with some effort, stood and made her way towards the living room. She walked over to the window and looked out onto the street below. Had she drunk that champagne after all? She certainly felt as if she had. The whole bottle. Outside, in the late afternoon sun, life seemed to be going on as normal. Except everything wasn't normal, was it?

Lucy turned away from the window and dropped into the nearest chair. Her thoughts, usually ordered, were flitting in all directions. It was as if her mind had been shocked into a state of confusion, a mayhem that she was struggling to understand and, far worse, failing to bring under control and she was, whether she was prepared to admit it or not, scared.

The images, some brief and indistinct, others clearer and far more disturbing, were increasing in intensity and it seemed that the more she tried to push against them the more they fought back with a ferocious determination. Had she had a nightmare? Were these 'memories' some kind of backwash from a deeply disturbed sleep?

Where was she? The moment she thought she could make out something that seemed to be familiar, it had disappeared, only to be replaced by another 'something' that proved to be equally elusive. It was as if each scene was being carefully choreographed so that she might never see the whole. And then suddenly she had been in sunshine, embraced by a clarity and beauty that took her breath away. She had looked around her, at the meadows that rolled down to a river where some horses were grazing, and then up the shallow rise to the edge of a large wood. She wanted to walk towards it but seemed unable to move from where she stood. It was as if, for some reason, she was just being shown this place, but nothing more. Beside her feet a small pink flower grew, its petals and golden heart glowing bright in the morning sun. And it was the last thing Lucy saw before the scene disappeared. She felt the terror rising inside her. She had never experienced fear like it and wanted to run but somehow knew there was no escape….

Lucy looked down at her hands which were visibly trembling, and she felt her clothes clinging to her body, wet with perspiration. She rose from the chair and walked through to the bathroom. After removing her damp clothes, she turned the shower on and stepped into the cubicle, closing her eyes as the warm spray washed over her.

She remained in the shower for less than a minute. After stepping out, Lucy selected one of her largest, most luxurious towels and was equally hurried in drying herself. In no time she was searching through her wardrobe for fresh clothes, her one goal to be out and on her way back to Mattie as quickly as she possibly could. She had long since ceased to worry about what she was going to say to her. That particular bridge could be crossed when she came to it. All that mattered to Lucy now was to put distance between her and the cause of all her pain. If it transpired that she was left with no choice but to return then so be it but now, right now, she wanted nothing more or less than to return to Mattie.

After collecting together one or two essentials in a small bag, including the two photographs that she had decided to retrieve from under the bed and take with her, Lucy was out into the corridor and locking the door of her apartment. This time she did take the lift down to the foyer, past the flowers and out to where she had left the Porsche. Throwing the bag onto the passenger seat, she fastened her seat belt and guided the car out of the parking space and into the quiet side street, all remaining memories of her fractured nightmares gone, if indeed they had ever existed at all.

As she skilfully negotiated the London traffic, Lucy welcomed the distraction that driving in the capital provided. Weaving in and out of lanes, avoiding cyclists with suicidal tendencies, and getting herself away as fast as safely possible, was keeping her mind sufficiently occupied and preventing it from dwelling on darker things.

Once clear of the city and on the A road that would take her to within a few miles of her destination, Lucy pulled into the first layby she saw. It was occupied by two large articulated lorries and another car, but there was room to park at the furthest end. As soon as she'd stopped, she removed her mobile phone from a side pocket in the bag and switched it on.

She had felt guilty when, much earlier in the day, she had turned it off but she knew that there was a strong possibility that Mattie would have tried to call her, and she didn't want, or need, that complication. She knew she had probably put her dearest friend through a day of hell, but hadn't intended being so late returning. Why had she slept for so long? She couldn't recall the last time she had fallen asleep during the day. As she continued to think about that, Lucy selected Mattie from her contacts and placed the call.

Chapter 18

Before Lucy had the chance to press the bell, the door was thrown open and Mattie had launched herself, flinging her arms around her. It took a few moments for the inevitable embarrassment to set in and Mattie to release her embrace.

"Good to see you too, Matts!"

Mattie took her by the hand and pulled her into the apartment.

"I've been really worried."

Of course she had.

"I'm so, so sorry. I should've called earlier. To begin with, I didn't want you trying to talk me out of anything because you might have succeeded and then, to be honest, I didn't want to talk about it at all. I still don't, not right now. Is that ok?"

Lucy wasn't happy taking what she felt was the coward's way out but, for the time being, she couldn't bring herself to tell Mattie about her discussion with the CEO.

"It's ok."

That was all Mattie could give her. Obviously she was desperate to know what had happened, but her respect for Lucy's wishes outweighed everything, and she attempted to deflect any awkwardness that she might feel by asking if she had eaten.

"I could do us something with pasta?"

Lucy smiled. It was good to be back.

"Would you like an assistant?"

Mattie beckoned her to follow her to the kitchen where, for the next half an hour, they set about producing a meal while conversation remained light and inconsequential, the mood helped along by the opening of a bottle of Chardonnay. By the time the bowls of pasta, Mattie's version of a carbonara, were dished up, both women were feeling quite relaxed with only a third of the bottle of wine remaining.

"Trays?"

Mattie enquired and received a nod of approval. So, with trays on their laps and the television on in the background, they sat together in the living room, each enjoying their meal and each other's company. It wasn't until they were back in the kitchen, Lucy tidying up while Mattie found some fruit for dessert, that Lucy decided she couldn't remain silent about her day any longer.

"He had me followed here, Matts. He knows about you."

There was little point in trying to sugar the pill. Mattie deserved better than that.

"I wondered if he might."

Mattie said, softly. Had Lucy expected such a measured, calm response? It somehow made her feel worse for dragging her friend into something which was nothing to do with her. All Mattie ever wanted was to get on with her life as best she could, and now her safe, predictable little world was under threat through no fault of her own.

"I'm so sorry."

Mattie seemed genuinely puzzled by Lucy's apology.

"Why? I want you to be here. I want to help you. If you hadn't come here what would you have done?"

"If I hadn't come here you wouldn't have been involved."

"And I'd never have forgiven you. What would it have said about our friendship if you'd stayed away?"

"But I've put you at risk, Matts."

And, of course, while she had been talking, Mattie had already worked out the implication of what Lucy had told her.

"I don't care about that, but I do care about you. He's using threats against me to force you back, isn't he?"

Lucy looked away, and that told Mattie all she needed to know.

"You can't go back there. I won't let you."

There, for the first time, was an emotional edge to her voice.

"I'm sorry. I've already agreed to return. He has my next target lined up. I won't allow you to come to any harm because of me."

But Mattie had no intention of accepting that.

"He won't do anything. He wouldn't dare. It'd be too much of a risk."

"That thought had occurred to me, but I think we have to consider the chance he's already taken with me. If things don't pan out the way he wants he may feel he has nothing to lose. He's made me an asset and a threat in equal measure, and he has to ensure that I remain onside. You're the deterrent, Matts, and please believe me when I say that he won't hesitate if he feels cornered. If I don't show when he calls, he can only come to one conclusion, and I can't let that happen."

She could see from Mattie's expression that she was considering her next counter-argument, and knew she had no intention of letting it go, so….

"I'm tired, Matts. Can we talk about this tomorrow?"

Actually, her words weren't just intended to close the subject. Lucy truly did feel exhausted. She could recall that she had slept for some time in her own apartment, and there was something about a dream, but any details had long since faded into nothing.

"Will you come to the shop in the morning?"

Mattie's question, while ignoring Lucy's, was almost bordering on a plea, because she knew that if she had to eventually give her friend back, then that would make whatever time they had left together even more precious.

"Just try and stop me!"

Lucy gave her, what she hoped, was a convincing smile but, whether it had had the desired effect or not, Mattie's answer was to present her with a small wicker bowl containing a selection of fruit, an offering that said 'Ok, I accept the subject's closed, for now'. So they returned to the living room and allowed the television to do most of the talking for the rest of the evening. It wasn't what some might call an 'awkward silence'. It was doubtful that such a thing could exist between them. No, the minimal conversation was born out of a mutual respect and understanding for each other. Lucy appreciated Mattie's concerns and Mattie, in turn, recognised Lucy's position and her lack of options, and to continue with any discussion that evening, both knew, would have achieved nothing.

As it transpired, both women enjoyed their night together, in the company of a very light, inconsequential rom-com (yes, Mattie managed to find one and convince Lucy she need not check the Horror Channel on this occasion). And it was near midnight when they embraced before going to their bedrooms, saying nothing but just taking comfort from each other, both knowing that their world, and the future that they both wanted so much, was under threat as never before.

Chapter 19

Mattie lay in her bed, staring at the ceiling. She had known that sleep wasn't going to come easily that night. Although she had held it together when she'd been with Lucy, and kept the demons at bay for the sake of her friend, it had been inevitable that the shadows would wait until she was alone, as they always did. And it was with a weary acceptance that she knew she could no longer control the thoughts and emotions that were preparing yet another onslaught, given a renewed momentum by her deep concerns for Lucy and what she feared the future may hold for them both. Mattie closed her eyes, inviting sleep to take her because there, at least, was a refuge from an unkind, hostile world.

"Follow me."
Sarah took Mattie's hand and led her away from the cottage and back through the trees. She walked quickly and Mattie struggled to keep up.
"They'll be just through here. You'll see."
She laughed as Mattie had to duck to avoid a low hanging branch that brushed against her hair.
"Who will?"
Mattie's question was answered with a smile, as if Sarah was enjoying keeping her guessing. In moments they had cleared the trees and were out into another clearing, the early morning sun not yet high enough to give it the direct light that it would enjoy later in the day. Sarah let go of Mattie's hand and pointed over to the far side of the glade where two horses, one chestnut and the other grey, stood, heads down, enjoying the lush grass.
"Come on! You can choose which one you want to ride!"

Before Mattie could reply, Sarah had broken into a run towards the horses, who both looked up and began to walk slowly in her direction.

"Are they yours?"

Mattie asked as she caught up with Sarah, who already had her arms around the neck of the grey.

"No! They're not *mine*, silly, they're *ours*! Don't you remember?"

As Sarah looked at her so, for just a moment, Mattie *did* remember. Their childhood together, galloping their horses over the meadows, through the wild flowers and along the river. She recalled their excitement as the water was thrown up by the flying hooves, soaking their simple cotton dresses, but knowing that the summer sun would dry them before they returned home to their mother.

As Mattie ran her hand down the chestnut's forehead, a question suddenly occurred to her. If these beautiful horses had been theirs as children, how was it that they were not only still alive, but looking as young and strong as they had in those wonderful, carefree days? But, no sooner had that thought struck her than it was lost as Sarah leapt onto the back of the grey.

"We can swap if you want!"

Mattie shook her head.

"The chestnut's my favourite!"

'It always was' Sarah whispered, as Mattie lowered herself onto her horse's back before reaching out to take hold of the mane. Instinctively, she used her legs to squeeze the chestnut's flanks, and it walked forward to stand beside Sarah and the grey.

"Ready?"

Sarah asked before urging her horse into a trot, not waiting for a reply and leaving Mattie wondering what it was she was supposed to be ready for. This time the chestnut didn't wait for a command from its rider, and quickly caught up with the grey. Together they followed a wide path through the wood, both horses picking their way between the trees and dropping back to a trot when the gaps narrowed, so that they could negotiate a safe route and giving their riders time to avoid the larger boughs that occasionally stretched across the path in front of them.

It took some minutes to reach the far edge of the wood and to leave the half-light and the cool shadows behind them. Mattie blinked as they emerged into sunlight and, even though it was early in the day, she felt the warmth on her skin. Sarah brought the grey to a halt and turned to Mattie.

"Race you down to the river!"

She pointed out across the meadow to where, in the distance, Mattie could just make out the dip of the riverbank, and she felt a rising sense of fear as her horse tensed, ready for the gallop.

"I....I can't. I've never done anything like this! I'll fall!"

Sarah coaxed her grey over to her side, bringing it round next to Mattie.

"Trust me when I tell you we've done this so many times and you've never fallen. In fact, you're a better rider than I am."

Should she believe her? Before she had time to answer her own question, Sarah gave a yell, pushed her legs against her horse's flanks and, in the blink of an eye, they were gone. Mattie's reaction was immediate. She tightened her grip on the mane, but before she could give any further signal to the chestnut, it was off in fast pursuit of Sarah and the grey. And, suddenly, the fear was gone, replaced by an exhilaration and excitement as she felt the power and speed build until they were matching the grey stride for stride.

With the summer breeze rushing though their hair, they galloped through the meadows, side by side, their horses perfectly matched for speed and stamina. Every few seconds Sarah would glance across to Mattie, and her broad smile soon became infectious. Suddenly Mattie realised that she was actually having fun! The fear, the trepidation, all those things which were forever at her shoulder, waiting for their moment, had disappeared without trace.

The riverbank, which had been so far in the distance just a short time ago, was now looming in front of them and they had just seconds to veer away or face the drop into the water. Mattie looked over to Sarah, who had already begun to bring her horse round to run parallel to the river, all the time slowing it until it had come back to little more than a fast trot. Without a great deal of input from Mattie, the chestnut had followed, dropping in perfectly behind the grey.

"Shall we get wet?"

Sarah called over her shoulder, and Mattie shouted 'Yes!' without giving it a moment's thought.

"Then follow me!"

Sarah yelled as she pushed the grey on to where the riverbank's incline became slightly shallower for a short distance. Both horses, without hesitation, made their way down through the tall grasses and into the water. Sarah checked that Mattie was safely down before kicking the grey on into a canter, following the river's course, and showering Mattie, who was just a few yards behind her, with the cool, clear water. Together they made their way downstream to the sound of splashing hooves, birdsong, and the breeze through the long meadow grass and if, right then, Mattie had been asked her one desire she would have answered instantly. It would have been to stay in that moment, with Sarah, forever.

They walked on for another few minutes before Sarah urged the grey up out of the river and onto the mossy riverbank where she dismounted and allowed her horse to begin to graze on the meadow grass.

"Here we are...."

Sarah said as she lay down on her back, staring up at the clear blue sky.

"....I sometimes come here when I just want to...."

Mattie waited for her to finish the sentence but, after several silent seconds, thought she should try to help.

"Think?" she offered, hopefully.

"....be somewhere else, of course."

Of course. Why hadn't she thought of that? She looked over to where Sarah lay. Was there the hint of a smile on her lips? Mattie dropped down onto the grass next to her as the chestnut joined Sarah's horse in the meadow.

"Do you understand now? About us? About what we were? About what we are?"

Mattie turned to look at Sarah as she lay beside her, her eyes now closed. Her sister. And, yes, she now understood. As the memories flooded in on her, so she felt tears well and, instinctively, she reached out for Sarah's hand.

"Please don't leave me. I don't want to lose you again."

Sarah opened her eyes and looked into Mattie's.

"I never left you. I told you I would always be with you."

"But I never knew, and why have you waited until now?"

Sarah looked away, back up to the sky, where faint wisps of cloud had momentarily drifted over the sun,

"Perhaps I shouldn't have. Perhaps if I'd been with you from your earliest days I might have been able to spare you the worst of the darkness that follows you."

Mattie wiped away a tear that had found its way onto her cheek.

"I would've liked you there. You have no idea how scary it was, being like me in that world. It can be so cruel, so unforgiving."

"But I didn't allow you to be on your own, Mattie. Surely, by now, you've realised that?"

"Lucy?"

Mattie whispered her name, suddenly aware, as if she had forgotten, that there was another love. A love that belonged to another world and another time.

"I found her for you and, to answer your next question, no, she is unaware."

"But how can that be right, Sarah, to use someone like that?"

Sarah smiled.

"I haven't used her. I gave her purpose."

Mattie somehow couldn't bring herself to argue because she now felt hopelessly torn, and found herself longing for a time before Sarah had revealed the truth of their life together so many years ago, in all its beautiful joy and heart-breaking sadness.

Chapter 20

"Don't you want your breakfast?"

Lucy watched as Mattie reluctantly took another small mouthful of toast. She couldn't have looked less enthusiastic about the food in front of her if she'd tried.

"I'm sorry. I'm really not hungry at the moment."

"Ok."

Lucy decided against any further comment and continued to eat her bowl of granola, trying to look anywhere but at Mattie, who had now pushed her plate away and stood up.

"I'm just going to get ready. We'll leave in about ten minutes, ok?"

Lucy nodded as Mattie made to leave the room but, as she reached the doorway, she stopped and turned back.

"I'm so sorry, Lucy, it's just that I'm thinking about stuff and the more I try to stop thinking about it the worse it gets."

Lucy walked over to her.

"Matts? Don't forget, I know you. I know how it works with you and I'm fine with that."

She put a hand under her chin and lifted her head, forcing her to look directly into her eyes. A smile slowly found its way onto Mattie's lips and Lucy knew that represented a small victory.

"Go and make yourself beautiful for your adoring customers. I'll clear up in here."

Mattie threw her arms around Lucy, holding her for several seconds before making her way back to her bedroom. It had been a spontaneous act, catching Lucy by surprise. She watched as Mattie closed the bedroom door behind her. She then set about picking up all the breakfast things from the kitchen table and doing some general tidying up before returning to her own room.

Mattie sat on her bed, staring at the wardrobe mirror. The memories that Sarah had revealed to her were proving to be an unbearable burden, and she was unsure whether the coping strategies that had served her in the past would prove any match for the knowledge that she now possessed.

Why had Sarah done this? She wouldn't want her to suffer, surely? Perhaps she'd had no choice. But how Mattie wished for the ignorance that she had once had, for the ghost-like, elusive images that had receded into nothing when she had returned to this world. Because she now had to live with the memories that Sarah had given her.

And then there was Lucy. Should she talk to her about Sarah? No. Whatever the cost to herself she decided that, until there was no other choice and however much Lucy asked, she would say nothing. But Mattie knew that might prove very difficult. No one had a better understanding of Mattie's psychological problems than Lucy and it would be bordering on the impossible to hide the fact that something was troubling her. Mattie was sure Lucy already had her suspicions, and it wouldn't take long for those suspicions to turn into awkward questions. So be it. But maybe they would be busy in the shop and Lucy's day would be spent charming the plastic out of customers' wallets and handbags.

"Ready?"

Lucy was waiting by the door, looking every inch as good as ever.

"I am, but I'm not sure the general public will be."

"Sorry?"

Mattie smiled as she gestured to the silk blouse with its low v neck and the skirt with its hem several inches above the knee. It was then that Mattie felt a sudden sadness wash over her as she had the realisation that, in all probability, this might be one of the last days that Lucy would be accompanying her to the shop.

"Where are the sunglasses?"

Lucy gave her a look of mock indignation.

"You wouldn't want me to become too predictable, now would you, Miss Hayes?"

This had the desired effect of forcing another smile onto Mattie's lips.

"Oh, perish the thought, Miss Foster. Your car or mine?" she asked as she closed and locked her apartment door.
"The Porsche?"
"Fine."
They made their way to where Lucy's vehicle was parked. Mattie, deep down, would have preferred they had taken her far more modest little hatchback. She couldn't look at the Porsche without resenting what it represented, and hesitated when Lucy unlocked it and opened the passenger door for her. Although Lucy couldn't have failed to notice she made no reference to it, but walked around to the driver's side and climbed in. There was nothing to be gained by referring to Mattie's fears at that moment.
"Can you do the shop again if I sort out the online orders?"
Lucy swung the car out onto the main road.
"No problem. I dressed for the meet and greet."
She glanced at Mattie and smiled.
"I had noticed. I do like it, by the way."
"I'm sorry?"
"The Porsche. It's nice."
Lucy wasn't sure if that was what they called 'damning with faint praise'.
"You don't have to say that."
"No, really. I'm jealous."
Lucy gave a her a wry smile.
"No you're not, but I appreciate the attempt, Matts."
The fact that Mattie didn't reply, making no effort to deny her insincerity, confirmed Lucy's suspicions that the 'stuff' that she had earlier said she was thinking about, was now in control to such an extent that it had succeeded in stifling her natural kindliness and perfect manners.
As she drove on to the shop, Lucy made several attempts at conversation but she received very little back from Mattie and decided that it would be best to let the radio provide the soundtrack to the rest of their short journey. However, once they had arrived and she was able to immerse herself into her overnight orders and various other admin tasks, Mattie seemed to relax a little and was happy to let Lucy prepare everything front-of-house, ready for opening. When she was sure all was up

to Mattie's high standards in the shop, she walked through to the back office.

"Another good night?"

Lucy perched herself on the corner of the table, close to Mattie and her laptop, with one of her legs actually across part of the keyboard. Mattie, no longer able to concentrate, sat back and looked up at Lucy, desperately hoping that she wasn't blushing.

"Good enough. I think I can afford you for another few days."

Any other time and she would have punctuated such a remark with a knowing wink or grin. But, somehow, not today. Today it wouldn't have felt right.

"You'd better not try and pay me. You know I won't accept it. It's been fun, Matts. It really has."

Lucy immediately regretted using the past tense but, much to her relief, it seemed that Mattie hadn't picked up on it.

"More limited editions?"

Lucy asked, hoping to move the conversation on.

"Yes. I have a contact in Tokyo. She gets hold of JDM watches for me…."

Mattie saw the question that had appeared on Lucy's expression before she could turn it into words.

"….JDM. Japanese Domestic Market. Models that only get released in Japan. There's a real demand for them over here."

"A contact in Tokyo? Wow! Get you Matts. I'm impressed!"

"Friend of my mum's actually. So are the ones I have in Geneva and London. When she heard I was going into specialist watches she organised various contacts. Well, she knew full well I wouldn't be able to."

"So? You still have to make it work. Good for you!"

Don't go along with Mattie's insecurities. Always praise and encourage, even if, like today, it seemed to fall on deaf ears.

"Lucy? Does the name Sarah mean anything to you?"

She was momentarily thrown by the non-sequitur but, well, this was Matts, so normal rules didn't apply. Lucy thought for a second.

"Don't think so. Sarah who?"

"Just Sarah" Mattie replied, helpfully.

She shook her head slowly.

"Not a name I recognise. Should I?"

A very good question. Should she? Should Mattie have even mentioned the name to her? Perhaps it didn't matter, one way or the other. Had she even considered that Sarah only existed in her dreams? No. She was real. She was sure of that now.

"No. Not necessarily. I just wondered."

"Where did you get the name from?"

Another good question. How ought she to answer? With the truth this time? Had the moment come for that?

"It doesn't matter. I must have imagined it. Forget I said anything."

Inside, Mattie was angry with herself for not having the courage to at least try to give Lucy something better than that.

"Ok. I'll go and open up then, shall I?"

Lucy stood and made her way out into the shop. Of course, she knew that Mattie hadn't imagined the name. Sarah. It had come from somewhere. She tried to think back, to anyone in their past, to someone she might have mentioned in passing, but on each possibility she drew a blank. Mattie was obviously keeping something from her. She knew her too well to be fooled by the 'I imagined it' line. Why would she not want to tell her? They had shared so much over the years. Maybe, given time, she'd change her mind. But one thing was certain. She wouldn't press her for an explanation.

Lucy flicked the sign around so that it said 'Open' and unlocked the door. It was as she turned away that she heard the screech of tyres. As she spun round so there was a scream from somewhere down the street. She pulled the door open and ran out onto the pavement. A short way down the road a van had come to a stop. It was slewed across onto the wrong side of the road and had hit a lamp post.

Lucy began to walk along the pavement with a rising sense of trepidation, and it was as she neared the van that she first saw the young man lying in the middle of the road. He was completely still and there was a growing pool of blood around his head. She wanted to look away but somehow couldn't. Someone, an older man, rushed past her to where he lay and knelt beside him. As she looked on so the man removed his phone from his jacket and placed the call for an ambulance.

Although Lucy had initially been unaware of them, a small group of people had gathered around her. She could hear their murmurs and the hushed tones of a woman whispering something about the van driver. She said something about him seeming to be in shock. Lucy looked over to the vehicle, a huge dent in the middle of its bonnet. Behind the windscreen the driver, still sitting in his seat, was staring ahead, his eyes unblinking. Several people were trying to talk to him but there was no response. Drink? Drugs? Somehow Lucy didn't think so.

The activity all around her seemed to blur into a kaleidoscope of voices and colours. Somewhere in the distance there was the sound of a siren, several sirens, that became louder and louder. Lucy felt as though she was in the eye of the storm, surrounded on all sides by whirlwinds and chaos but none of it touching her. Out of the corner of her eye she saw two men, dressed in their green paramedic uniforms, run towards the young man. But she knew they were too late. She knew he was dead.

"Lucy?"

She recognised the woman's voice before she turned to see the young policewoman walking towards her. What was her name?

"Vicky."

She remembered a split second before it would have become obvious that she'd forgotten.

"Did you see this happen?"

Lucy shook her head.

"I was in the shop and heard the van brake."

She looked over to where the two paramedics were still working hard on the young man. They had to, of course they did. But Lucy knew.

"If it's ok, I'll go back now. I don't want Matts coming out to find me."

Vicky smiled.

"Of course. I may need another word later. You'll still be there?"

Her question was tinged with more than a hint of hope.

"I'll still be there."

Lucy threw over her shoulder as she walked past her and back to the shop, where Mattie was waiting for her in the doorway.

"What's going on?"

Lucy put an arm around her and gently guided her away from the door.

"Someone's been hit by a van. It happened a little way down the road."

"Is it serious?"

"I'm sure he's dead, Matts."

There was the merest waver in Lucy's voice and it was apparent to Mattie that she had been more affected by the incident than she was letting on. She didn't reply but led her through to the back office and sat her down in the office chair. As she removed a bottle of water from the small fridge near the safe so her thoughts turned to another death they had so recently witnessed. A heart attack. A random, chance event that could happen anytime and anywhere. And now a tragic road accident. Again, a totally arbitrary incident involving a complete stranger. Lucy took the bottle from Mattie and smiled her thanks.

"Do you want to talk about it?"

She shook her head.

"Ok. Stay in here as long as you want. I'll go out front. Join me when you feel up to it."

Mattie allowed her hand to brush Lucy's shoulder as she walked past, sure that the best thing for her friend right now was some time alone. She'd look in on her in ten minutes or so if she hadn't appeared. Walking over to the door she looked out. From her vantage point she could just see that there were now several police cars and two ambulances, all with their blue lights flashing, parked on the opposite side of the road.

Mattie opened the door and took a couple of paces out onto the pavement. There was a paramedic helping the van's driver away from the vehicle and towards one of the ambulances. As he was assisted into it, so the first ambulance drew away. Not wanting to intrude further on another's misery, unlike some members of the public who were still showing no sign of leaving the scene, Mattie returned inside. There, leaning against the counter, looking as if nothing had happened, was a now smiling Lucy.

"I'm fine now, Matts. Honestly" she said, in answer to Mattie's unasked question.

Of course she was, even if she wasn't. She should have known that Lucy wouldn't allow herself more than a few brief moments to bring her thoughts and feelings back under control.

"Ok. Good. Well, I'll get onto the orders then. It's all yours."

Mattie returned to her laptop, leaving Lucy in the shop. Perhaps any visiting customers might not find her at her best today, but Mattie didn't care. She was where she wanted her to be. Hopefully there would be enough customers to keep her preoccupied, and there were, she had ensured, a few small tasks that she could busy herself with in the meantime.

As it transpired, throughout the day, there had been a steady flow of customers. Some wanted to talk to Lucy regarding the accident that they'd heard about, but she seemed to take everything in her stride and always, sooner or later, turned the conversation towards a particular watch or piece of bespoke jewellery that they hadn't realised they desperately wanted.

On one occasion, when Mattie had peeked out from the back office, she had seen a middle aged man, with more than a hint of wealth about him, standing at the counter. He had his attention firmly fixed upon Lucy's legs, which she'd skilfully ensured were positioned perfectly in his eye line, while she proceeded to confidently extol the virtues of a wristwatch that he'd expressed an interest in. A lamb to the slaughter.

"Pretty good morning, all things considered."

Lucy took the sandwich that Mattie offered her and pulled up a chair she had brought through from the shop.

"Pretty good? At this rate we'll be floating on the London stock exchange soon!"

Mattie realised she had used 'we'll' instead of 'I'll' without thinking, but made no attempt to correct herself.

"Oh, almost forgot...."

Lucy reached into the pocket of her skirt and removed a scrap of paper.

"....a guy asked me to give you his mobile number. Wants you to try and source him an Omega Seamaster 300 Spectre. Will you let him know?"

Mattie took the piece of paper from her and laid it next to her laptop.

"Sure. They're going for around seven and a half k on the second hand market right now. Should be able to find one."

Lucy continued to dispatch her sandwich while Mattie busied herself on her laptop.

"You ok for the afternoon, or do you want a break?"

She glanced over her shoulder as Lucy took another water from the fridge.

"I'm fine, Matts. Bring it on!"

Before Mattie could say anything else she had picked up the chair and taken it and herself back into the shop. As there seemed to be a pause between customers, Lucy busied herself with some minor housework in the form of going through the various brochures distributed on the counter and around the shelves. It would be highly unlikely that Mattie didn't give these a look on a regular basis but it wouldn't hurt just to check for anything out of date or superseded.

She gathered up a selection of jewellery and watch leaflets and catalogues and laid them out on the glass counter. She began to sort and discard, making a small pile of those she intended to ask Mattie about before consigning them to the recycling bin. In fact, Lucy became so engrossed in her task that she didn't, initially, react to the bell as the door opened.

"Lucy."

She looked up to see Vicky standing in the doorway.

"Hello. Good to see you again. Is this business, or a social call?"

"Might I have a word with you and Miss Hayes, in private?"

The young policewoman threw a glance towards the shop's door and Lucy took the hint. She dropped the catch down into the 'lock' position and turned over the 'Open/Closed' sign before following Vicky into the back office. As Lucy watched her remove her hat and greet Mattie, she couldn't help thinking that any persistent interest from the police right now, for whatever reason, was a very unwelcome development.

Chapter 21

Mattie got up and offered Vicky her chair.
"No. That's fine. I'm ok, thank you."
Without a moment's hesitation, Lucy dropped into the vacated chair, deciding to make herself comfortable by slowly, and with great care, crossing her legs. This had the effect of briefly destroying Vicky's train of thought, much to Lucy's amusement. Mattie threw her a 'look' that spoke of her disapproval.
"You had something you wanted to tell us?"
Lucy prompted, helpfully.
"I….er….yes, that's right."
Vicky removed a small notebook from the pocket of her stab vest, flicking over the first few pages before finding the information she required, clearly now fully back in 'on duty' mode.
"Regarding the accident this morning, you told me you heard the sound of the van's tyres as the driver applied the brakes?"
Lucy nodded.
"How is he...?"
"He died before he reached hospital."
"I'm sorry to hear that."
"However, certain facts have come to light since the accident and I need to clarify one or two points, if that's ok?"
During the few seconds of silence that followed, as Vicky quickly consulted the next page of her notes, neither Mattie or Lucy quite knew where this was going.
"Had you ever seen the accident victim before?"
Lucy shook her head.
"No, not that I can recall. I mean, I didn't look at him for long but, no. Should I have?"
Vicky ignored the question.

"Ok. So, I'll get to the point. We now have reason to believe that the deceased man had every intention of robbing your shop when you opened up this morning."

She allowed them a few moments to take that in before continuing.

"Obviously I can't go into detail but, at the hospital, he was found to be carrying a knife and a subsequent search of his flat has given us further evidence regarding his intention, hence my question about whether you'd seen him before. He may have been keeping your premises under observation and I wondered if either of you had seen anything suspicious recently."

Lucy and Mattie both shook their heads.

"I'm sorry, I don't think we can help you."

Mattie's voice was quiet, and she had obviously been shaken by what she'd just been told.

"We will, of course, be checking local CCTV and talking to all of the other businesses in the street."

"Of course."

Lucy found herself sitting up a little straighter, any further attempts at levity put well and truly on hold.

"Presumably you have security measures in place, in view of your high value stock?"

That was directed at Mattie, who seemed to be struggling to come up with an immediate answer. Once more, it was Lucy to the rescue.

"As you can see, we have a modern safe, two CCTV cameras in here and the shop, and infra-red detectors strategically placed around the property...."

Lucy stood up, now warming to her new role as the owner's spokesperson.

"....and, obviously both myself and Miss Hayes are well-versed in the more common sense precautions that are required when working in our line of business. So, I believe we have all obvious bases covered, as I'm sure you'll agree."

She punctuated this with her best reassuring, confident smile as Mattie nodded in solemn agreement, looking at her friend with an even greater respect and admiration, if that were possible, impressed at how quickly Lucy had gone up through the gears. And her use of 'we' and 'our' hadn't gone unnoticed, although

Mattie knew that would only have been for the present audience and, in reality, probably meant nothing. But she would hold onto Lucy's words for as long as she could keep alive some kind of hope.

"I'm sure I would."

Vicky replied, now finding she was going to have to revise her initial impressions of Miss Foster. Not that said revision would make her any less attractive.

"Excellent. Is there anything else we can help you with?"

Although Lucy seemed to be looking to bring this to an end without much further discussion, it was clear that Policewoman Traynor was in no hurry at all.

"Well, maybe yes, maybe no."

Lucy resumed her seat, this time without the cabaret. She glanced across to Mattie who had a concerned expression. She gave her a quick wink that had the desired effect of nudging a smile onto her lips.

"We're intrigued. Do go on."

Another flick through the notebook, which Mattie found strangely reassuring in this high tech, cyber world that she was forced to inhabit.

"Right. Yes. Here we are. It's about the other night. The fatal heart attack?"

She asked the question as if either of them might have forgotten.

"We remember" Mattie confirmed.

"He stopped you to ask the time? That's what you told me, isn't it?"

They both nodded.

"Is there a problem with that?"

Lucy enquired, sensing that there might be.

"Not a problem as such. It's just that since then certain information has come to light regarding those two men."

"Such as?"

"Well…."

Another glance at the notebook.

"….it appears there have been several allegations against them. No police action required or taken, but I just thought it might be relevant to mention it to you in case you wanted to, er, adjust your story."

"Allegations?"

"Of harassment. Part of my job is to liaise with local pubs, nightclubs, wine bars and their clients. Just to check on any problems that might need our attention and, on a couple of occasions, these two were mentioned. Nothing more than that. No one I spoke to wanted it taken any further."

It now became clear that she expected them to offer *her* something, and she was clearly prepared to wait.

"There might have been one or two words exchanged."

Mattie looked to Lucy, now regretting her decision not to give the whole story at the time.

"We felt...."

Lucy, once again, was not going to let her take this on her own, even though she had argued against Mattie's 'asking the time' lie.

"....that they had enough problems without adding to them. It was an omission made for the best of reasons. Compassion."

She looked to Mattie and smiled. And Mattie knew then just how much she loved her.

"So they *were* paying you unwanted attention?"

It was plain that Vicky wasn't ready to let this go just yet.

"Yes, but it doesn't matter now, does it?"

Equally, Lucy intended to make it clear that they had no desire to pursue it. Vicky took one last glance at her notebook before replacing it in her pocket.

"Well, I suppose from one standpoint that's a valid argument in so far as one of them isn't going to do it again."

"So you could just have a quiet word with his friend and let it go at that, couldn't you?"

Lucy sensed that there was something more behind Mattie's question, more than just that there was 'no point' in taking it further. Mattie's concern that the matter should be closed was being driven by something deeper. There was an edge of urgency in her voice, an insistence that this should be finished with here and now. Had Vicky picked up on that too? Lucy hoped not.

"Yes. We could do that and, between you and I, that'll probably be what will happen. But hasn't it occurred to you?"

"Hasn't *what* occurred to us?"

"Well, it's almost as if fate is looking out for you two, isn't it? Not that I believe in that sort of thing but, well, it's quite a coincidence, don't you think?"

"But coincidences happen all the time, don't they?"

Lucy was eager to draw a line under the discussion for no reason other than Mattie's barely hidden unease. Maybe it was because she had known her for so long that she had sensed her growing anxiety, and hoped that because Vicky didn't know her at all she would fail to pick up on it.

"Yes, I expect they do. Ok. Well, I just thought you ought to be kept informed of developments. If there's anything further we need, or if anything else occurs to me, I'll contact you."

Lucy leapt to her feet, keen to see Vicky off the premises before anything else had the chance to occur to her. She put a guiding arm around her and steered her back out into the shop.

"Miss Hayes seemed a little 'on edge', didn't you think?"

Lucy shrugged.

"Can't say I noticed."

Don't offer anything more than that. Vicky took one last look towards the back office as Lucy unlocked the door, pulled it open and turned the Open/Closed sign back around.

"Well, good to meet you again, Lucy."

"You too, Vicky."

She hesitated, as if trying to make up her mind about something. She then quickly reached into one of her uniform pockets and removed a piece of paper. Before Lucy could react, Vicky had pressed the folded note into her hand and turned away, heading back to the police car that was parked a little way down the road. Slowly pushing the door closed behind her, Lucy walked back through to where Mattie sat, behind her desk.

"Don't look so worried. She's gone. Why *are* you looking worried, by the way? There's no suspicion attached to us. Never could be. Could there?"

Lucy perched once more on the edge of the desk.

"Why do you ask? They were both clearly random and entirely unconnected incidents. And what did Vicky give you?"

Lucy had to admit that was as good a way as any of changing the subject, and although she wanted to get to the bottom of exactly what was troubling Mattie, it could, and should, wait. She unfolded the piece of paper and read it.

Lucy. If your relationship with Miss Hayes is of an intimate nature, please destroy this note now. But if, as I hope, you're just good friends, maybe you'd like to give me a call or message me and we could arrange to spend some time together? Whatever you decide, I'll rely on your discretion.

"She's included her mobile number."
Lucy handed the note to Mattie.
"Well, you've just failed the discretion bit, haven't you?"
"What do you mean? I've only shown you, and you're the most discreet person I know."
Mattie handed it back to her.
"I told you, didn't I?"
Lucy frowned.
"Yes Matts, you told me. Well done you. So maybe you can help me compose a 'let her down gently' message."
Mattie leant back in her chair.
"She's nice. I think you should arrange to meet her. See what she's like 'out of uniform'."
She failed to prevent a smile creeping its way onto her lips.
"You're enjoying this!"
Lucy returned to the shop, but not before she'd flicked the lever under Mattie's chair with her foot, causing it to suddenly plunge downwards.
"Tell her you'll meet her!"
Mattie called out as she readjusted her chair's height before returning her attention to her laptop. Of course she didn't want Lucy to contact Vicky because Mattie knew the undeniable truth. That *she* was now experiencing the most private, deepest desires towards Lucy. But by seeming to approve of, and encourage, Lucy and Vicky's prospective date she might, just might, be able to hide, suppress and, ultimately, deny those desires, because to express them could mean that she lost her beloved Lucy forever.

Chapter 22

"So can we talk about it now?"

Lucy asked as she handed Mattie a bowl of hot carrot and coriander soup. She tasted it and gave her a nod of approval.

"I wouldn't be too impressed, it came out of a carton" Lucy said, in the interest of full disclosure.

"Nevertheless, it's nice."

Lucy sat down next to her on the sofa, both had trays on their laps and an undemanding quiz show quietly on in the background.

"Talk about what?"

Mattie took another mouthful of soup as Lucy gave her a sideways glance.

"Have a think and then you tell me."

"Have you contacted Vicky yet?"

"No, and changing the subject won't work this time. Something's on your mind, Matts, and before you answer, remember how long I've known you."

Any thoughts that Mattie might have had of further avoiding the question lasted only a moment. Lucy wanted to know, and so she would tell her.

"You recall when I asked if the name Sarah meant anything to you?"

Lucy nodded.

"I think I knew it wouldn't, but I had to ask. You see, I know her but I'm not sure she exists."

Mattie lifted the tray from her lap and placed it on the floor to the side of the sofa, prompting Lucy to put her bowl on the coffee table in front of her. She was unsure where this was going to go but knew that, whatever Mattie might be about to say, she needed and deserved her undivided attention.

"I meet her in my dreams. It's where I go to when I sleep, and I find her in that beautiful place where I know I'm safe, and I feel I'd like to stay there forever, but I know I can't."

She paused, and Lucy could see her fighting back the tears. When she had virtually demanded an answer from Mattie she hadn't considered that there might be an emotional cost attached to her explanation. Should she stop her? Tell her it didn't matter? Even the smallest degree of upset wasn't worth the price she was now paying.

"Matts...."

Mattie shook her head.

"No, I want to tell you. I want you to know."

Lucy put an arm around her shoulders, as she had done on so many occasions in the past, only this time was different. This time Lucy didn't know what she was going to be able to say that would make everything alright. And that scared her.

"Then I'm listening" she whispered.

Mattie took several shallow breaths, her gaze fixed upon a small painting on the wall opposite. It was a fairly nondescript print, a landscape. Not something Lucy would have imagined Mattie buying. She had asked her about it one day, and Mattie had told her that she couldn't recall where she'd found it. But Lucy had the feeling that, at that moment, Mattie wasn't seeing the painting. As she spoke, her eyes were seeing something else, something from another place and another time.

"There aren't any bad things there. And if there were, Sarah would protect me. I know she would, she told me. She told me other things too. Or did I already know them? I'm not sure now. And it doesn't matter, does it, how I know them? But it hurts so much, Lucy. It's wonderful and it hurts so much."

Lucy tightened her hold around her, and she felt her body shuddering as the tears threatened to come again.

"Sarah and I were so happy together. We played in the meadows and by the river. We would ride our horses. They could run so fast, and we would gallop them through the water, and we would be soaked and our mother would tell us off for coming back drenched! But she wasn't cross really. We knew she wasn't."

"*Our* mother?"

Mattie nodded.

"Yes. Sarah's my sister."

Lucy fought the urge to tell her she was, and always had been, an only child.

"Our cottage was in the woods, in a clearing. I used to pretend that no one knew we were there although, of course, they did. But it was our own little world and we didn't care about anything else. Just me, Sarah and mother."

"Where was your father?"

As Lucy asked the question she saw a cloud pass over Mattie's expression, and a few moments passed before she continued.

"I just want to talk about Sarah."

Mattie turned to Lucy and smiled. The cloud had gone.

"Ok Matts. That's fine. But could you tell me more about this place? Did your horses like to graze near the river? And the woods, were they at the top of a rise?"

Only seconds before, Lucy had been listening to Mattie tell her about a vivid dream, a product of her own imagination. But, as Mattie had spoken of a river, and meadows, and the horses, so something had been triggered in her own memory. A memory of a dream she had experienced, and it had suddenly come flooding back. She had been in her London apartment, after her meeting with the CEO. She had fallen asleep and seen the same place that Mattie was now describing. And she knew it was the same place, even before Mattie answered her question.

"Yes. You stand on the edge of the wood and look down, across the meadows to the river and you can usually see the horses by the riverbank. You talk as if you've been there!"

Mattie laughed as Lucy shook her head.

"No, Matts. That isn't possible, is it? It's your dream, not mine. Please tell me more about your life with Sarah. It sounds idyllic."

Lucy's thoughts were now racing, trying to make sense of something that couldn't possibly make sense.

"Idyllic? Yes, it was."

The look on Mattie's face suddenly changed as other memories flooded in. Memories that Sarah had given her that last time, and the sadness they brought with them was almost too much for her to bear.

"What happened?"

Lucy whispered, somehow knowing that Mattie not only wanted to tell her, but *had* to tell her. She had no choice.

"They said they didn't kill him. But we knew they did. The whole village knew they did…."

Mattie's voice had become harder, almost angry.

"….they were cowards, all of them. Not one of the villagers tried to stop it. Not one."

She paused, staring ahead, expressionless.

"Who did they kill, Matts?"

She turned to Lucy, the tears now falling freely from her eyes.

"Our father. They murdered our father."

Lucy got up and moved so that she could sit on the floor in front of Mattie. Gently she took her hands and held them, more uncertain than ever about how she might begin to rescue her from what now appeared to be the darkest of all her demons.

"Why would they have done that?"

Perhaps if she didn't abandon her to the dream memories, perhaps if she asked questions, kept it as a conversation, then maybe she could hold onto her, keep her closer and thereby stand a better chance of protecting her from the worst of her darkness.

"They were saying things about Sarah. Bad things."

"What did they say?"

Mattie looked directly into Lucy's eyes as she replied.

"They said she was a witch."

"Why would they think that, Matts?"

Lucy deliberately used her pet name, trying to hold her in the here and now. Mattie shrugged.

"We lived away in the woods, so we were 'outsiders'. They didn't like us, but we didn't care. We were happy to be left alone. But sometimes father would have to go down into the village, when we needed something we couldn't grow or make. They said some cattle had died and they didn't know why, so they blamed that weird family who lived up in the woods. Mostly father would ignore their stupid whispers and accusations. But one day he couldn't bear it any longer. He should have kept ignoring them, but these three, they continued to say things about Sarah.

They said she was the only one of us who had black hair, that someone had seen her in the woods surrounded by imps and demons, and that they were going to send a message to the Witchfinder. And when he came, he'd hang her. Father couldn't let them do that. He'd heard what the Witchfinder did, and he knew that he would kill Sarah."

"But they had no evidence against her, did they?"

Mattie gave a quiet, humourless laugh.

"They didn't need evidence. Their suspicions and superstitions, that's all they needed, and father knew it. He tried to reason with them. But you can't reason with blind ignorance and hatred. They wouldn't tell us what happened, but a while later some villagers carried his body up to the edge of the wood and left it under one of the yews. When he didn't return, mother set out for the village to see where he'd got to. She found him and ran back to our cottage. Together we brought him back and laid him in the stone chapel. I remember that mother just sat next to him in silence. Sarah and I tried to comfort her. We wanted her to cry, to get angry, to do something, but she just sat there holding his hand."

Lucy felt her own tears beginning to well and quickly wiped them away. She had been drawn into the world Mattie was describing and somehow felt a part of it which, of course, was impossible. What connection could she possibly have?

"Mother was broken, her world destroyed, and for what? I grieved in my own way. I would take myself off into the wood, or sit with the horses as they grazed, sometimes from sunrise to sunset."

"And Sarah? How did she cope with her father's death?"

Lucy's question had an immediate effect on Mattie. She let go of Lucy's hands, stood and walked over to the window. She pushed the curtain aside and looked out, staring across the street to the rows of houses beyond. Lucy waited for a few moments before she made her way over to her and, standing just behind her, she rested a hand on her shoulder. Mattie turned and smiled.

"This isn't just a dream, Lucy. I'd forgive you for thinking that, but I know it's not."

Lucy gently pulled her around so that she faced her.

"I believe you, Matts. Ok? I believe you."

Did she? Or was she just saying what she thought she wanted to hear? Lucy's thoughts briefly returned to their school days. What had some of the girls called her? 'Mental Mattie'. Well, they *had* called her that until the first time Lucy heard them, and then they hadn't called her that anymore. But was all of this a product of the issues she had coped with for most of her life? Had her demons found another way in, another way to unsettle and undermine? If so, then they had decided to include Lucy in their unfolding nightmare because, no matter how she might want to put all of this down to Mattie's darkness, there was no way she could deny her own visions of the place Mattie described.

"Come and sit beside me again, yes? I want you to tell me how Sarah survived the loss of her…your….father."

Lucy led her back to the sofa and together they sat, with Mattie's hands once more in hers. She could see that Mattie was fighting to keep her emotions in check but Lucy remained silent, believing that any intrusion at that moment might only serve to make it that much more difficult for her. Finally, Mattie looked directly into her eyes.

"She didn't."

"I'm sorry?"

"She didn't survive the loss."

"Tell me, Matts."

Again, Mattie had to gather herself before she could continue.

"The three men, those responsible for killing our father. They all died."

Lucy fought to keep her expression impassive.

"And what did that have to do with Sarah?"

Mattie smile had no warmth in it, just a coldness that shocked Lucy.

"I want to tell you how they died."

Should she say she didn't want to hear it and stop this now? No. Lucy knew that she had no choice but to listen to the whole story.

"The first was thrown by his horse. His neck was broken as he hit the ground…."

As Mattie spoke, so Lucy sensed something in her voice, something bordering on pride. Was this still Mattie, or was she now listening to Sarah?

"….and he died there and then. He didn't suffer."

There was disappointment etched into those last three words.

"The second though, he took days to die. I used to sit out of sight on the edge of the village just to hear him scream."

A small shiver ran down Lucy's spine, but this had to continue.

"What did he die of?"

"Terror. Just pure, inescapable terror."

Mattie said it with a disturbing indifference.

"And the third?"

Get this over with. Get Mattie back from wherever she was now.

"Oh, he was the best…."

Another cold smile.

"….they were worshipping inside their chapel when he jumped from its roof. He didn't hit the ground, though. The rope around his neck saved him from that!"

She laughed at her own little joke, but Lucy wasn't laughing. She took hold of Mattie's shoulders and pulled her around in an attempt to force her to look into her eyes.

"Matts. Finish this now. This isn't you. You would never be like this."

But Mattie pushed her hands away and stood up.

"They deserved it! For what they did to our father, they all deserved it!"

Lucy jumped to her feet, now knowing she had to try to keep Mattie with her. Whatever more there might be to tell, it had to come from the Mattie she knew and loved, not the Mattie of the dream, or whatever it was. She took her hand and led her through to the hallway.

"Get your shoes on. We're going for a walk."

For a moment Mattie seemed ready to argue but the look on Lucy's face was that of someone not in the mood for an argument, and no more words were spoken until they were out onto the street.

"Where're we going?"

Mattie eventually asked in a voice that, much to Lucy's relief, had lost its edge of anger.

"The park."

Considering that, when they had left Mattie's apartment she had had no idea where they were going, Lucy was quite pleased with herself for coming up with that. The sun was setting behind the furthest line of trees as they walked through the large iron gates. It would be another hour or so before they were closed for the night. Time enough.

"Here looks good, don't you think?"

Lucy sat down on a bench near the lake's edge. Several ducks flew over and landed on the island in the centre of the lake, preparing to settle down for the night.

"You can say it…."

Mattie sat next to her.

"Say what, Matts?"

"That I'm going mad, because I'd probably agree with you. But when I was telling you about those men, about my father, I knew what I was saying but, it's difficult to explain….I felt I wasn't the one choosing the words. I wasn't in control."

"I know for a fact you're not going mad, unless I am as well."

Lucy hadn't intended to tell her, at least not yet, but now it was clear that Mattie was becoming distressed and Lucy knew, from past experience, that there was a chance she could fall into a downward spiral if she wasn't steered away from her darkness.

"Matts, your beautiful place. I've been there too."

Lucy waited for her to take that in.

"I think I know why."

Not 'that's not possible!' or 'oh my God!' but - she thinks she knows why.

"Go on" Lucy whispered.

"The last time I was with Sarah, she talked about you. She said she had given you purpose, and that purpose was to look out for me, protect me. So you have a connection, don't you?"

Lucy took a deep breath, unsure now of anything at all.

"Matts, how about we sit here for a while and just watch the ducks and the sunset? Then we'll go back to yours and you can tell me what happened to Sarah. Do you think that'd work?"

Mattie turned to her and smiled, and this time it *was* Mattie's smile, warm and honest and perfect. And so, for the next half an hour, they sat together on the park bench, hearing only the breeze in the trees and the gentle lapping of the lake against the water's edge.

Chapter 23

As it happened, they ended up remaining by the lake until the park attendant informed them that he would be locking the gates in about ten minutes. The peace and quiet, together with the gradually dying daylight, had kept them on their bench by the waterside well after they had intended to leave.

"We must do that more often" Lucy said as they made their way back to Mattie's apartment.

"Yes, we must" Mattie replied, trying to forget the fact that in a few days, in all probability, Lucy would have returned to London and the opportunities to 'do that more often' would become very few and far between, if they were to exist at all. But, in saying those words, perhaps they could both deny Lucy's impending departure for just a little longer.

On arrival back at her apartment, Mattie wasted no time in making them both a mug of coffee, which was accompanied by a slice each of a particularly moreish chocolate gateau. The cake had been Lucy's idea. Although not particularly hungry she had felt that the presence of anything that represented 'normality' could only be a good thing. And what could be more normal than the two of them together with some food and a drink?

As Mattie settled back into her chair, with Lucy sitting opposite her, very little was said between them until both coffee and cake had been finished. Although Lucy had said she wanted to hear more of Sarah and her fate, she didn't want Mattie to go through the earlier trauma of actually seeming to live the narrative. How could she prevent that? In truth, she had no idea, except maybe to watch her closely and to intervene should she see something in Mattie's demeanour that she didn't recognise or that worried her.

"The villagers knew that those men died because of Sarah."

"They might have suspected but they couldn't *know*, could they?"

Mattie laughed softly.

"They knew….and I hope those three knew before they died."

Get the discussion away from them, and try to keep Sarah in the third person.

"What did they do, Matts?"

The question made her hesitate.

"They were angry. A group of them came to our cottage and demanded we give them Sarah."

"Wasn't she with you?"

Mattie shook her head.

"She was alone in the little chapel behind the cottage. They didn't take long to find her."

"And they took her?"

Mattie looked down and Lucy's immediate instinct was to comfort her, but she remained in her chair.

"Matts? They took her?"

She prompted.

"There was a man among them. He wasn't like the rest. He was from their church. A priest. He came with them to try to calm their anger. He tried, but they wouldn't be dissuaded, of course they wouldn't. And yes, they took her. Mother and I did everything we could. We begged, offered them money…."

"Take your time, Matts. It's all ok. I'm here. I'm here."

Could she keep Mattie with her? Lucy knew that her mental state was almost certainly not robust enough to cope with 'living' this tragic dream, or story, or whatever it was. Must keep her 'here'. Must keep her 'now'.

"Where did they take her?"

"Down to the village. She was taken to the meeting hall. They dragged her, and even when she fell and they hit her to make her get up, she didn't make a sound. She didn't scream, or cry out. She was completely silent."

Lucy wanted to react but knew she had to keep her own emotions in check if she were to stand any chance of seeing Mattie through this.

"She was delivered to the four wisest of the village. I knew of them. They were evil. I'm told they held some kind of trial. Of course, it wasn't. They knew the verdict was guilty before they'd even begun. It couldn't have been worse for Sarah if they had called for the Witchfinder."

And so, of course, there was a question that needed to be asked, wasn't there?

"Matts, do you believe Sarah was a witch?"

Did Lucy even think such a thing as a witch existed? Of course not. But still she asked.

"I thought those men died because they had done something evil. I thought it was some kind of divine retribution. That's what I thought then."

"And what about now?"

Mattie considered this for a moment.

"She's very special, and she loves me like only a sister can."

The present tense.

"What happened after the trial? Can you to tell me?"

Mattie nodded.

"The priest tried to take myself and mother away but we wouldn't go. If Sarah were to die we would be there with her at the end…."

She paused and took a breath.

"….so, they took her to the woods and hanged her from one of the yews."

And so there it was in that simple sentence. No elaboration, but just a straightforward statement of the incident. Lucy felt the pain in her words, and could only imagine what it had cost Mattie to say them.

"Mother begged them to take her instead but they wouldn't listen. I wanted to look away but I couldn't and I'm glad I didn't, because just before she died Sarah looked at me and smiled. And I knew then that I'd see her again. So it didn't matter, did it? Nothing mattered. And when all the villagers had gone, the priest helped us take care of her body. She looked so peaceful, and perhaps I felt thankful that they couldn't hurt her anymore. Is that a bad thing to say?"

Lucy shook her head.

"No, Matts. It's what a sister who loved her very much would say."

Mattie smiled sadly.

"The priest said that they wouldn't allow us to bury her anywhere near the village. That included our cottage and chapel. He told us that, if we would consent, he would take Sarah to a nearby town and ensure that she was buried in consecrated ground."

"Did you give that consent?"

"Yes. We could do nothing more for her. But this man could."

Mattie sat back in her chair and closed her eyes. In the moments that followed Lucy continued to watch her carefully, looking for any sign of undue stress or anxiety. Of course, anxiety ruled Mattie's life. It always had, it always would. But what Lucy had seen in her recently had been something else. Something very worrying. At last, Mattie opened her eyes.

"Can you tell me what happened after that, Matts?"

Lucy had so far succeeded in her aim of keeping her outside of the story, but could that continue?

"He left us with Sarah and said he'd return before sunset. He was as good as his word. He came back with a small carriage and a beautiful coffin with the most wonderful, shiny brass handles. We carefully laid Sarah in it, wrapping her in one of her shawls that I fetched from the cottage. She had embroidered it herself. I don't know how, but he had hitched the carriage to our own two horses and though they'd never done anything in harness before, they were perfectly behaved and pulled the carriage as if born to it. I like to think they understood. We journeyed for a good part of the night to the churchyard in the nearest town. When we arrived we could see some flickering lights in the farther side of the graveyard. The gravediggers were still working and so we waited. I remember that they finished just as the sun began to rise, and we laid Sarah to rest. The priest said some prayers and then I dropped a flower into the grave that I had picked from the meadow. I remember seeing it laying on top of the coffin. It was such a bright, wonderful pink, with a golden heart."

Had Lucy recently seen such a flower? She was sure she had. Where had it been?

"We stayed as the gravediggers completed their task. The priest told us that he would arrange for a simple headstone. Mother and I thanked him with all our hearts and asked him the cost. He would take nothing from us. We had never experienced such kindness...."

Lucy could now see the tears on her cheeks and got up from her chair. Gently lifting Mattie to her feet, she put her arms around her and held her. There was no taking away the hurt she was feeling, but Lucy knew she could do what she had done in the past. Just be there for her. After some moments of silence, Lucy guided Mattie to the sofa where she could sit beside her and keep the physical contact.

"We wanted to return to our cottage...."

Mattie wiped away another tear.

"....but the priest told us that, for our own safety, we shouldn't. He found us dwellings in the town. We were well cared for and wanted for nothing. But it wasn't home, was it? Eventually, the priest accompanied us back to the cottage. We found that the villagers had partly destroyed the small chapel. They had even managed to dislodge some of the larger stones, and the roof was gone. Fortunately, our home was untouched, and mother and I returned there."

Lucy kept her arm around Mattie's shoulders as she waited for her to continue, but after a minute or so she said softly

"What then, Matts? Can you tell me?"

She turned to her, her eyes still moist and ready to give up their tears.

"I can't. I don't know anymore...."

Lucy could see her struggling with her thoughts, searching her memory for something that wasn't there.

"Now is the time to come back to me, Matts. Yes?"

She looked directly into Mattie's eyes, hoping to find her there. When, at last, she smiled Lucy breathed a sigh of relief. At times that evening she had felt she was losing her. Had it been nothing more than a bad dream, a fantasy world given life by Mattie's own personal darkness, then Lucy might have stood a chance. However, this was so much more. This was a past that she had also been allowed to see. Was that because Sarah had needed her to know?

"It's real, Lucy. It happened. All of it."

Lucy nodded.

"And it's just come back to me, Matts, in my vision of that place, I saw a flower, just like the one you describe putting into Sarah's grave."

Mattie smiled, this time with a heartfelt warmth that Lucy hadn't seen for a long time.

"I think, deep down, I always knew someone had sent you to watch over me."

"Why would you say that?"

Lucy looked slightly bemused.

"Because you're just so perfect for me."

Mattie embraced her.

"You could use many words to describe me, Matts, but 'perfect' isn't one of them."

Mattie pushed her back, holding her at arms' length.

"Well, you are to me...."

She leant forward and kissed her on the cheek, the simple gesture taking Lucy by surprise, and then added

"....and I'm really tired, so I'm going to bed and you're going to ring Vicky."

Mattie, after another quick kiss, turned away and was gone from the room before Lucy could come up with any kind of reply. For some minutes afterwards Lucy sat in her chair, needing the silence that surrounded her. And now she understood. Mattie's darkness drew its strength from her grief and sorrow for Sarah, and that grief and sorrow would be all pervading and all powerful, no matter what Mattie did in this life, no matter how many times she would tell herself that she *should* be happy. Could she ever hope to escape that?

Lucy looked at her mobile that lay on the coffee table, unable to get past the feeling that to ring Vicky, whatever Mattie might say, would seem like a kind of betrayal. The men and women she had formed relationships with in the past, they had just been a means to an end. An emotion-free transaction under the direction of her CEO. But what she was now considering, that was something different entirely. If she picked up her phone and called Vicky she had no way of knowing the consequences of such a personal, potentially emotion laden relationship for her, for Vicky and, of course, for Mattie. Was that a risk she was ready to take?

Mattie lay on her bed. She hadn't yet drawn her curtains and, through the window, she could see the night sky. The first stars were beginning to appear, just faint pinpricks of light against the ever darkening blue. Her bedroom door was slightly ajar and through it she could just hear Lucy's voice. She was only catching the occasional phrase or word but one thing that she did hear clearly was the end of the conversation and Lucy saying 'Ok Vicky, I'll see you there.'

Those words ran over and again in her mind, and each time they did she felt as if her heart would stop. She fought back the tears as she heard Lucy's footsteps approaching. She rolled over so that she faced away from the door and closed her eyes. She heard the door open as Lucy pushed it a little wider.

"Matts?" she said quietly. When she received no reply she gently pulled the door closed. Seconds later Mattie heard Lucy leave the apartment and she began to sob uncontrollably.

Chapter 24

The late summer sun was low in the sky and just dipping below the highest trees, its rays throwing long shadows across the higher meadow. Mattie ran up the gentle incline, the tall grass brushing against her legs as she approached the edge of wood. She ran on into the shadows, lifting an arm to brush aside the lower branches. But, by the time she reached the clearing, there were flecks of blood on her face where she had been cut by smaller, sharper twigs that she hadn't seen in the failing light. As the cottage came into view Mattie stopped to look around her.

"Sarah!"

She called out, looking in all directions for any sign of her sister. Hearing only the dusk birdsong and the breeze in the trees, she walked on towards the cottage, looking for any movement within as she walked up the short path to the door. It was closed. Tentatively Mattie pushed it and it slowly swung inwards. Once inside, she called out again.

"Sarah? Are you here?"

She was met only by an unnerving silence. Slowly she began to walk from room to room, every so often saying Sarah's name but knowing that, had she been there, she would have heard her when she had first walked in. On the back of a chair there was a half-finished piece of embroidery, something she had seen Sarah working on when she had last been in the cottage. She picked up the shawl and held it to her face, sensing Sarah's presence within its delicate pattern.

Where could she be? Mattie had seen the horses, including the chestnut and the grey, in the meadow on her way up to the cottage, and so knew she wasn't with them. She made her way through to the bedroom and sat down on the bed, still holding the part embroidered shawl. The last of the day's sunlight was just managing to find its way through the window beside the bed, the rays falling on a painting on the opposite wall. It was a landscape. When she had last been in this room she had failed to notice it. But now, for the first time, she saw it and the recognition was instant. It was the same painting that hung on the lounge wall in her apartment.

Mattie stood and walked over to it. She could now see that it depicted a scene from the top meadow, looking down to the river and there, lying on the riverbank and surrounded by horses, were two small figures. As she moved closer to the painting she saw that they were two young girls. Mattie thought back to her apartment, to where the picture hung, and tried to remember if she had actually ever looked at it, even once. It seemed to her that it had always been there. She recalled Lucy had asked her about it once and she had told her that she had no idea where it came from, and that had been the truth. It just 'belonged'. It always had. It always would.

Mattie returned to the bed and picked up the shawl, draping it over her shoulders. Taking one last look at the painting, she left the bedroom and walked along the hallway to the rear of the cottage. She opened the door and stepped out into the garden. Looking over to the ruins of the chapel, she thought she saw a weak flicker of light coming from behind one of the larger stones. Without hesitating she began to run towards it, calling Sarah's name as she neared the ruin.

"I wasn't sure if I would ever see you again."

It was good to hear Sarah's voice once more. She was sitting on the lowest part of what was left of one of the walls. A candle, in its brass holder, burnt with a small, dancing flame beside her. Mattie sat down next to her.

"Why would you say that?"

Sarah smiled sadly.

"Because you know everything now. You know what I am. You know what I did."

Mattie took her hand in hers and squeezed it tightly.

"Do you really think that anything you've let me see would turn me away from you?"

Sarah's head lowered for a moment, causing her jet black hair to fall forward and cover her face.

"I failed you and I failed our mother. I allowed my anger at our father's death to eclipse all else. I couldn't think past getting revenge and the worst of it is, I'm still not sorry for what I wished upon those three men."

Mattie reached out, slowly pushed Sarah's hair back over her shoulder and gently turned her head so that she faced her once more.

"But you paid a terrible price for your anger, Sarah. And you didn't fail us. Please don't ever think that."

Mattie put her arms around her and held her close and, in that moment, she felt she never wanted to let her go.

"But I paid no price at all. It was you and mother who were condemned to suffer all those years, to move out of your home, to lose everything you knew and loved….because of me."

There was a barely concealed anguish etched into every one of her words.

"Lucy asked me if I believed you were a witch."

Sarah said nothing. She stood, picked up the candle, and beckoned Mattie to follow her. Together they carefully made their way over the stone strewn ground. Every so often Sarah would turn to Mattie and give her a reassuring smile as they left the confines of the ruins and walked out into the half-light and towards the wood at the rear of the cottage. They continued on for several minutes, the candle's solitary flame barely adequate now that the sun had set. Sarah took Mattie's hand to guide her between some waist high undergrowth before stopping and lifting the candle shoulder high.

"This is the oldest yew in the wood…."

The candle seemed to glow brighter as she held it up in front of the tree.

"….it was already fully grown in those days when we were happy."

Mattie instinctively put out a hand and rested it on its massive trunk, feeling its rough, peeling bark against her skin.

"Can you sense it?"

Sarah whispered, with more than a hint of awe in her voice. Mattie moved closer to the yew and immediately felt an intensity of emotion that she had never before experienced. It seemed to be reaching out to her, its power drawing her in and she was unable to resist.

"What is it telling you, Mattie?"

"I don't know. I don't understand...."

She became aware of Sarah beside her. Her presence gave her comfort, and her growing fear seemed to recede just a little.

"You don't need to be scared. It doesn't want to hurt you. It just wants to give to you."

Mattie took a step back, her unease getting the better of her despite Sarah's words of reassurance.

"What does it want to give to me?"

Any pretence of calm that Mattie might have been trying to hold on to was now completely undermined and betrayed by her voice, every syllable betraying an increasing anxiety. It took only another moment for her courage to fail her completely. She turned away and begun to run back in the direction of the cottage. Despite it being almost dark Mattie ran on, blindly plunging through the undergrowth. Several times she almost lost her footing, falling to her knees before pushing herself back up and continuing on, running as fast as she could until, finally, she tripped and was thrown forward, her head hitting the ground hard as she landed. She remained conscious for only seconds before her vision closed down into blackness and she lay motionless on the woodland floor.

"Mattie?"

She opened her eyes and saw Sarah sitting beside her on the bed. She tried to push herself up, but Sarah took hold of her shoulders and gently eased her head back down onto the soft pillow.

"How do you feel?"

"I'm sorry. I'm sorry I ran away. I know you told me not to be scared but I couldn't help myself."

Sarah gently rested a hand on her arm.

"Ssh. It's alright. Everything's alright. You should try to sleep now."

"But I want to tell you, Sarah. When I was out there with you, by the yew, it was so wonderful, so perfect. And so frightening."

"It's natural to be scared by something that you don't yet understand."

Mattie looked into Sarah's eyes and saw nothing but love and compassion.

"I need to know about the men that died."

Sarah lay down beside her on the bed, and Mattie could feel her breathing.

"They deserved their fate, for what they did to our father."

Mattie turned to look at her, and time seemed to stand still. She found herself struggling to concentrate on what she wanted to say, her mind a maelstrom of emotions.

"No, I don't mean….not those men. The men who died in my time. The heart attack, the road accident."

"Why are you asking *me*, Mattie?"

"I'm sorry?"

"Why would you ask *me* about them?" she repeated.

"Because you've been looking out for me. You saw those men were a threat to myself and Lucy, didn't you?"

Sarah remained staring up at the ceiling but a smile was now creeping its way onto her lips.

"You still don't understand do you, my dear, darling Mattie? I knew I was right to send Lucy to stop that big bad world eating you up."

Mattie pushed herself up from the bed and stood beside it. Sarah slowly turned to face her, but remained with her head on the pillow.

"I'm not sure what you're saying."

"I think you are."

Their eyes met and an inescapable, dreadful realisation began to creep in upon Mattie.

"Do you recall what you asked me before we visited the yew?"

Mattie nodded.

"I said Lucy asked if I believed you were a witch."

"And you do believe that, don't you?"

Another nod.

"But what do you believe about yourself, Mattie? Have you ever asked *that* question?"

She dropped to her knees, feeling the strength drain from her.

"I didn't wish those men dead! I didn't even know that the second one...."

This prompted Sarah to sit up and swing her legs around so that she sat facing Mattie. She opened her arms and Mattie fell into her embrace. She held her close, knowing that all her sister needed at that moment was to feel loved.

"We are each a servant of our power. We are not its mistress. It channels through us, and around us, but we cannot control how it chooses to protect us."

"You have to help me, Sarah. I don't think I can live with this, with what I am. I wish I'd never been given my new life. I don't want it and I don't want to live without you."

Sarah tightened her hold, knowing that this moment would inevitably come but, even with that knowledge, she was still at a loss as to what she might say to her precious, beautiful, vulnerable Mattie. Had it been right to want her to have this second chance, to give her this new experience of life? Or was it the unkindest thing she could have done to the one she loved the most? Her desire for something better for Mattie, in safer, kinder times had been heartfelt and sincere. But Sarah couldn't have foreseen that the darkness and cruelty would merely take a different, subtler, more insidious form.

"You will never live without me, Mattie. I'll always be watching over you. I'm so sorry for the demons that have followed you, that make you feel so scared. But we will keep them at bay. They won't defeat us. They couldn't then. They won't now."

Were those words enough? Could mere words ever be enough to express what she felt for Mattie? And how was she to tell her that she had to return, that there was no eternal haven for her here? Sarah now wondered if her wish to bring Mattie back to this ethereal paradise had been driven by something darker masquerading as love. That was a question that she didn't want to ask, because she feared the answer.

"I don't want to go back."

Mattie's voice was now quiet, almost a whisper.

"But you have to Mattie. I just wanted you to know. I just wanted to feel your love one last time. You were never going to be able to remain here."

She looked into Mattie's eyes and felt that her heart might break.

"But I can't let you go, Sarah. I can't say goodbye."

"Then visit me. Visit me every day. And bring me roses. I love roses."

"To where? Your grave? No! I want to talk to you, laugh with you. Cry with you. But what I don't want to do is mourn for you."

"And I wouldn't want that. What I do want is for you to live your new life with happiness and contentment, and free of the fear that has brought you so much misery…."

"Sarah! You can't leave me! You don't understand. I think I'm losing Lucy and I don't know what I'll do! Sarah!"

As the tears filled her eyes, so Sarah's image began to fragment and shatter and, just moments later, Mattie knew she was alone.

Chapter 25

Lucy had considered walking to the wine bar but, unsure if that would turn out to be the evening's final destination, decided a better option might be to have her own transport. She climbed behind the wheel of the Porsche but didn't immediately start the engine. Her thoughts, although superficially drifting towards the night ahead and Vicky, were still very much focussed on Mattie, who need only to have expressed the smallest hint of misgiving regarding Vicky and she would have, without hesitation, sent a polite refusal. So why had Mattie seemed so keen that she should go? Did she fear she'd already lost her? If that was the case, then maybe pushing her towards Vicky was her way of drawing some kind of line, and knowing Mattie as well as she did, Lucy knew it would be the uncertainty that would be hurting her the most.

With the shadow of her imminent return to London, and a future that would surely mean opportunities for them to be together would rapidly become fewer and fewer, maybe what Mattie really wanted was a clean break and an end to the doubt. Encouraging a relationship with Vicky might represent Mattie's version of a strategy to cope with that. But could Lucy simply assume that? Of course she would never abandon Mattie, and Mattie must know that. She had promised her, many times, that she would always look out for her, and she would never go back on that promise. Not ever. And Mattie needed her. She knew that. So, no, that couldn't be the reason, could it? Therefore, what exactly was it that Mattie, with her apparent enthusiasm for a potential relationship between her and Vicky, was seeking to prevent?

It was with that question running through her mind that Lucy started the Porsche and guided it out of the parking space, along to the end of the side street and out onto the main road.

The wine bar was, as always, buzzing. As Lucy entered she looked around the room, which was now full of all the bright young things enjoying their money and each other's company. She couldn't see Vicky at first, and it was only when she moved a little further into the bar that she glimpsed her sitting at one of the tables near the far wall. The moment she saw Lucy she jumped to her feet and waved, a broad smile on her face.

"I wasn't sure you'd come!"

Lucy had just about managed to make her slow, tortuous way to the table without knocking anyone's drink out of their hand.

"Well, here I am."

Vicky pulled out the chair next to her and Lucy sat down. It wasn't until she was settled that she had the chance to take a proper look at the woman who sat next to her. It certainly wasn't 'Policewoman' Vicky Traynor. She wore a striking crimson skirt that came to just a few inches above the knee. Short enough, but not too short. On her feet were a pair of black kitten heels and the look was completed by a conservative light grey blouse. Lucy was forced to admit that she approved.

"Yes. Here you are."

There followed a few seconds of what could only be described as an awkward silence before Lucy asked

"Do you come here often?"

It took just a moment before Vicky laughed. Lucy hadn't heard her laugh before, and it came as a pleasant surprise. It was gentle, unforced and genuine.

"Shall we order something? I decided to wait until you arrived, just in case you didn't want anything to eat."

Fortunately, a waiter was clearing glasses from a nearby table and Lucy, with consummate ease, managed to attract his attention. They decided, after a short discussion, that they should stick to non-alcoholic drinks for the evening and, despite Vicky's insistence that she wasn't very hungry, an assortment of olives, toasted almonds and other lite bites were also ordered.

"Sorry I'm not drinking but I'm on duty at lunchtime tomorrow."

Lucy smiled.

"And I've got my car, so…."

Minutes later Lucy was picking up a carafe of the wine bar's own non-alcoholic cocktail, a blend of various fruit juices and crushed ice, and filling both their glasses.

"This tastes good" Vicky commented after taking several sips.

Lucy shrugged.

"On me. I'll take the bill tonight."

"But I can't let you...."

"Yes you can. Look on it as compensation for all the anxiety you suffered wondering if I'd turn up."

Lucy noted that, as well as an attractive laugh, Vicky had a very beautiful smile.

"Does your friend know you're seeing me?"

"Matts? Yes, she knows. In fact, she insisted I came."

Vicky took another sip.

"So what exactly is the relationship between you two, if you don't mind my asking?"

Lucy put her glass back onto the table and took a toasted almond from the small bowl.

"I've no problem with you asking. Answering, however, might prove to be more of a challenge."

Vicky leant in a little closer.

"Now I really am intrigued."

"Oh, don't be. It's, um, I'm her friend. Always have been, always will be. She doesn't have many friends, you see...."

Vicky regarded her with more than a degree of scepticism.

"I sense there's a subtext to that. Am I right?"

Lucy gave her a wry smile.

"She's my friend. Beginning and end of story."

Vicky picked up a large green olive and looked at it for a moment before putting it into her mouth.

"Mmm."

Lucy shifted a little in her chair.

"Is that 'Mmm' for the olive or...."

"Do you know what I think? I think your reluctance to discuss your relationship with Mattie Hayes is not just a respect for her privacy. I think there's more to it than that."

"Oh really?"

Lucy hoped that had sounded sufficiently casual and indifferent, but feared it hadn't.

"And it might somehow involve those two deaths. They have to be a coincidence, don't they? And yet…."

"Is this why you asked me to meet you this evening? Just for another opportunity to interrogate me about them?"

"Interrogate? No, absolutely not. Please don't think that. I'm just interested, that's all."

Could Lucy believe her? She had certainly considered the possibility that Vicky may still be in full 'policewoman' mode and she had no intention of being lulled into saying more than she was prepared to about Mattie.

"Then can we talk about you? All I know is that you look good in uniform, and out of it."

That not only had the desired and calculated effect of momentarily causing Vicky some degree of embarrassment but, Lucy hoped, might also test whether she was merely making conversation or if there indeed might be a professionally based ulterior motive to the evening.

"Thank you for the compliment. I, of course, haven't seen *you* in a uniform but I imagine you would wear it well. As for me, there's not much to tell. My father was in the force and I also decided I wanted it as a career. I went to uni and did my three-year undergraduate policing degree. Been in the force five years now. I'm good at my job. I'm ambitious but in no hurry and not to the exclusion of all else. I'll take the promotions when they come. I'd like to do firearms training, maybe Armed Response or Close Protection one day. We'll see. Oh and, by the way, I'm lesbian, as you might possibly have already guessed. Your turn, Lucy Foster."

She picked up the carafe and refilled their half empty glasses.

"You want to know about me? Ok. I work for a company in the City. I use my talents to obtain certain information for said company, and that information helps to make them, and its CEO, richer. As for my sexuality, let's just say that if I like what's on offer I'll go for it, regardless of gender."

Lucy hoped that her brevity wouldn't be mistaken for rudeness, but she still felt very much on her guard, waiting for the question designed to catch her out. As if she had read her mind, Vicky said

"You seem very defensive. You don't have to be. I'm not about to arrest you. I'd just like to get to know you, that's all."

Lucy immediately felt guilty that she was turning what should be a pleasant evening into some kind of verbal chess match.

"I'm sorry, but if I'm honest, I find talking about myself quite boring."

She tried to look sincere as she said that.

"I think you're far from boring. You fascinated me from the moment I first met you."

It was Lucy's turn to be faintly embarrassed.

"I'm flattered. And I thought you…."

Vicky laughed.

"You didn't think anything about me! You wouldn't have given me another thought if I hadn't given you that note with my phone number on it."

Lucy sat back, and took another long look at the attractive young woman sitting next to her.

"But I'm so glad you did" she said softly, realising she was enjoying Vicky's company more than she had expected to. Perhaps she had been too ready to believe there was something behind the invitation and had been too much on the defensive. But, as the evening progressed, so she found herself warming to Vicky. She was fun, interesting and undeniably attractive.

When, eventually, Lucy glanced at her watch she was surprised to see that it had just gone eleven. It was then she felt guilty that, for a good part of the evening, she hadn't thought about Mattie and, just for a moment, she wanted to be back in the apartment, with her. Being there for her. She should be there for her.

"Do want to come back to my place?"

Vicky's question stopped any further thoughts of Mattie dead in their tracks and it was the logical conclusion to the evening, wasn't it? Was the answer equally obvious?

Vicky fumbled in her handbag for her front door key as Lucy waited by her side. Seconds earlier she had parked the Porsche behind Vicky's car, having followed her from the wine bar to her house on the outskirts of the town. Eventually the elusive key was recovered from the depths of the handbag and they entered into a dark hallway. Moments later Vicky found the switch and the hall was bathed in a soft, warm light.

"Come through."

Vicky dropped her bag onto a small table and led her into a beautifully furnished and decorated living room. Lucy could see that it had been put together by someone, presumably Vicky, with a good eye and even better taste. The furniture was modern and blended perfectly with the deliberately understated colour scheme. There were several works of art on the walls, and some sculptures carefully placed equidistant on the window sill. Lucy found the overall effect stylish and pleasing. Vicky pointed to one of the chairs and Lucy sat down while continuing to take in her surroundings. Had it been what she had expected? Perhaps not. Perhaps she had brought with her some preconceived ideas as to what a policewoman's home should look like. And this wasn't it.

"Do you like it?"

She asked as if Lucy's approval was, right then, the most important thing in the world to her.

"Very much. You have exceptional taste."

This was met with a barely disguised look of scepticism.

"No. Truly. You have a beautiful home. I never say stuff for the sake of it."

Vicky smiled.

"I believe you."

"And would the rest of your home be equally as gratifying?"

Lucy punctuated her question with a carefully calculated flick of her hair.

"Would you like to see it, the rest of my home?"

She pushed herself up from the chair.

"Nothing would give me greater pleasure."

"I hope that's not true."

Vicky beckoned her to follow as she led her back to the hallway and began to climb the stairs.

"Shall we start with my bedroom?"

She threw a glance over her shoulder and saw the look of approval in Lucy's eyes.

"That would be a very good place to start."

Chapter 26

"That was fun!"

Vicky propped herself up on one elbow so that she could look down at Lucy who lay, with her eyes closed, next to her.

"It was….exceptional."

She lazily opened her eyes and smiled.

"Yes. Yes it was. But now it's time that you went back to her."

"I'm sorry?"

Vicky lay back down so that her head was next to Lucy's on the pillow.

"Tonight was wonderful, from the moment you walked into the wine bar, and I'll treasure it always. But it's not who you are, Lucy. Maybe you won't admit it, even to yourself, but I can see it as clear as day."

She could have said that she had no idea what she meant and, perhaps, even a few days ago there might have been a modicum of honesty to such a denial. But Lucy's silence confirmed to Vicky that she understood and, more importantly, accepted the truth.

"Give Mattie my love, and tell her she's very lucky."

Lucy kissed her softly on the lips as she pushed back the duvet and walked over to the chair where she had left her clothes. Silently she got dressed as Vicky looked on. Finally, she picked up the Porsche's key and made her way over to the bedroom door.

"Lucy?"

She turned back to her.

"If I promise not to mention coincidences again, could we remain friends?"

"Of course. I'd like that."

Vicky heard her descend the stairs. Seconds later, the Porsche roared into life and she listened until she couldn't hear it anymore.

Lucy swung the car into the same parking space she had vacated earlier that evening. She switched off the engine and headlights but remained sitting in her seat, staring out through the windscreen at the street lights.

Of course Vicky was right. Perhaps she had always loved Mattie, but that love had been hidden from her by what? A sense of duty? Had she seen it for so long as her duty to try to protect Mattie that she couldn't see their relationship for what it truly was or, at least, what it so desperately wanted to be?

She climbed from the Porsche. As she approached the apartment block she looked up to Mattie's windows. Her apartment was in darkness but, by the time she had reached her door, a light had been turned on in the lounge. She removed the door key from her pocket, a spare that Mattie had given her the previous day but, before she could put it into the lock, the door was pulled open.

"Matts. I thought you were asleep."

Mattie, wearing her dressing gown, walked back into the lounge and sat down on the sofa.

"I heard your car pull up. I've been listening for it to return ever since you left."

Lucy sat down next to her but said nothing as she put her arm around her. Mattie's response was to rest her head against Lucy's.

"I didn't want you to go. I know I said I did, but I didn't."

"I know. But I'm glad I did because Vicky made me admit something to myself."

"And what was that?" Mattie whispered.

Lucy took a deep breath, knowing that she would remember this moment for as long as she lived.

"My true feelings for you, Matts."

She allowed Mattie time to take in those words before she spoke again.

"Even when we've been apart, and God knows we've spent more time apart than together in recent years thanks to my own greed and conceit, you've never left my thoughts. I'd convinced myself that I was still the Year Nine girl looking out for the little Year Seven, that my feelings hadn't evolved from that scenario. Don't ask me why because, right now, I can't think of anything more wonderful than to tell you how much I love you."

She felt Mattie's body give a gentle shudder and realised that she had begun to silently cry. When, eventually, Mattie spoke Lucy could feel her fighting hard against the tears.

"I've never stopped loving you, and that scares me so much."

Perhaps that should have come as no surprise to Lucy. To have to now confront something so intense, something she had put behind a barrier for so long, would be one of Mattie's worst nightmares.

"I don't want this to frighten you, Matts. I'm here and we'll face the bad things together. Ok? You and me."

She felt Mattie edge away from her.

"But we won't be together will we? Any day now you'll be going back to London and I'll have no one. Not you. Not Sarah. She doesn't want me anymore. No one does."

This was close to being the lowest that she had ever seen Mattie.

"But I've been away before Matts."

She turned to her and Lucy saw the fear and hurt in her eyes.

"But this is different, isn't it?"

And, of course, she knew it was.

"Sarah told you she'll always be watching over you. You have to believe that. When I'm not here…."

Mattie gripped her arm, and she felt her fingernails bite into her skin.

"How do you know?"

"I'm sorry?"

"How do you know what Sarah said to me? You weren't there."

"I…."

Lucy realised that she couldn't possibly answer Mattie's question because she had no idea how she knew. She had been desperate to offer some kind of comfort and the words had just come to her at the moment when she needed them most. Now Mattie wasn't the only one who was scared.

"….I imagine that's what Sarah would say."

"How do you expect me to believe that when you don't believe it yourself?"

Perhaps Lucy had briefly forgotten that the empathy was mutual.

"Then what *do* you believe, Matts?"

"Everyone's asking me questions! You! Sarah! What do I believe? Who am I? It might be me. I might be responsible for those deaths and I can't face it, Lucy! I can't face the truth because I've been running from it my whole life!"

Mattie pushed herself up from the sofa and walked over to the painting. She stood in front of it for some seconds, and it seemed to Lucy that she was being held by it, transfixed by the scene. Finally, she turned back to her.

"I'm sorry. You didn't deserve that."

Lucy was relieved to see that she seemed calmer, and that the anxiety that had threatened to overwhelm her had subsided.

"What does love mean?"

Mattie seemed briefly confused until the penny dropped and the beginnings of a smile touched her lips as the realisation dawned that Lucy was recalling a night in, over a year ago, when they had watched 'Love Story' and both ended up in tears by the end of the film.

"Never having to say you're sorry."

Lucy stood.

"Come here."

She held her once more.

"We have tonight Matts, and that's all that matters right now. Isn't it?"

Lucy had never felt closer to her, and yet she couldn't escape a growing fear that their impending separation would now be so much more painful. During her return to Mattie's apartment she had gone over and over in her mind how she might be able to lessen some of that pain. She had even considered returning to London that night, thus avoiding telling Mattie of her true feelings for her. Might it have, in the longer term, been the kinder thing to do? As she held her, there was a part of Lucy that was still unsure. But, feeling the warmth of her body as it pressed against her own and her breath on her skin, she gave thanks that she had decided to stay.

"But can you make this night last forever?"

Mattie asked as she pushed herself away from Lucy and walked towards her bedroom. Following her, Lucy kicked off her shoes in the doorway before leaning against the door and softly closing it behind her, watching as Mattie undressed and climbed back into bed.

"I can try, Matts. I can try."

Chapter 27

Earlier that day the CEO had opened the folder to the first page and re-read the introduction. He knew most of what it contained, but there would be no harm in reacquainting himself with certain relevant details. The fact that this information was in physical form, and not buried in cyberspace, was an indication of its sensitivity. From the outset he had ensured that he and he alone had, under his own control, all the details of Lucy Foster's work and the results of that work. On numerous occasions he had been assured that his company's computer systems were protected by the most robust, state-of-the-art security that rendered them impregnable even to the most accomplished of hackers, and on numerous occasions he had nodded his acknowledgement whilst knowing that he had no intention of testing that assertion, at least not with the Lucy Foster project. In fact, he had recently ensured that she had been erased completely from the company's personnel database, retaining just her security pass, its existence hidden behind layers of encryption, that gave her access to the building for their infrequent meetings. Her high salary was funded through his own private Swiss account, making sure Human Resources didn't ask any awkward questions regarding how much was being paid to this ghost of an employee.

Various staff were now engaged on data gathering in connection with Foster's latest, and probably last, target. He had been careful to ensure that none of them had more than one piece of the jigsaw. It would only be when all the disparate reports were brought together that their true purpose would be apparent, and he would be the only person to see the completed whole. Preparations were almost complete. He would soon be in a position to recall her and instruct her to engage the target.

Given the information he already possessed, it seemed to him that this target wouldn't present any major difficulties. Knowing

Foster as he did, and knowing how good she was at her job, he was as certain as he could be that it wouldn't be long before sensitive intelligence regarding a major rival was appearing on a mobile that he owned for the single purpose of contacting Foster and receiving messages from her.

He sat back in the plush leather chair and looked across the room at the ridiculously expensive abstract that hung on the far wall. He recalled that Foster had once asked him about it, and that she had laughed when he had told her how much he'd paid for it. It had been a laugh that had owed nothing to humour and everything to a mocking incredulity. She had been, as far as he knew, loyal. But respect? That had always been questionable. Even common courtesy had, at times, seemed almost beyond her. He knew that she saw the work she did for him as merely a means to an end, and that their professional relationship had always been, at best, fragile. Therefore, it hadn't come as any surprise to him that she wanted out. But, of course, that could never be an option.

Lucy Foster was an intelligent woman. She would have worked out that, if she wanted to walk away, she would need to play the 'mutual destruct' card. She agrees to remain silent over her work for him in return for her freedom, whilst accepting that if she didn't, she would have to face the consequences, whatever they might be. But that scenario presented too much of a risk. Revenge of any kind, after his professional reputation and that of his company had been consigned to the gutter, would be small recompense and the irony of the situation was not lost on him. Had he not built his, and his company's, reputation upon the bedrock of an overtly honest and ethical philosophy, then the damage that Foster could do would have been much more limited in its destructive potential. Perhaps he should have given that a little more thought before he had instigated the project, but there was little point in regretting what couldn't be undone. He had to accept that his desire for even greater profit and success had led him into a misjudgement and, regrettably, he could only see one solution. That solution would, of course, come with its own difficulties and risks, but reputations had to be protected at all costs.

The CEO closed the folder, got up from his chair and walked over to the window that made up one wall of the room. Often, when he needed to think, he would stand and look out over the City. Today the sun was shining, glistening off the sea of glass and metal that stretched away into the distance. He was already running through his options, all variations on a theme.

His threat to the life of Foster's friend (he couldn't now even recall her name) had been merely a lever to get her attention, to concentrate her mind and prevent it from wandering too far in the wrong direction. It seemed to have served its purpose, for now. But that was all he needed, just to get her back onside one last time.

However, once Foster had been finally removed he would have to ensure that no evidence remained of their arrangement. He quietly congratulated himself that, due to his foresight and planning, that would not prove a difficult task. With everything locked away in his own private safe in that very room he could be certain, when the time came, that he had easy access to all incriminating documents. They, together with that dedicated mobile phone, represented the whole story and could be disposed of without too much difficulty.

It would even be true to say that Foster's own professionalism would also make the task of evading investigation that much easier. She had been discretion personified throughout the whole undertaking. There had been no whispers of anything untoward in the company, either in the boardrooms or the offices, and he prided himself on the fact that nothing was said in that building without him getting to hear of it. But then a thought struck him. Might she have spoken to this friend of hers? It was possible, of course. Perhaps more than possible. He considered this for a moment before deciding that, ultimately, it would be of no consequence. In fact, matters could be neatly tied up by them both meeting with an unfortunate accident.

He returned to his desk and picked up the folder, taking one last glance at the first page before taking it to the open wall safe behind the chair. He placed it into the safe, closed it and pressed a button on the small keypad he carried in his jacket pocket. He heard the lock click and, a second later, the confirmatory beep.

The CEO sat down once more and removed his business mobile from an inside pocket. He began to scroll through the phone's contact list, just wanting to be sure he still had the details of the individual whose services he would probably be requiring in the not-too-distant future. Once confirmed, he placed the phone on the desk, staring at it as he contemplated the day when he would have to make that call.

Chapter 28

Lucy opened her eyes and could see through a small gap in the bedroom curtains that it was still dark. Beside her Mattie stirred, rolled onto her side and, in the same movement, draped an arm across Lucy's body. She was about to say something to her but realised that she was, in fact, still asleep and so lay as motionless as she could. She looked at her face and saw that, finally, she seemed to have found some sort of peace. Perhaps their new found intimacy had given her a kind of emotional release. Lucy felt grateful to Vicky for her perception and the courage it must have taken to voice it. Had she said nothing, had she not forced Lucy to face the truth of her feelings, a longer term relationship with Lucy would have been almost inevitable. She had given Lucy up for Mattie's sake.

But was Mattie now in that beautiful place once more, her sanctuary from the darkness? She had told Lucy she thought that she would no longer find Sarah there and that, for some reason, she had now forsaken her. Could that be true?

Lucy began to think of Sarah, trying to recall all that Mattie had told her. She closed her eyes, wanting to reach out and find again those brief images that she had seen in her London apartment. Outside, the black sky was beginning to give way to a dark blue as the sun began to creep its way up towards the eastern horizon. Lucy rested a hand on Mattie's arm, and could feel her body against her own as she took shallow, even breaths. Just before sleep took her once more, she thought she could hear the first notes of the new day's dawn chorus.

The first thing Lucy saw was the yew tree. She took a few hesitant steps towards it, somehow unsure if she should move nearer as fear began to take hold. Should she be frightened? She looked around her at the trees and grass. Wild flowers grew in random drifts, giving the scene a rare, almost perfect, beauty.

"That yew, it's the one from which I was hanged."

Lucy spun round to see the young woman with jet black hair standing just yards away.

"Sarah?"

"I'm pleased you're here, Lucy. You are welcome."

Lucy looked beyond her, to where she knew there were meadows and a river.

"You brought me here?"

Sarah held out a hand, beckoning Lucy to approach. Lucy slowly made her way to her side and took the hand that was offered. Sarah felt so warm, so alive.

"Let's walk. Perhaps you'll feel a little less anxious away from the woods. I suppose some people might find the dark shadows and the tall trees quite unsettling."

She led her along the grassy path, back past the cottage and ruined chapel and on to a small clearing.

"We shall sit here, I think."

Sarah had chosen a place where they were surrounded by the most colourful, fragrant flowers and, as she sat down beside her, Lucy saw the two horses standing some distance away. She watched them as one followed the other, grazing and occasionally looking up to where Sarah and Lucy now rested.

"Did you bring me here?" she asked again.

Lucy turned back to her, noticing for the first time how her black hair shimmered in the morning sun.

"Yes. I wished to talk with the one person to whom I owe so much."

For the first time, she smiled.

"You owe me?"

"You have been my darling sister's salvation in a world that holds so many demons for her and I want you to understand that this role was not given to you by chance. I need to explain to you...."

Lucy shook her head.

"You don't. I don't want an explanation. I accept it...."

"You fear what I might tell you?"

"Maybe. Yes. I fear it."

Sarah reached out and held her hand once more.

"There is no reason to. There are no demons lurking within the explanation. It is simply told. I wanted someone to be there for Mattie in her new world, as it soon became apparent to me that she would not be capable of surviving it alone. It was my wish in the moment just before I died that she had another chance, a chance of something better, because I knew that the rest of her life here, in this time, would be forever darkened by sorrow. I didn't foresee that the shadows would follow her to her new beginning. But when I saw her suffering, it broke my heart. I felt as though I had given her nothing in return for her love and her lifetime of tears. So I looked to those around her, near her. Who could I choose to help her where I couldn't?"

"But why me?" Lucy whispered.

Another warm smile.

"Look into your heart, Lucy Foster, and answer your own question. Your kindness and understanding was already there, I merely guided you towards my darling Mattie. So you see, it's all you Lucy. Nothing more, nothing less. Just you. You were destined to be her guide and her friend."

"You've suffered more than anyone, Sarah. Why didn't you find another life for yourself?"

Lucy's question caused a fleeting look of sorrow in her eyes.

"There was only one new life to be given and I chose that it should be for Mattie. I don't regret that. I'll never regret that."

Lucy squeezed her hand as she struggled to comprehend what it would have cost Sarah to make such a decision.

"Mattie believes she can never come back here."

Sarah nodded sadly.

"I just wanted to be with her again, and that was selfish of me. It was a mistake and I know that now. Showing her this place only made things worse for her. It's best she doesn't come back."

Lucy looked into Sarah's eyes and saw only sorrow.

"Mattie doesn't believe that and she's hurting so much. She's also scared. Really scared. She believes those two deaths, the heart attack and the road accident, are somehow linked to her. Is that true?"

As she waited for Sarah to answer, the only sounds Lucy could hear were distant birdsong and the breeze in the trees.

"I tried to explain, to say it without frightening her, but...."

Sarah lowered her gaze, feeling unable to look at Lucy at that moment.

"....it could have been either one of us that they hanged. Does that answer your question?"

As Sarah lifted her eyes to meet hers so Lucy saw her pain once more. A pain that had not been dimmed by the centuries, but had been fed by Sarah's eternal love for her sister. How much had it cost her to keep this hidden for so long?

"I lied to Mattie. At least, I didn't tell her everything. I couldn't. You see, there *was* witchcraft in that village. But, as I explained to her, we were merely its channel...."

"We?"

"She had forgotten it all, everything, as I hoped she would. Therefore, I knew I didn't have to tell her the whole story. You see, they wanted to hang us both."

"Matts....Mattie told me that after your father was killed, there were deaths in the village. That was you....wasn't it? You lied to her, please don't lie to me."

"I wished them dead, and they died...."

Sarah hesitated before adding

"....but what Mattie wished for, I don't know."

Even now, she was still protecting her sister.

"They wanted to hang you both, you said. Why didn't they?"

Sarah smiled sadly.

"Because I talked to them. I convinced them it was just me. They wanted their witch. I gave them their witch."

"You sacrificed yourself for Mattie?"

"And for our mother. I couldn't let her lose both daughters. Mattie believes what I have told her. Please, she must never know the truth. It would be more than she could bear."

"You 'talked' to them?"

Sarah looked away again as she nodded.

"The truth, Sarah. What was the true price of sparing Mattie's life?"

"You must promise me. You must never tell her. She must never know. Promise me."

And now Lucy understood the pain that she saw in her eyes.

"Tell me" she whispered.

It was a simple request, but it was clear that the memories she was asking Sarah to recall were distressing and all Lucy felt she could do was hold her in her arms and wait. But, as she held her, Lucy began to question whether she should have pushed Sarah this far, into a place where there was nothing for her but darkness and despair.

"There was a meeting hall on the edge of the village. I was taken there and they were waiting for me."

"Who was waiting?"

"The four. They were the men that the village turned to for wisdom and guidance. I was left with them and they were to question me."

Lucy felt her breathing get heavier and her body was now trembling.

"Sarah, you don't have to do this…."

She gently pushed herself away from Lucy's embrace.

"I do. I can't tell Mattie. I couldn't tell our mother. Who is left to listen?"

Of course. Why hadn't Lucy seen that? She had probably been waiting for this moment for so long, and Lucy now knew that she was destined to serve another purpose, a purpose that went beyond her relationship with Mattie.

"Then I'm listening."

Sarah closed her eyes, as if needing to summon the strength to say what she so desperately wanted to say. When, seconds later, she opened them they seemed to radiate with a renewed determination and resolve.

"You have to understand that I believed I had no choice. They gave me one chance to save Mattie. If I didn't agree to their 'bargain' they said they would have Mattie brought before them too, and told me she would suffer the same fate that faced me. My humiliation for the life of my sister. What would you have done, Lucy?"

"Did you consent to what happened?"

Sarah thought for a moment before she replied.

"I agreed to the bargain for Mattie's liberty. Would I have chosen to do this? No, of course not. I would never choose to allow my body to be used in such a way in the absence of love."

Lucy attempted to hide her own discomfort at hearing those words.

"How could you be sure they would honour the bargain?"

"I used their own superstition against them. They were convinced of my powers. They made their bargain understanding that if they reneged then...."

A momentary darkness seemed to possess her.

"....they would face horror and torment without end."

The sudden change in her demeanour shocked Lucy and she could see how those four men might well have believed there would be a terrible price to pay for breaking their side of the arrangement. Sarah, seeing Lucy's fearful expression, reached out and brushed the back of her hand gently down her cheek.

"I see you too have a little of their superstition...."

Her eyes softened.

"....and recoil in the face of a threat imagined."

She paused to take a deep breath.

"They each took their turn. When they had finished with me I was taken back into the woods. I felt so angry and scared, and I was hurting so much...."

Up until that moment she had referred to it as 'a bargain', a simple arrangement mutually agreed. However, as her words hit home, Lucy understood the stark reality of what Sarah had sacrificed in the last hours of her life in order to save her beloved sister.

"....but I was determined that mother and Mattie wouldn't see my pain, and I held my head high as they put the rope around my neck. I even managed to smile at Mattie."

Lucy could see she was determined not to cry and, perhaps now, there were no more tears to shed.

"That village, those people, took away everything we had. Our family, our beautiful life, our happiness. But I want Mattie to know love and contentment again, Lucy. I want you to give her the happiness back."

How could she respond to that? With the truth? She had demanded it of Sarah. And yet, after everything, how could she say that her future with Mattie was far from certain?

"I love Mattie more than life itself and I'll do anything to keep her safe. Please believe that. However, I think you know that happiness for her won't be easily found. But I'll do everything I can for her, Sarah. I promise you, I'll do everything I can."

Sarah turned away from her and picked one of the flowers that was growing nearby. She held out her hand so that Lucy could take it, its beautiful bright pink petals and golden heart glowing bright in the sun.

"And there's something else I need to tell you, Lucy...."

Sarah leant forward so that she could whisper.

"....your mother and father both loved you so very much."

Chapter 29

"Is it your turn or mine?"

Mattie offered Lucy her bag of doughnuts that she'd just bought from the bakery opposite the park gates.

"For what?"

Lucy asked as she stared into the bag, clearly torn between wanting to be able to still fit into all of her designer clothes and the sight of the golden brown, sugar dusted delights that nestled in the large paper bag. Her resolve lasted at least a couple of seconds before she reached in and removed a doughnut, still leaving another three for Mattie who, although believing in the value of a good, healthy diet, would more than occasionally opt for the 'it's delicious so who cares' option.

"To prepare dinner tonight."

Lucy was unable to reply immediately, having to first swallow an exceptionally large piece of gorgeously warm doughnut.

"Two choices. We could either do it together, or go out. Choose the latter and I'll pay."

Mattie licked the sugar from her fingers before considering dipping into the bag for one last time.

"Oh, no contest then, we'll book the table when we get back to the shop!"

They were sitting in the park on what might be termed their 'usual' bench. Everything was present and correct. The swans, ducks and moorhens were on the lake, the children were amusing themselves in the play area while their parents sat beside the swings and roundabouts, their attention fixed firmly upon their mobile phones, and the weather had obviously read the script. The sky, apart from the odd wisp of high cloud, was a clear, brilliant blue.

Both Mattie and Lucy wanted to make the most of the time they had together, and both needed, for as long as possible, to at least maintain the pretence of normality. Now that their relationship was not only very close emotionally but also physically intimate, time spent in each other's company seemed more precious than ever.

On waking that morning, Lucy had said nothing to Mattie of her time with Sarah. She had made a promise and she would keep it. There was no reason to cause Mattie the further distress that knowing of her sister's true suffering would undoubtedly bring, and the coming days and weeks would be difficult enough when, once more, Lucy would have to leave her and return to London.

She had gone over it again and again in her mind and, whichever way she looked at it, Lucy could see no alternative but to continue to play the game while she and the CEO held a metaphorical gun to each other's head. She hoped that there would be opportunities to return to Mattie but, as before, she knew that in reality they would be parted for long periods, and she would just have to hope that Mattie would be able to deal with that. She had in the past, hadn't she? But that was the past. Things had moved on and Lucy was still asking herself if she should have allowed last night to happen.

"I have some more online orders to deal with when we get back. Could you give the window display a quick look? I was thinking of moving the watches in with the jewellery rather than having them separated. Mix things up a bit maybe? Give it a revamp? Do whatever you think looks good. I trust you."

It was clear to Lucy that Mattie was making her best 'I'm fine, don't worry about me' effort, and she couldn't decide whether to go along with it or cut straight through it and try, once more, to help her face up to her fears and anxieties.

They returned to the shop with one surviving doughnut remaining in the bottom of the bag, having decided they would probably share it later that afternoon. Mattie immediately returned to the back room and her laptop to continue dealing with her online orders, leaving Lucy to focus her skills on the window display.

After having spent a few minutes standing outside on the pavement studying the current layout, Lucy made her way back inside, picked up a notebook and pencil and began to jot down some ideas that had occurred to her. Although Mattie seemed to have more confidence in her ability to improve on the status quo than she did, Lucy applied herself to the task that would occupy what promised to be a rather slow afternoon and that, she was sure, was the reason behind Mattie's request. Keep her busy and she wouldn't have the opportunity to discuss all the bad things, a conversation that, clearly, Mattie so desperately wanted to avoid.

The arrival of a customer took Lucy's attention away from her notebook, and immediately put her into full saleswoman mode. He approached the counter and received the warmest of welcome smiles. Mattie, still seated in front of her laptop, listened through the half open door, and heard him express an interest in the G Shock Full Metal Titanium digital watch that he had seen in the window. She was about to return her attention to the screen when she heard him ask Lucy about the watch's STN display. Mattie quickly made her way to the door, knowing that Lucy would now be well out of her depth but before she had the chance to intervene....

"Oh yes, the Super-Twisted Nematic display. It offers a much higher contrast in comparison with the usual LCDs that you find in most digital watches. Another advantage is that it can be viewed clearly at much shallower angles. Were you also aware that this model has the new core guard structure inside and a Diamond Like Carbon coating on the titanium? It makes the watch exceptionally scratch resistant."

Mattie looked on in disbelief as Lucy caught her eye and gave her a quick wink before returning her attention to the customer, who was on the point of surrendering and already reaching into an inside pocket for his wallet.

"Were you impressed, just a little bit?"

Lucy asked some five minutes later when the gentleman had left with his new watch and a somewhat lower bank balance.

"More than a little bit. When did you become an expert in STN displays and DLC coatings? Been doing some homework?"

She leant back against the counter and gave her hair an exaggerated flick.

"You know me, Matts. Ever the professional."

"I'm going to miss you."

As soon as she had said those words, Mattie returned to the back room and was already seated once more in front of her laptop when, seconds later, Lucy walked in. She didn't look up but kept her concentration firmly fixed upon the screen, even though the tears were rolling down her cheeks.

"Matts...."

"There's nothing you can say, is there? We both know you're going to go, and you can say anything to try and make me feel better, but we both know the truth."

Lucy turned away and walked back into the shop. Seconds later she heard the door lock click and, moments after that, Lucy was kneeling beside her. She closed the laptop's screen and took her hand, gently holding it in her own.

"We're on a tea break for ten minutes."

"We don't close in the afternoon."

"We do *this* afternoon."

Lucy stood and, as she lifted Mattie to her feet, they embraced. Maybe there was little more to be said. Their friendship, throughout its evolution over the years, had always had its foundation in truth and so one thing was certain, there were going to be no empty 'everything'll be alright' promises. Lucy was not about to offer them, and Mattie would immediately see right through any such meaningless attempts to placate her.

"Of course I realise, in my absence, that your profits may take a hit, but I'm sure you can weather the storm."

Mattie gave her a playful dig in the ribs.

"You haven't mentioned last night, Matts. Are you still ok about it?"

Lucy spoke softly, asking what she had wanted to ask since she had woken up with Mattie lying next to her that morning. Had she said nothing because she had her own concerns that it shouldn't have happened?

"*Ok?*...."

Mattie pushed herself back so that she could look into her eyes.

"....Am I *ok* about it? It was the most wonderful thing that's ever happened to me."

Coming from anyone else, those words could have sounded hollow and clichéd. But Lucy knew just how much genuine emotion Mattie had invested in that one simple sentence, and her response seemed obvious to her now.

"And for me, Matts. And for me."

"But...."

"What are you going to say? That with all the sex I've had there must've been something better somewhere along the line?"

Mattie shook her head.

"No. I mean, not really. I don't know...."

Lucy, seeing Mattie's embarrassment, held a finger to her lips.

"Before, with all the others, there was always something missing."

"I still don't...."

"Love, Matts. You're the first person I've gone to bed with that I've loved, and that love will be with you even when I'm not here to remind you of it."

Was that going to make things worse for Mattie when the 'goodbye' moment eventually came? Perhaps, but it was the truth, and it was a truth that Lucy, whatever the future held, needed her to know.

"And will you remember the love I have for you when you're....with someone else?"

Lucy pulled her close once more.

"That, my darling Matts, is when I'll treasure it the most."

For some seconds they held each other, taking whatever comfort they could from those few precious moments.

Chapter 30

As soon as they had returned to her apartment, Mattie wasted no time in reminding Lucy of her offer to pay for dinner out that evening. They quickly agreed that they both fancied pizza and a call was made to one of the town's several Italian restaurants. With their table booked for eight o'clock, that left a couple of hours before they would need to get ready for their night out. With a look that failed miserably to hide her embarrassment that she was even asking, Mattie hesitatingly suggested that they might spend at least one of those hours in her bedroom. To spare Mattie another moment's discomfort, Lucy took her by the hand and, without saying anything, led her through to the bedroom and sat on the bed, pulling her down beside her.

"Do you know what I love most about you?"

Mattie shook her head.

"Your beautiful innocence. And all the bad things that try to make your life so difficult, they never have, and never will, take that away from you."

Lucy put her arms around her and gently laid her down, softly pushing her hair away from her face as she brought her lips down onto Mattie's. And, as their lips touched and she felt the warmth of her once more, Lucy became Mattie's universe and the outside world, with all its lurking horrors, ceased to exist.

"That was wonderful but it's really made me sweat!"

Lucy looked at what was left of the chilli topped pizza on the plate in front of her.

"Surely you don't sweat, you perspire?"

Mattie enquired as she took another slice of her own, much more benign, margherita. Lucy threw her a knowing look before taking a sip of her spritzer.

"You should know, Matts" she whispered under her breath as she decided whether or not to finish the last slice of chilli pizza.
"I'm sorry?"
"Nothing. Enjoying yours?"
"Mmm...."
Mattie nodded.
"....I'm so hungry. I can't think why."
Lucy looked away, wanting to avoid her seeing her smile.
"Room for a dessert then?"
"Absolutely!"

It was good for Lucy to see Mattie able to enjoy another simple evening out. Of course this setting, with just the two of them in the relaxed atmosphere of the restaurant, was well within Mattie's comfort zone. Lucy knew how important it was that Mattie felt in control and now was not the time to try and push the boundaries again.

Twenty minutes and two outrageously indulgent chocolate desserts later, they both sat with their cups of coffee. Lucy reached down for her handbag and removed her debit card from its place in one of the zipped up side pockets and placed it on the small silver plate.

"I'm impressed. You haven't checked your phone once this evening."

"Left it in your apartment, Matts. Didn't want it interrupting our time together."

Mattie reached out and rested her hand on Lucy's.

"I know you're going to get that message anytime now. I can handle it, Lucy. It'll hurt when you go, of course it will, but I'll be ok."

At that moment the waiter appeared with the card reader and Lucy gave her attention to entering her Pin into the machine. Finally, after the payment had gone through and the generous tip gratefully received, she turned back to Mattie.

"Even if I believed you, what makes you think that *you* handling it will be the problem?"

Lucy didn't wait for a reply but got up and removed her jacket from the nearby stand. With Mattie following, it wasn't until they were once more sitting in the Porsche that they spoke again.

"Let's stay here, just for a short while."

Mattie whispered as Lucy had been about to start the car.
"What do you want me to say, Matts?"
Mattie smiled.
"I want you to know that it's ok, that you can talk to me. You've given me so much of yourself, and for so long I haven't seen the price you've paid for protecting me, for pulling me out of the shadows for the thousandth time. If I ever did take you for granted, then I'm sorry and I want to help you if you'll let me."
Lucy looked away, back towards the restaurant, still full of light and life. What should she say? Should she tell her about Sarah, about finding her in that beautiful place? Lucy recalled her promise to never let Mattie know the truth of her sister's last hours. She wouldn't break that promise, but there was something that she so much wanted to share.
"Sarah told me that my mother and father *did* love me."
"You've met her? You found her?"
Lucy leant back against the headrest.
"I believe she found me."
"Tell me. Please."
She turned her head to look at Mattie.
"Do you think she would know, Matts? About my mother and father, would she know?"
"She wouldn't lie to you."
Wouldn't she? Sarah hadn't told Mattie the complete truth, had she? But that had been to protect her because, had Mattie known of the sacrifice her sister had made in her darkest moment so that she might live, Sarah knew it might have destroyed her.
"She understood the significance of what she was telling me. I've only ever told you about my mother and father, about what happened, about how much it hurt...."
Although Lucy had momentarily fallen silent Mattie said nothing, not wanting to intrude upon thoughts that she knew to be deeply personal and about something that cut so deeply.
"....she said she chose me to look out for you, Matts, and I feel so privileged that she did. I'm sorry, I'm making it worse for you, aren't I?"
Mattie shook her head just a little too emphatically for Lucy to be convinced of her denial, and she began to regret mentioning her encounter with Sarah.

"She'd know about your parents, about your worries and fears. She just would. We're irrevocably connected now, you see. All three of us."

Mattie said it in a matter-of-fact way and, for a moment, Lucy felt it might have been Sarah speaking. She looked across the street and saw a couple leaving the restaurant, huddled in their coats, they hurried along the pavement. Rain had begun to fall on the windscreen causing the lights from the buildings opposite to flicker and shatter as their rays passed through the many rivulets that had formed on the glass. Lucy started the engine and drove the Porsche out of its parking space, the wipers clearing the screen in one sweep. Mattie had been braced for a right turn onto the high street but instead Lucy steered the car left to take them towards the town centre.

"Short diversion. Don't worry Matts, won't take long. I know you're not fond of anything spontaneous."

In less than a minute they were coming to a stop once more, this time outside the off licence.

"Won't be long!"

Lucy slipped her seat belt and jumped from the car. Mattie watched from the passenger seat as Lucy entered the shop, seemingly knowing exactly where she was heading. A short time later she was back in the car and handing Mattie what looked like a very expensive bottle of champagne.

"We'll take this home and finish the evening off in style! It was the best they had."

Lucy performed a perfect U turn and in moments they were on their way back to Mattie's apartment.

"It looks pretty good to me" Mattie said as she studied the label, hoping she sounded as if she had some idea of what constituted a 'pretty good' champagne.

"It'll do."

Lucy smiled as they pulled up in one of the 'Residents Only' parking places opposite the small apartment block. With Mattie clinging onto the champagne, they arrived back at her front door where Lucy relieved her of the bottle as she hunted in her jacket pocket for the key. Once inside the apartment Lucy wasted no time in putting the champagne into Mattie's fridge.

"Should be good to go soon, it was already chilled" Lucy said on her return to the lounge. Mattie had kicked off her shoes and was lying full length on the sofa.

"Are we celebrating something?"

Mattie moved her legs to make room for Lucy as she sat down next to her.

"Us, Matts. Let's celebrate us. I think we should, don't you?"

Mattie lay back, letting her head rest on one of the large cushions that lay at either end of the sofa.

"You don't have to pretend anymore Lucy."

"I'm sorry?"

"At the restaurant, you said you left your phone here and yet you haven't checked it since we returned."

"We haven't been back more than a couple of minutes."

Mattie didn't reply. She didn't need to. The look on her face told Lucy that there was now no point in attempting to feign ignorance.

"You don't need to check it because you've already received the message you've been expecting, haven't you?"

"How long have you known?"

Mattie smiled.

"While you were in the off licence I started to think about why you wouldn't have brought your phone with you. Then when you returned with the champagne, I knew. When do you go?"

"First thing tomorrow. He'll expect me in London by nine."

"You do what you have to do. I'll be fine."

How many times had Lucy heard her say that? She had lost count. All she knew was that she no more believed it now than when she heard it for the first time. Mattie would survive, of course she would. But that didn't make it right, did it? She deserved so much more than that and, for a brief time, they had both been afforded a glimpse of what a happy life together might look like. And that glimpse, those precious moments, were now undeniably making their imminent parting so much harder to bear.

"You know I'll be back just as soon as I can."

"I know."

Another smile, this time a little more forced, and Lucy had been about to attempt more words of comfort and reassurance but instead she pushed herself up from the sofa and disappeared in the kitchen, appearing a few moments later with a tea towel, two glasses and the champagne.

"Might not be quite ready but I think we need it now, don't you?"

She held out one of the glasses for Mattie to take and placed her own on the table. With the confidence of someone who was well used to opening bottles of champagne, Lucy removed the foil and undid the wire that held the cork. With the towel over the bottle, thereby respecting Mattie's ornaments and décor, she carefully eased the cork out until there was the satisfying 'pop'. With only the minimum of spillage, Lucy filled their glasses and sat back down next to Mattie.

"Do you know where you'll be going this time?"

Lucy took a sip from her glass before replying.

"We don't have to talk about this, Matts. We can find a film or something...."

"I want to."

She placed her glass on the table next to the bottle and folded her legs under her.

"Ok. Well, I know the 'who', but I'll find out about the 'where' tomorrow."

"Do you ever think about the people you've been with when it's all over? I mean, can you just switch it on and off?"

Lucy could see where this was going and knew that what Mattie was really asking for was reassurance. Her insecurities were threatening to crowd in on her, and her darkness would feed upon any and every anxiety.

"It's what I'm paid for, Matts. It's like an actor giving a performance and then they move on to their next role. No more than that. But I don't think it's my work you're interested in, is it? I think you want to know if I might treat you in the same way, if I'll forget you when I'm with my target."

The use of the word 'target' had been a deliberate attempt to dehumanise, to not refer to them as 'him' or 'her'. She hoped it might help to set their relationship apart in Mattie's eyes.

"So will you?"

And that question confirmed Lucy's fears. Mattie was losing the battle, one of so many over the years, and what had been clear and certain in her mind just a short time ago was now suddenly shot through with fear and doubt.

"Never, Matts. Never."

Lucy put her arms around her and pulled her close, knowing that the stakes for her were higher than they'd ever been and, silently, she cursed that man for taking her away from her dear, vulnerable, precious Mattie.

Chapter 31

They had taken what was left of the champagne into the bedroom and had made love with an extra tenderness and quiet intensity. Mattie's earlier anxieties seemed to have receded as she lay in Lucy's arms, remaining there for much of the night, and as the dawn's first light appeared through a small gap in the curtains, Lucy had tried to quietly climb from the bed without disturbing her. However, as she attempted to gently roll away from Mattie's embrace, she stirred and was awake before Lucy had managed to push herself up from the bed.

"Is it morning already?"

Lucy smiled sadly as she picked up her dressing gown and made her way over to the bedroom door.

"I'm afraid so, Matts. But you stay there. I won't go without saying goodbye. I promise."

Mattie closed her eyes as the door clicked shut, unsure if she had the strength and courage to face that 'goodbye' moment and she felt her fear beginning to grow. In the past, when Lucy had been away, she had been able to run to a special place in her mind, her own storm shelter, where she could hide whenever life threatened to overwhelm her. Even as a child, she could recall going there and waiting for the darkness to pass. But today, right now, she didn't seem to be able to find it.

She knew that Lucy would keep her promise and wake her to say goodbye but, although she tried to find sleep again, it proved impossible. Mattie pushed back the duvet and swung her legs over the side of the bed. She walked over to the window and pulled back the curtains, looking out onto the empty street below. From her vantage point she could just see Lucy's Porsche in its parking space. Might it fail to start this morning? Might she be unable to make that drive to London?

Mattie left the bedroom and made for the kitchen where she flicked on the kettle and began to assemble various cereals, and fruit from the fridge. When Lucy appeared some ten minutes later she was already dressed in one of her best designer outfits, the honey blonde hair didn't have a strand out of place, and the look was completed by the reappearance of the Ray Bans perched on the top her head. Behind her, Mattie saw the small travel case by the front door.

"Wow. You look wonderful."

Mattie spoke the words without any trace of enthusiasm, as if saying them was a requirement rather than a pleasure.

"Thanks Matts. You didn't need to get up. I could've got my own breakfast. I don't want much anyway."

"I couldn't go back to sleep and, besides, I wanted to be with you for as long as possible before you go."

Lucy sat down at the kitchen table and helped herself to a small bowl of muesli and a glass of orange juice.

"I'll try and call you tonight."

Mattie took a slice of toast from the toaster and half-heartedly began to spread some honey onto it.

"I won't be expecting you to. I know it'll be difficult and you'll have enough to worry about."

Lucy knew she was right. She had no idea where she might be or in what situation, but she had needed to say something.

"But I will contact you as soon as I can."

"I know you will. I'll be fine. I'll have enough at the shop to keep me occupied, especially as now I'll have to serve customers as well as deal with the website orders!"

Mattie forced an unconvincing smile before taking a bite of her toast. Lucy could see how hard she was trying and, until this moment, she had placed all of her faith in the empathy between them. Surely past experience would tell her how she should best deal with this? Except now, as she put down her empty glass, everything she thought she could rely on had suddenly deserted her. Lucy stood and carefully placed her chair back under the table.

"I'll be on my way then. Take care Matts and remember, it's only you who'll ever have my love."

At first it seemed that Mattie might stay in her seat as she stared at what was left of her slice of toast. But, as Lucy turned to leave she stood, ran to her, and threw her arms around her, all pretence of a calm acceptance now gone. But it wasn't until minutes later, when Mattie lay alone on her bed, that she let her tears come.

Lucy pushed down on the accelerator at the same moment she flicked the steering wheel, causing the Porsche to dart into the outside lane and power its way past several cars. In moments they were mere dots in her rear view mirror. Saying goodbye to Mattie that morning had been one of the hardest things she'd ever done. On every previous occasion when they had parted she had left her sure in the knowledge that she'd be ok. And Lucy had always been fine with just 'ok'. 'Ok' had always been enough to see Mattie through. But this time was different. The dynamic of their relationship had fundamentally and irrevocably changed. Had that been completely down to Sarah? Lucy believed not. It seemed obvious to her now, but the more she thought about it, the more it seemed to her that it was inevitable that their friendship was destined to evolve into something more.

And what of Sarah? Mattie had seemed certain that she wouldn't see her again. Lucy hoped that wasn't true because where Sarah was, and who Sarah was, represented something so vital to Mattie. She had found a refuge in her, a place where the modern world couldn't touch her. Lucy recalled how, even back in their school days, Mattie would talk of a place where she could go when her darkness came. What had she called it? Her storm shelter, where she had been able to shut everything out and weather the storm. Lucy so wanted to believe that Mattie might be able to discover some kind of sanctuary until she could find a way to return to her. However, as the miles to London counted relentlessly down, Lucy felt that the day when she might see Mattie again was further away than it ever had been.

Her impatience began to grow as she neared the familiar office block. The Porsche crawled its way through the heavier than usual traffic. Apparently, according to the traffic reports, there was a road closure in the area 'due to an earlier accident'.

Lucy sat back in her seat, attempting to resign herself to the joys of the City's roads, although her frustration and annoyance at having to be there at all threatened to eclipse any attempt to think better thoughts.

Eventually she arrived at the turning into the side road that led to the underground car park directly beneath the company's office block. The Porsche's nose dipped as she drove down the short ramp and into that concrete and neon world. The barrier lifted as she held her security pass up to the scanner and, seconds later, she was climbing from her car and making her way to the lift in the far corner.

As soon as she arrived in the foyer Lucy, without hesitation, made her way straight past the reception desk and the bright young thing behind it, with her smile so sincerely insincere that Lucy wondered if there was a factory somewhere that produced these receptionists to a set template of perceived perfection. She headed to the lift at the furthest end of a row of four. As she approached it she saw the female security guard that she'd met on a previous visit. Tanya, wasn't it? Preparing to produce her security pass, she threw a smile in her direction but received nothing in return, not even a demand for her ID. She wasn't surprised. Although always ready to be asked for sight of her pass, no one had ever challenged her and she suspected that the CEO had, somehow, ensured she had full clearance without challenge, thus helping to keep her profile as low as possible.

She stepped into the lift and, with no button press required, the doors swished shut almost immediately. Lucy, in the short time it would take to reach the top floor, tried to clear her mind of everything but the task in front of her. The CEO would be interested in nothing but her total commitment and professionalism, and delivering anything less was not an option. She had always been able to set aside any ethical misgivings, instead concentrating on the bottom line which had always been, for her, the joy of a very healthy bank balance. It had never been about anything but the money and everything that came with it. Did that make her a bad person? Up until now she had never cared.

The lift doors opened. She stepped out into the CEO's private office and the doors closed behind her. He was standing over by the massive window, looking out across the City, his back to her.

"Lucy. Thank you for your punctuality."

So, it was to be 'Lucy' today. Ok. Perhaps that was a good thing.

"I aim to please."

He turned to face her and beckoned that she take a seat. As she lowered herself into the chair she saw the folder he had placed in the centre of his desk.

"You may open it. As you will see, it now contains far more detail than when you saw it initially. Flesh on the bones, so to speak. Of course, the usual protocols apply. Take as long as you wish to study it, ask any questions you may have, but I'm sure I don't have to remind you that it does not leave this room."

"You don't."

Lucy reached out and pulled the folder towards her. She opened it and saw the photograph attached to the first page. It showed an attractive woman, probably mid-forties, auburn hair cut to the shoulder. Lucy noted the necklace she was wearing. It looked very expensive and probably was.

"As I previously mentioned, it's rumoured that her husband is currently involved in the planning of a hostile takeover bid for one of our main rivals. Get close to her and do what you do. I want to know anything and everything."

Lucy didn't reply but continued to read the notes relating to her target. She set about memorising such details as usual haunts, set routines and the names and addresses of close friends, lesser acquaintances and other associates. She read on, learning more personal details about her. Although she recalled that the CEO had previously described the target as bisexual, her preference definitely seemed to be for female company. It seemed to Lucy that her marriage was merely for convenience, for whatever reason. Probably money.

The CEO remained silent as Lucy turned the pages, absorbing details of each and every fact and rumour. He had watched her do this many times before and he almost found himself beginning to regret that, at the conclusion of this assignment, he would be terminating her employment. Permanently. When, finally, she closed the folder he spoke.

"When will you make contact?"

She didn't answer straightaway, instead taking her time to slowly push the folder back across the desk towards him.

"That's my decision and I haven't made it yet."

Lucy sat back in her chair clearly indicating that, as far as she was concerned, the meeting was over.

"Then I trust you will inform me when you have. I needn't remind you that the clock is now ticking. I gave you a few days with your little friend, but your holiday is now over. I want you in place sooner rather than later. How is Miss Hayes, by the way?"

Lucy's expression hardened at the mention of Mattie's name.

"If that was meant as a less than subtle reminder it wasn't necessary. I haven't forgotten your threat…."

"Merely an insurance for your cooperation."

Lucy's nails dug into the leather arms of her chair as she fought to keep her temper under control. There was nothing to be gained by any outward display of anger, however much she may, at that moment, desperately want to put her hands around his neck and squeeze the life from him. She recalled something she had always recommended to Mattie in times of stress and took several deep breaths before replying.

"If you have nothing more to add, I'll be on my way."

She got up and walked over to the lift, but its doors remained closed. She stood in front of them, waiting, not wanting to turn back into the room and face him. Eventually, after what seemed a lifetime, they sighed open and she stepped forward, not turning around until she heard them close again.

The CEO picked the folder up and returned it to the wall safe. As he sat back down he removed his mobile from an inside pocket and placed it on the desk in front of him. He had a feeling that it wouldn't be too long before he would make the call. Knowing Lucy Foster as he did, and for all her pretence of indifference, he was sure she would waste no time in engaging the target and obtaining the information he required. Once that information began to come through he would know when he had all he needed, and that moment would signify the end of the line for both Lucy Foster and Miss Mattie Hayes.

Chapter 32

If Mattie had hoped for a busy day at the shop she was to be disappointed, although in financial terms it had been very successful. She had obtained a rare wristwatch for a customer and that one transaction had brought in a very healthy profit, but as Mattie had accepted the man's debit card she recalled that it had been Lucy who had taken the original order.

The shop had always been a refuge for Mattie, a place where she felt safe and in control. But today, whenever she looked around her all she saw was Lucy, either charming the customers with that smile, or giving her the benefit of her disgracefully risqué sense of humour and, with her online orders completed with very few interruptions, there had been little to take her thoughts away from Lucy.

It had just begun to rain as Mattie locked up for the day and took the short walk to her car. During the drive home she tried to lift her mood by considering what she would cook for her meal that night, and maybe there might be a good film on one of the cinema channels. But, whatever she prepared and whatever she watched, Lucy wouldn't be there with her.

She opened the door to her apartment and walked into the empty lounge. After switching on the television Mattie made her way through to the kitchen. She spent over a minute staring into her fridge, but her mind was as far away from food as it was possible to be. She closed the door and sat down at the kitchen table. Past experience told her that the more she tried to push back against the gathering shadows the stronger they would become.

Eventually, having lost track of the time, Mattie found herself back in the lounge but, unable to settle to anything, she decided she would go and lie on her bed for a short while. As she lay there, still in the clothes she had worn all day, she tried to find her storm shelter but it wasn't there. She wanted to cry but had no tears left. And, as she closed her eyes, the darkness crept ever nearer.

What was it that she could hear? Something that hadn't been there a moment ago. It was a gentle, peaceful sound that was so familiar. Mattie opened her eyes. She was still lying on her back but instead of seeing her bedroom ceiling she was looking up through the branches of a large tree and the sound was coming from the leaves rustling in the summer breeze. As she sat up her eyes took a moment to focus, and then she saw the meadows and the river and by the riverbank a small figure was sitting, looking up towards her. She jumped to her feet and began to run as fast as she could down the gently sloping meadow. At one point she almost fell as her foot caught in a small dip hidden by the long grass.

"Sarah!"

Mattie called out as she ran on, her breaths coming in rapid, short gasps. As she neared her Sarah stood and in seconds Mattie was with her once more and being held in her arms.

"I thought I would never see you again."

Mattie whispered through her laboured breathing. Sarah didn't reply but simply tightened her embrace. Beside them the river flowed over its pebble bed, the larger stones causing the water to ripple and eddy as it rushed over them.

"I want to stay here with you. I don't want to go back. I try to survive, to make it work. But I can't. I'm sorry…."

Sarah gently guided her down onto the long grass before sitting beside her.

"You can't remain here, my darling. You and I no longer belong in this place. Our time here is over and you must return."

Mattie shook her head.

"No. This is our home. This is where I feel truly safe."

Sarah cradled her head in her hands, looking into her eyes.

"This *was* our home, my love. But you have a new home now, and there's a person there who loves you very much."

"But she's not there, is she? She's abandoned me, just as you're going to abandon me."

"But I've told you, Mattie. I'll never leave you, and neither will Lucy. We haven't abandoned you."

Mattie turned to look back towards the woods, in the direction of the cottage they had once shared.

"We were happy here and where you say I now belong, I just feel so scared, and I can't fight it anymore."

Sarah sensed her trembling in her arms and felt, more than ever, that using their gift to give Mattie another chance of happiness might have been the most awful mistake. All it had given her was more suffering. How could it have come to this? The power that they both possessed should have been their salvation, their friend and their protector. Instead it had ultimately brought them nothing but fear and death.

The sun had dropped below the trees to the west and dusk was not far away. Already the air was cooler and the sky was becoming a deeper shade of blue. Sarah removed the shawl she was wearing and wrapped it around Mattie.

"The night is coming, my love. It's going to get cold very soon."

She felt Mattie shiver but knew her reaction had nothing to do with the rapidly approaching night.

"Can we stay here until the stars come out? I want to be with you when the darkness comes."

And, as Sarah looked into her eyes and saw how utterly lost Mattie was, she thought her heart might break.

The two horses, silhouettes in the moonlight, made their way slowly along the riverbank towards Sarah and Mattie. They stopped as they reached their owners' side, waiting. Sarah lifted Mattie to her feet and led her over to where the horses stood.

"Shall we?"

Sarah grabbed the grey's mane and swung herself onto its back. Mattie hesitated for only a moment before she climbed onto the chestnut.

"Where will we go?" Mattie asked.

Sarah smiled, nudging the grey into a gentle walk.

"Somewhere. Anywhere. It doesn't matter, does it?"

Mattie smiled and shook her head as together they followed the course of the river, the moonlight flickering and dancing on the flowing water. On the edge of the furthest meadow, the wood loomed, dark and forbidding. Mattie looked over towards it as they rode on, knowing that if she were alone imagined terrors would now be gathering, ready to drag her back into the shadows. But she wasn't alone, and Sarah could protect her. She could protect her forever.

The two horses walked on, seemingly knowing where they were heading, their gentle rocking motion lulling Mattie into a feeling of sleepy contentment. And, as the minutes passed, so any residue of fear that might have been lurking, waiting for its moment to take her, had gone. How long since she had felt such a release from the darkness that was always at her shoulder?

"There's a place I've never taken you, and it's not too far from here."

Sarah pointed ahead and, as they continued, so in the distance Mattie could just begin to make out that the river was widening. But it wasn't until they had walked on for a little longer that she saw where Sarah had been pointing.

In the middle of the river, equidistant from both banks, was a small island. As they approached, Mattie could make out trees and undergrowth, moonlit and breathtakingly beautiful. Sarah walked the grey forward a few further strides until she reached a place where the bank sloped in a shallow, short path into the water. She urged her horse along it and down into the water, shattering the moon's reflection as they made their way across the river and up onto the island. Mattie's chestnut needed no encouragement to follow and she felt the cold water splash against her legs as they made the short crossing, taking just moments to join Sarah and the grey on the island's shore.

As soon as she saw that Mattie had made it safely to the island, Sarah dismounted and allowed her horse to amble away into the trees. She walked over to Mattie and held the chestnut as she climbed down. The horse remained still until Sarah released her hold, and as soon as she did it trotted off, eager to join the grey.

"I kept this special place a secret, even from you, but I'm pleased we have this chance to be here together."

Mattie took a moment to look around her. Even though the only source of light was the bright full moon, she could see enough of their surroundings to appreciate that this was somewhere of exceptional beauty, with the sound of the flowing river providing the backdrop to the sight of trees, low undergrowth and small clearings that ran along the shoreline, free of larger vegetation, where grass and flowers grew.

Sarah waited as Mattie stood in silence, seemingly hypnotised by the island's magic. When at last she turned to her, Sarah took her hand and led her along the path that the horses had taken, into one of the clearings at the concealed heart of the small island.

"Do you like it?"

Sarah stepped aside, letting Mattie make her way past her so that, for the first time, she might see the glade, a natural shelter bordered on three sides by trees that created a canopy of leaves and branches. The ground beneath was covered with grass, moss and chamomile, its apple sweet scent hanging in the night air.

"It's beautiful. Can we stay here until morning?"

Sarah beckoned her into the shelter and they lay down, the ground warm and yielding beneath them.

"Yes. Until morning."

Sarah took her in her arms and they lay together saying nothing but both drawing strength from the love they had for each other. But, as Mattie slept in her embrace, Sarah found her sadness and regret threatening to eclipse the happiness she felt being with her sister once more. She knew that with the coming of the dawn she would have to say goodbye again, for the last time, and thinking about what that might do to Mattie was almost too much to bear. She began to ask herself what she could possibly do to make things right. Mattie's new life had to work for her. It had to. It couldn't just become another tragedy, filled with nothing but fear and sorrow. Sarah recalled the look of horror on her face when Mattie had come to realise that she had been unconsciously responsible for the deaths of those two men who, in different ways, had posed a threat to her. That had told Sarah that for Mattie to continue to use their gift to clear herself a path in her new life would clearly be impossible for her and, consequently, she would always be at the mercy of the ever present darkness.

Sarah didn't sleep at all but, instead, spent the night looking up through the trees at the stars, while all the time cradling her beloved Mattie, feeling every breath that she took. But, as the sky to the east began its slow but inevitable transition from night into day, Mattie began to stir and Sarah knew that the moment had come. Was it cowardly to let her go now, before she woke? Perhaps.

"Goodbye, my darling Mattie" Sarah whispered, kissing her softly as she gently laid her down and released her embrace for the last time.

Chapter 33

Mattie pulled back her bedroom curtains and looked out on the grey overcast sky. She had already gone through her morning routine and had, seconds earlier, finished her one piece of toast that she had spread with the merest hint of strawberry jam. She hadn't wanted to eat anything, and even that one pathetically thin slice had been almost too much for her.

The trauma of waking and finding herself back in her own bedroom, alone in the deafening silence, had brought more tears. She had thought she had done all her crying. She had thought she couldn't be dragged down any further. She had thought she had seen what the depths of despair looked like. But she had been wrong. And the more she fought to hold onto the memory of lying in Sarah's arms, on her island, in that beautiful place, the further away the images drifted. It was as if she was to be denied even the comfort of her dreams, to be cut loose and allowed to drown in the frightening, cruel, uncaring world to which her new life had been consigned.

Walking over to her wardrobe, Mattie slid the door back and began to half-heartedly look through the 'shop' end of her outfits, the ones she kept solely for work. In fact, they comprised about three quarters of all her clothes, as she had little need for what might be called 'evening wear'. And, today, she felt as if she didn't have any need for the rest either, as she wasn't even sure she would bother to open the shop. What was the point? What was the point in anything anymore?

She lay back down on the bed still wearing her night clothes, having no desire to either make the effort to choose an outfit or put it on. She could hear rain against the window and watched as the water drops gathered and ran down the glass in thin, random rivulets. Maybe if she closed her eyes again sleep would take her and Sarah would be waiting. If she could just find her again everything would be alright. Except sleep wouldn't come, and the more she willed it the more it defied her.

As Mattie lay there, alone, she knew that she had nothing left to fight this battle. She knew that the darkness would take her and she was ready to let it. She could see the approaching storm on the horizon, and it was moving inexorably towards her. She had no shelter, nowhere to run. Even that had deserted her. Of course, this was just one of many that had sought her out, and she had survived them all. But she knew that this one was different. This one, she was sure, had the potential to rip away all hope and hurt her more deeply than anything that had gone before.

Was this because of Sarah and Lucy? Had the intensity of her love for them, perversely, made her fears and anxieties grow stronger and given that prowling dread a new purpose? Would everything have been alright if Sarah had never found her, if Lucy hadn't taken their love to another place? Mattie wanted to tell herself 'no', that all of that had made no difference. But, of course, she would always be asking herself that question. She tried to fight the doubt by recalling all of the beautiful moments she had known with Sarah and Lucy, and those memories caused her to smile, just briefly. Was that, perhaps, where her salvation lay? But would those memories endure when the darkness surrounded her, when the storm was at its height?

She held her eyes closed as she sought to find again Sarah's warm embrace and the touch of Lucy's lips on her own. If she could just hold onto all the beautiful things, those moments that had told her life was worth living, then she might be able to rediscover her storm shelter and find the sanctuary she so desperately desired. And, even though she felt the shadows gathering around her, she managed to focus her thoughts upon Sarah and Lucy.

Mattie rolled over on to her side and drew her knees up into her chest. With her eyes still tightly shut, she knew that the storm was nearly upon her and all she could do was wait and hope….

The ringing of the bell was incessant and getting louder. Mattie tried to shut it out but it wouldn't stop and it was all pervading. She put her hands over her ears but there was no escape and, after what could have been seconds or minutes, the sound succeeded in dragging her back into the here and now. She sat up and climbed from the bed. As she walked through to the lounge so her doorbell continued to ring. Before she released the chain and opened the door she took a quick glance through the spyhole. As she pulled the door back so Vicky took a step forward.

"Hi Mattie. You ok?"

She was used to seeing her in her police uniform and so this, coupled with her still semi-conscious state, meant that Mattie took some moments before she recognised the young woman standing in front of her wearing a pale blue blouse and distressed, well-fitting jeans.

"Oh, yes, I'm....come in."

Mattie stepped aside and Vicky made her way past her and into the lounge.

"Please, have a seat."

Vicky chose the chair opposite the sofa and sat down, her eyes all the time fixed on Mattie.

"If you want Lucy, she's not here at the moment and I'm not sure when she'll be back."

Vicky shook her head.

"No. I'm here because of you."

"Why?"

Mattie was rapidly regaining her senses and Vicky saw the look of suspicion that accompanied her question. Vicky gave her, what she hoped, was a reassuring smile.

"I'm off duty, well, fairly obviously."

She looked down at her clothes.

"Then....?"

"I drove past your shop this morning and I saw it was closed so I stopped to take a look. There was no notice on the door, or any sign that it was a planned closure...."

Once again, another wary look was thrown in her direction.

"....forgive me, I can never switch the 'police mode' off these days. If something doesn't look right, I feel the need to check it out. Your shop being closed didn't look right, and I remembered your home address from that incident the other night. So here I am."

She completed the sentence with a shrug, as if to say 'over to you'.

"That's really kind of you but, as you can see, I'm fine."

Vicky nodded slowly.

"Of course you are. Well, in that case I'll go then, shall I?"

Mattie had been about to reply, but her expression changed and any pretence of being 'fine' evaporated as quickly as it had appeared.

"I, um, I get a bit down from time to time and today's one of those times. That's all. I'll get over it. I always do."

The glance away told Vicky all she needed to know. She stood up and looked around her.

"Your kitchen through there?"

Mattie nodded.

"Ok. Stay right where you are. I'm going to make us both a coffee."

Mattie looked on as she disappeared into the kitchen. A short time later she heard the sound of the kettle and the clink of coffee cups.

"How do you take it?"

"Milk, no sugar, thank you."

In other circumstances Mattie would have been in there with her, not expecting a relative stranger to wait on her in her own home. But, right then, she had to admit that she felt nothing but gratitude both for the forthcoming coffee and for the company.

"There you go."

Vicky handed her a large, steaming mug before sitting back in her chair. Mattie took several sips, all the time watching and waiting for a question that she didn't want to answer, or a comment that she didn't want to respond to. But instead....

"I lied to you earlier."

"I'm sorry?"

Vicky leant forward and carefully placed her coffee on the table.

"When I told you that it was my police officer's instinct that brought me here. It was a lie. Not that I intended it to be. Don't think that. It was just that I'm not totally sure why I came to find you."

"I don't understand."

Mattie's words prompted a smile from Vicky.

"Well then, that makes two of us."

"I still don't...."

"Would it sound really stupid to say that I felt compelled to come here and check you were ok?"

Her question was followed by a short silence as Mattie hesitated before replying.

"Sarah" she whispered.

"I'm sorry?"

"It was Sarah. She brought you here."

Vicky shook her head.

"No. I think you must be mistaken. I don't know anyone called Sarah, and no one told me to come here."

Mattie took another drink from her mug as she considered just what, if anything, she should say.

"Then I apologise. I must be mistaken. Thank you for making the coffee, by the way, it's perfect."

Vicky's every instinct told her that she wasn't hearing the truth, that Mattie felt she was far from mistaken but, for whatever reason, had decided she didn't want to pursue this 'Sarah' thing. Should she push it? No. She wasn't interviewing a suspect now. She was with, what looked to her, a very vulnerable, anxious young woman.

"You said Lucy's away at the moment?"

It was an innocent enough enquiry but Mattie knew that any conversation about Lucy had the potential to get more than a little awkward. How would it go? 'So what takes your friend away from you for such long periods of time?' 'Well, she fucks industrial secrets out of people'.

"Yes. But I'm used to it. I can cope, usually."

"Can we call her, maybe? Perhaps she can come back for a short while, just until you feel a little better."

"No. That isn't possible and she knows I understand that."

For a moment Mattie found herself wishing that wasn't so, but she managed to push away any such ridiculous notions before they took hold.

"And do *you* know just how much she loves you?"

The look on Mattie's face told Vicky that she did, but the sadness that was so clearly there just below the surface, was also painfully apparent.

"Do you know what I think?"

Mattie shook her head as Vicky stood and walked over to the window.

"I think...."

She pulled the curtain back and looked out.

"....that we should go out for a bite to eat. Nothing fancy and I won't argue if you insist on paying. I also promise I won't make any more clumsy attempts at pointless conversation. We can sit in silence if you want."

Mattie's first instinct had been to politely refuse but, if she had, what then? Go back to bed for the rest of the day, trying to hide from her darkness? She had done that too many times now and she feared that if she continued down that path then maybe, one day, she might not come out the other side. Although she had never put such a fear into words, she knew it had been there in her subconscious for some time. If she fought and lost then, at least, she would know she had tried and not merely surrendered to what she had, for so long, considered inevitable.

"Give me a few minutes, can you?"

Vicky nodded as Mattie made her way past her to the bathroom. She sat back down and picked up her coffee. There was a magazine on the table. She began to leaf through the pages, looking at each one but not really seeing it. Why had she come here? Yes, she had seen that the shop had been closed when it should have been open. But what had taken her on that route on that particular morning? It certainly wasn't on her way to....where had she been going? She really couldn't remember, and the more she tried the more elusive the answer became. Vicky replaced the magazine on the table and leant back in her chair, closing her eyes. Perhaps if she could just think, try to recall....

"I'm ready if you are."

Mattie's voice broke through the silence and dragged Vicky back from wherever she had gone.

"Good. My car's in the next street. There's a really nice tearoom on the outskirts of town. I go there sometimes."

"Sounds good."

"And then maybe back to the shop?"

Mattie smiled.

"Yes, maybe."

As good as her word, Vicky remained silent as they walked the short distance to her car. It had stopped raining and the sun was making a valiant attempt to break through the ever thinning cloud. Mattie climbed into the passenger seat and it was as she looked down to fasten her seat belt that she noticed something lying on the dashboard.

"Where did that come from?"

"What? Oh, that. I'm not sure. Quite strange really. It was there when I got in the car this morning. Here, you can have it if you want."

Vicky picked up the small, bright pink flower with its golden heart and offered it to Mattie.

Chapter 34

"I'm so sorry! How clumsy of me."

Lucy knelt at the feet of the elegant, middle aged woman and proceeded to gather up the contents of her handbag that, moments earlier, she had 'accidentally' knocked from her grasp and onto the floor of one of the more exclusive London fashion boutiques. The woman watched as the rather attractive young lady fumbled around the carpet, gathering up various lipsticks and other cosmetics, several credit cards, a compact mirror and a small bottle of Kilian - Good Girl Gone Bad perfume, the latter two fortunately undamaged.

"Please don't apologise. It may have been my fault" the woman said, knowing full well it wasn't. Lucy picked up the last item, a pencil eyeliner, and placed it back into the Gucci handbag with all the other things that had been scattered in all directions. She slowly stood and her skirt, that she had surreptitiously encouraged to ride up when she knelt, fell back into place.

"I think everything's there."

She returned the handbag and the woman took it without so much as a glance inside, her gaze instead fixed firmly upon Lucy.

"I'm sure it is. Thank you."

Lucy smiled as she gave her honey blonde hair a flick, already knowing that the woman had taken the bait. But getting to this moment had taken careful planning and close covert observation. Experience had shown Lucy the value of detailed preparation and now it had become second nature to her. For this particular target she had noted how the woman always carried her handbag in such a way that, if she were accurate in her approach, she could not only knock it from her grasp but also release the clip so the contents would be scattered as it fell. Making it seem like an accident was the most difficult part and Lucy had turned it into something approaching an art form. She had used variations on this particular theme on several occasions in the past, achieving the desired result every time.

"I'd like to make amends in some way. Would you allow me to buy you a drink, or something?"

Lucy followed that with the warmest of well-practiced smiles.

"I might, if you think that such an insignificant mishap warrants such a thing."

"If you'd rather not...."

"I didn't say that."

Lucy realised that, although she no longer wished to be involved in these emotional games, there was still a perverse kind of pleasure to be derived from playing her target like a fish on the line. Even now there was a part of her, a part she had hoped to bury for good, that enjoyed the hunt and capture, and just a short time later they were sitting in a restaurant just a few doors down from the boutique, at a corner table away from the hustle and bustle elsewhere in the room.

"One of your regular places?"

Lucy looked around her at the clientele, noting the various designer labels and bespoke jewellery on display.

"I've been here a few times."

"Mmm. Is that how we just happened to get the best table without even asking?"

The woman looked over to the waiter who had ushered them to that table moments earlier. She received a broad smile and it was obvious that he was acknowledging a valued customer.

"Ok. Guilty as charged. I come here pretty much every week."

"Why didn't you say so?"

She looked a little embarrassed and so Lucy added

"I'm not intimidated by wealth, if that's what's worrying you. And my name's Lucy, by the way."

The woman laughed, realising that they hadn't yet introduced themselves.

"Angela. So pleased to meet you."

"Good to meet you too."

Lucy offered her hand which was taken gently, with a slight awkwardness that Lucy found strangely endearing. So, as the world continued on around them, Lucy began to learn more about Angela, and as she listened to a woman who seemed to be in need of someone to listen, she realised she was experiencing something she had never felt with any previous target. Guilt.

Here, sitting in front of her, was someone who appeared to have everything anyone could want. A wealthy, successful husband and a lifestyle that many would envy. She had an apartment in Knightsbridge and, she told Lucy, a 'place away from the City', set in several hundred acres of Berkshire countryside. And yet, Lucy sensed, there was an emptiness inside her, a longing which she was trying, and failing, to hide. She was desperate to be loved. Lucy was certain of it.

Having read the dossier, listened to the CEO outline Angela's situation and character, and formed her own conclusions from the reports, Lucy now saw, not the theory, but the harsh, sad reality of a human being who had it all and had nothing. And she, Lucy Foster, was about to exploit this woman's vulnerability in a way that could only result in further heartbreak and hurt. Yes, she felt guilty.

Over two exceptional glasses of wine and a salver of the most exquisite cakes and pastries, Angela continued to drive the conversation and Lucy remained mostly silent, listening and learning until

"If you'll excuse me...."

Lucy said when there was a natural pause.

"....I just need to visit the ladies room."

Seconds later, as she closed the cubicle door, she removed her mobile from the inside pocket of her jacket and from her contacts she selected the only one that consisted purely of a number, with no name or title attached. She was about to type in the short message, but hesitated. She wanted to call it off. Make her excuses and leave and never see Angela again. But she then thought of Mattie and remembered why she had to see this through. Quickly, she entered the words 'Target acquired' and touched the Send icon.

On her return to the table Lucy found that Angela had already settled the bill.

"But this was supposed to be my treat by way of an apology."

"Oh, I had no intention of letting you pay."

"Then?"

Her gaze dropped for a second, and she seemed almost embarrassed by the answer she was about to give.

"The moment I saw you I knew I wanted us to spend time together. I'm attracted to you, Lucy. There, is that honest enough for you?"

In the past, when Lucy had heard something similar, she would have felt an inward satisfaction that the hardest part was over. Once the target accepted her and wanted her, and provided she played the long game with patience and sensitivity, then success invariably followed. However, it was not only guilt that was overshadowing any feelings of accomplishment, but a sudden self-loathing. Angela had, without knowing, brought her face to face with a truth that she had managed to keep buried beneath the money and the conceit for so long. And the truth was she hated herself for doing this.

"We could take a walk, if you want."

"Do you have the time? I imagined someone like you would be dashing off for a terribly important appointment, or have something young and handsome waiting for her somewhere."

Lucy forced a laugh, and hoped it hadn't sounded too hollow.

"Absolutely not. My time is my own."

But it wasn't until they had left the restaurant that Angela asked the obvious follow-up.

"So what exactly do you do? Do you need to earn a living?"

Of course Lucy would always have had a credible, verifiable back story. She would have rehearsed it, tried to anticipate the questions she might be asked, and had every last detail nailed down. But that was then, wasn't it? That was when she cared little about anyone but Mattie. The bottom line for her had always been the money in the bank, the Porsche parked outside her apartment, the designer labels in her wardrobe, the best champagne in her fridge. But it was this encounter, with this target, that finally confirmed to Lucy that, for her, everything had now irrevocably changed.

She had not only Mattie's friendship, but her love. And that had given her a new purpose beyond the material, beyond the 'bottom line'. But, whether she was eventually to have the life with Mattie she now so dearly wanted or not, Lucy knew that, one way or another, this time, with Angela, it had to be different.

"I work in a small shop that sells artisan jewellery and select lines of wristwatches."

In that moment of spontaneous rebellion, dumping the cover story agreed with, and approved by, the CEO, Lucy felt an overwhelming sense of liberation. Perhaps that feeling was out of all proportion to its actual significance, but not for Lucy, not right then. All that mattered was that she had allowed the truth to momentarily subvert her world of deceit.

"That sounds…."

She could see Angela struggling to find an appropriately diplomatic response.

"….lovely."

Lucy nodded, ignoring the fact that Angela seemed less than overwhelmed with enthusiasm.

"It is, actually. I can honestly say I'm never happier than when I'm there."

She wanted to say more. To tell her of Mattie and the life she wanted so much.

"Then I'm pleased that there is somewhere where you can find happiness. Is there also some*one*?"

How should she answer that? If she continued with the truth she could well jeopardise everything and, as a consequence, endanger Mattie. Angela saw her hesitation and was quick to respond.

"I'm sorry. I didn't mean to pry. I've only just met you and it's none of my business. Could we take that walk you mentioned?"

Lucy nodded. She had been about to tell her that it wasn't a problem, but then thought that perhaps, after all, letting her believe that particular subject was off limits would be the better option, thereby keeping things as simple as possible.

"We'll take a taxi to the Embankment, if that's ok? It's one of my favourite places."

In response, Angela held up a hand to a passing black cab and seconds later they were sitting in the back of the taxi and on their way to the Southside of the Thames Embankment. As the driver expertly weaved his way through the London traffic, they said very little. Several times Angela threw Lucy a nervous smile, as if she needed some kind of reassurance that this young woman, who had suddenly come into her life, was still happy to be in her company.

"This'll do, thank you."

Lucy called through to the driver, who dutifully pulled into the kerb. Determined that Angela shouldn't pay again, she produced cash to pay the fare plus a generous tip.

"Why don't we walk a little way and then find an empty bench?"

Lucy asked as the taxi drove away in search of his next fare.

"That sounds perfect."

As they made their way along the footpath by the Thames, so London went on around them. Joggers, young couples, an elderly man walking his dog, tourists taking selfies, ensuring they got the Houses of Parliament in the background and, in the distance, the siren of an emergency vehicle.

"I can't remember the last time I did this. You know, just taking a moment to breathe."

Lucy pointed to a bench a little way in front of them.

"How about here?"

As they sat down Lucy noticed that Angela was taking care not to sit too close to her.

"They must pay you well at your little shop."

Lucy gave her a puzzled look.

"I don't follow."

"Where we met, I mean, I don't mean to assume but…."

Lucy laughed.

"You're right, I do have other means."

She had quickly realised that she had made a potentially catastrophic mistake by telling the truth. Angela would know designer labels if she saw her wearing them, and she would certainly recognise a Porsche. If she didn't offer her a credible explanation now it would become increasingly difficult to be believed later.

"My family is reasonably wealthy. The shop work is just a hobby really…."

Keep it as vague as possible. Don't offer detail when it's not asked for. Less likely to inadvertently contradict yourself later.

Except, of course, she had already decided that Angela was different from previous targets, hadn't she? But have to concentrate. Same rules must apply.

"….but I'd like to hear more about you, Angela. I've been fascinated by what you've told me so far."

As she listened to her, Lucy found the subtext of Angela's words confirming her initial thoughts. It was clear that just below a cool, contented surface, there was a woman who yearned to be loved. It appeared she was showered with everything but affection and this just served to exaggerate the barely hidden loneliness. There was also an emotional awkwardness and Lucy was gradually coming to the dreadful realisation that she liked her. That was neither helpful or desirable.

"I want to ask you, Lucy….I er, don't know if you'd like…."

When there was a short lull in their conversation, Angela attempted to take the opportunity to ask Lucy something that she had clearly been thinking about for some time. She was, however, not finding it easy.

"….to come back…."

Lucy, wanting to put an end to her embarrassment, decided to risk it.

"I'd love to see your apartment, if that's what you were going to ask."

The look of relief on Angela's face told her that she'd guessed correctly, and before she had the chance to begin a faltering, difficult 'thank you', Lucy had stood and was already looking for a taxi in amongst the steady flow of Embankment traffic but, as before, it was Angela who succeeded in hailing the black cab and, in moments, they were heading back over Westminster Bridge and towards Knightsbridge.

"Oh wow! I have to congratulate you. It's amazing."

Lucy had thought her company's Mayfair flat was something special, but the apartment in which she now stood was a perfect marriage of exceptional wealth and remarkable taste. The phrase 'less is more' was surely invented for a place such as this. From the understated décor to the artwork on the walls, everything seemed to work with everything else and the whole was, most definitely, greater than the sum of its parts.

"I'm pleased you like it, but I had no input. My husband employed one of London's top interior designers."

Of course he did. They wouldn't have sat down together and discussed it. He would have had no interest in what his wife wanted for the place, and the fact that the end result was so stunning was neither here nor there if it resulted in nothing more than a soulless show home. Lucy found herself quickly reassessing her first impression as she walked through to the living area. Angela sat down on the large sofa and beckoned Lucy to join her.

"I'm forgetting my manners. Would you like a drink, or something to eat?"

Lucy shook her head.

"I'm fine, but you go ahead."

"No, no. I just thought…."

She began to falter, her embarrassment threatening to overwhelm her once more as Lucy recalled her discussion with the CEO. She had asked him why she wasn't going after the husband. How she now wished she was, because she would have felt no remorse about betraying him. But Angela? Lucy reached out and rested a hand on her leg. It was a calculated move, intended to say 'don't worry, I know why you asked me here and I'm ok with that.' Had Lucy's experience served her well, or had she just made an error of judgement?

Angela looked away, just for a moment, before she turned back to her. Was there now something akin to relief in her eyes? She lifted a hand to touch Lucy's hair, letting the strands fall between her fingers.

"I was so scared" she whispered, her hand visibly trembling as she allowed it to brush softly against Lucy's face.

"Scared? What were you scared of?"

"Rejection. I wanted you from the moment we met, but I couldn't imagine a young woman like you…."

If Lucy had any lingering doubts about whether or not she should continue with her remit for this target, they had just disappeared. She had no love for her husband, or for his business interests, and couldn't give a damn whether he was damaged financially or not. But she was certain that if she were able to extract any information regarding his company's affairs and the leak was tracked back to Angela....

The game had now irretrievably changed but how it would eventually play out, Lucy could only guess. If she reneged on the deal with her CEO, thereby protecting Angela, then Mattie would be put at risk. But if she carried the job through, there was the real possibility that Angela would suffer. Of course she should, without further thought, choose Mattie over this relative stranger. But a decision like that took no account of the here and now. And here and now Lucy was sitting next to this woman, lost and desperate for affection, who was looking to her to bring something beautiful into her life. Lucy allowed her hand to move slightly, feeling Angela's skirt slide against her leg. Together they stood and, without another word, Angela took Lucy's hand and led her through to her bedroom.

Chapter 35

The CEO walked over to his drinks cabinet and poured himself a glass of his favourite thirty-year-old Macallan whisky. He had just re-read the message he'd received a few hours earlier from Foster and he was feeling like celebrating. Up until 'Target acquired' had appeared on his phone there had been the smallest of lingering doubts. Even though he considered he'd brought the right amount of well-aimed pressure to bear, he hadn't been sure that Foster would play the game. She, of course, didn't know that this was going to be the last time, but all good things….

The sun was going down over the London skyline as he made his way back around his desk and sat down, placing the glass almost reverentially down in front of him. He returned his attention to the screen of his laptop, entering the password that would reopen the file he'd been studying for the past hour. It contained in one place all of the available data, both factual and rumoured, relating to the possible takeover that might mean so much to the future of his company. As soon as Foster's reports had sorted those rumours from the facts and furnished him with all those golden nuggets of information that she had a gift for finding, then he would be ready to take whatever action might be required to gain a significant advantage over his rivals.

Below him, many of the offices would now be empty and most of his employees already on their way home if they weren't there already. Soon the cleaners and maintenance people would be arriving to prepare the building for another day. Sometimes he would stand in front of the huge window and look down onto the street below as evening turned into night.

He took a sip of his whisky, allowing himself time to enjoy its flavour to the full. It seemed a shame that he couldn't just sit there and slowly finish the glass, but there was work to be done. He wanted to have the entire contents of the file committed to memory before it was finally erased together with all other incriminating evidence. He couldn't afford to leave even the merest shadow of a doubt as to his company's ethical credentials, and had to be ready for when things began to move. When they did, thanks to his unequalled business intellect and Foster's own unique abilities, he would undoubtedly be word and number perfect and, above all, appear one hundred per cent trustworthy in the eyes of all of his business associates. Perhaps even, if this was as successful and profitable as he expected, and after the permanent removal of Foster and her friend, he may even consider handing over the reins and retiring. He had always had a desire for an exclusive villa in the heart of Tuscany, or perhaps something on the Amalfi coast. He took another mouthful of whisky, dimmed the office lights to their lowest setting, and then continued with his work. Whenever he stayed late he would always lower the room's ambient lighting as he liked to see the lights of the City gradually taking over from the setting sun.

It was minutes later, when he lifted his gaze from the laptop's screen, that he first noticed it. The large window, that had been clear when he had last looked, was now opaque. He didn't recall touching the small pressure switch located on the steel support frame that changed the glass from clear to opaque. In fact, he was sure he hadn't. He walked over and pressed the switch, but the window remained opaque. No matter. He shrugged and made a mental note to contact Maintenance in the morning to get it checked.

Returning to his desk, he scrolled down to the next page and yet another set of bullet points accompanied by figures and projections reflecting a range of various scenarios ranging from the possible to the highly improbable. It was important to have it clear in his own mind how he would react when faced with any one of these variants, because time would be of the essence and, when the moment came, he'd be ready to move decisively and turn the situation to his advantage before his rivals had even noticed there was a situation.

The sound of the lift didn't register at first. He had been so immersed in his work, almost mesmerised by the laptop screen, that it took some moments before he realised that it was a sound he shouldn't be hearing. He looked up and saw the floor indicator gradually counting up towards his office.

He stood and walked to the centre of the room, not taking his eyes off the lift doors, transfixed by something that should be impossible. The lift that was now in motion was a private one and was the only access from the main building to his office. As such it could not be in operation without his express permission. The office he now occupied was 'clean'. With no other employees having unfettered access he could be sure that all work done in that room, all conversations held, would not be in any way compromised. If someone had somehow bypassed the stringent security protocols and found a way to move that lift, which he still believed to be impossible, that someone would very soon be out of a job.

He moved a step closer to the lift doors. It was now just one floor away. He waited, hearing the soft whine gradually change tone as the lift slowed to a stop. Seconds later the doors slid open. The cabin was in complete darkness. He walked forward until he stood on the threshold and peered in. The lift was empty.

Confused, he turned back towards his desk. He then recalled the window that had arbitrarily changed from clear to opaque. Maybe that and the lift were in some way connected. Maybe they were carrying out some electrical work that he hadn't been told about. At least the second lift, situated in the further corner of the office, which was for his use only, seemed to be behaving itself. In the unlikely event of a mains and generator failure, there was, of course, the obligatory fire escape door beside the second lift but that was, against regulations and on his specific orders, locked so that only he could access it to leave. It couldn't be used to gain access.

The CEO, with one last disapproving glance at the recalcitrant lift, lowered himself once more into his plush leather chair behind the desk. Frustrated at having his attention taken away from his work, he muttered an expletive after he sat back down in front of his laptop. It was as he reached out for the glass of whisky that he saw her, standing in the shadow of one of the steel supports by the window.

"Who the fuck are you and how did you get up here!?"

The young woman remained where she was, perfectly still and hidden in the half-light.

"Come out where I can see you!"

Instinctively, as he was speaking he reached down to one of the drawers that were set in the right hand side of his desk. Without dropping his gaze, he quietly closed his hand around the automatic pistol and slowly withdrew it.

"If you don't come out where I can see you, you will regret it. I'll claim self-defence."

He raised the gun and pointed it, level and steady, in her direction. Could it be Foster? No. She wasn't the same height, or build, and he could just make out the shoulder length hair. It appeared to be very dark, maybe jet black although, as she remained in the shadows, he couldn't be sure.

Seconds passed and still she said nothing or made any attempt to move. Maintaining his aim, he stood and carefully made his way back around his desk, closing the distance between them. It wasn't until he was just feet away that he saw her head move slightly, her gaze following him but offering no reaction to the gun that continued to be levelled at her.

"You will do as I say! Move out now to where I can see you!"

He glanced at the automatic and then back to her. He knew, of course, that he couldn't afford to use the gun on this seemingly unarmed young woman, but he continued to hope that he might have sown a fragment of doubt in her mind. He had successfully bluffed many opponents in his time, but it seemed as if this one was not going to abide by the script. He was about to reach out, take hold of her arm and drag her into the centre of the room but, before he had the chance, she took a pace forward.

The first thing that struck him was what she was wearing. It was a simple, plain white cotton dress. There was no adornment on it at all. No fastenings, no pattern, nothing. He looked down at her feet. They were bare. He looked up. He had been right about the hair. It was jet black. And then their eyes met.

It was at that moment that his anger evaporated and was replaced by a feeling so alien to him that, at first, he didn't recognise it. Fear. Why did he fear this young woman who had said nothing and done nothing?

"Who are you?"

He asked again but this time in a whisper, all the aggression gone from his voice. In response, she took another step towards him. He wanted to back away but couldn't move, her gaze now unrelenting and unwavering.

"I am Sarah" she said as all of the lights in the room slowly flickered and died.

Chapter 36

Lucy pushed the sheets back and. as gently as she could, climbed from the bed. As she pulled on the dressing gown that Angela had given her the night before, she looked back to check that she was still sleeping. Quietly she left the bedroom, softly closing the door behind her.

It was early but Lucy had been awake for hours, lying beside Angela and staring at the ceiling, letting her thoughts and fears run where they would. Mattie had been the one constant in those hours, each and every strand always leading back to her. Every so often Lucy had turned to look at Angela, hoping that somehow she might be able to find the resolve to carry out her assignment. But all she felt was pity. She had had sex with her out of pity, not that Angela would have known. Lucy had given her usual five-star performance. Done all the right things. Said all the right things. Everything by the tried and tested playbook. Except for the denouement. There were going to be no clever leading questions, no soft nudging to talk about overheard conversations, glimpses of paperwork lying on desks or laptop screens inadvertently left on an incriminating page. And no ongoing relationship. But how to protect Mattie?

As Lucy stood under the hot shower she tried again to come up with some kind of workable answer. She had already decided that she was going back to the CEO that morning. Maybe some form of blackmail was a possibility. It would have to be carefully planned, with all bases covered. Or maybe just ask again to be released, appeal to any humanity he had kept so well hidden all these years. Yes, she could try to fool herself into thinking that might work.

She towelled herself dry and put on her clothes before making her way into the kitchen. Having found cartons of various fruit juices in the fridge, a couple of slices of bread and two eggs, breakfast was taken care of. Ten minutes later Lucy was sitting in the lounge with a glass of orange juice and two slices of toast topped with scrambled egg. Beside her, on a small coffee table, was the television remote control. She reached out and pressed the 'On' button. Seconds later the early breakfast news appeared on the screen with an interviewer discussing a doubtless important matter with some middle-tier, ten-a-penny politician. She muted the volume and returned her attention to her toast and scrambled eggs, which were cooked to perfection, even if she said so herself.

As well as the television remote there was the latest copy of Vogue on the table. Lucy picked it up and began to flick through its pages, stopping to speed read an article about a Milan fashion house and an interesting piece about Givenchy. She occasionally glanced up at the screen as the news headlines began, but it was the usual litany of conflict, argument and discord and her concentration was quickly back into the magazine.

It was a minute or so later, when she lifted her gaze once more, that the image on the television made her drop the magazine. Without letting her eyes leave the screen she slowly placed her plate on the coffee table and pushed herself up from her chair, turning up the volume as she did. She remained transfixed for the duration of the news item. When it had finished she turned the television off and ran through to the hallway where she had left her shoes and handbag.

Lucy hadn't planned to leave so suddenly and without so much as a word with Angela but, if what she'd just seen on the news was true, then everything had changed. She hurried back into the lounge and over to a desk that was positioned facing one of the windows. She began to quickly open each drawer in turn until she found what she was looking for. Removing the pad of monogrammed writing paper, she picked up the pen that sat in its holder on the desktop before sitting down and starting to write.

Dearest Angela
   Please believe me when I say I hadn't intended to leave without saying goodbye. But changing

circumstances mean that is what I must do. Thank you for last night. It was sensational.
If you'll allow me to offer you some advice you can take it or leave it, as you wish. I'll probably never know.
You need to give yourself the space to be yourself, to be what I know you can be. A wonderful, free thinking, independent woman. It may, of course, be that you want his money and all that it brings, or it may be that you just need someone to tell you that you can be so much more.
Ask yourself the question, Angela, and be honest with your answer.
I'll never forget you. Love, Lucy.

She replaced the pen in its holder and quietly made her way back into the bedroom, gently laying the piece of paper on the pillow next to the still sleeping Angela. As she reached the doorway she turned and whispered "Goodbye Angela, and good luck."

Outside, in the cool London morning, Lucy took no time in hailing a black cab. As she climbed in she gave the driver her Mayfair apartment's address. She wanted to return there and pick up her Porsche and a change of clothes before making the short journey to her company's building because, somehow, it was important to her that, before she made that journey, she was dressed in something as far away as possible from the labels and styles she would normally wear when 'working'.

As she sat back in the taxi she closed her eyes, but all she could see were images from the news bulletin and she knew she had to find out the real truth for herself. The driver was saying something about the weather and she replied with, what she hoped, was a polite, relevant response. But her thoughts were elsewhere, darting in all kinds of dark directions.

"We're here, Miss."

The driver's voice broke in on the maelstrom and returned her to the here and now. Lucy got out of the cab, paid the driver and wasted no time in getting up to her apartment. Once there, she selected a more casual outfit and shoes that owed more to comfort than style. It was just a few minutes later when she was pulling the apartment's door shut behind her and, with the Porsche's key in her hand, descending once more to the reserved parking spaces to the rear of the building.

Lucy gripped the wheel and guided the car out of its parking place. The ten-minute journey to the company's office block took a little longer than she would have liked, but road works and diversions notwithstanding, she still managed to arrive at the barriers to the underground car park in just on a quarter of an hour. She held her security pass in front of the laser scanner. There was a brief pause before the barrier lifted and for a moment she wondered if her access had, for some reason, been revoked. But, after the familiar whirr and click, the red and white barrier slowly raised.

Lucy drove into the nearest space, locked the Porsche and made her way to the lift. It wasn't at basement level so she had a short wait before the cabin arrived to take her to the ground floor reception area. When the doors opened onto the foyer the first thing Lucy noticed were the two policewomen standing over by the reception desk. Next to them was what looked like a plainclothes officer who was in conversation with the young woman behind the desk.

Lucy knew that this was not going to be easy. But, as soon as she'd seen that news bulletin, she had known that if she hadn't made an appearance at the company's HQ that morning it wouldn't have been long before there would have been a knock on the door of her apartment, or her car was pulled over. Better to face the music now than merely postpone the inevitable.

She took a deep breath before walking purposefully over to the desk. As she approached the receptionist Lucy gave her an assured smile, waiting beside the plainclothes man, who was in the process of concluding his conversation. Moments later he, together with the two policewomen, walked away, heading for one of the lifts. The receptionist was now ready to give Lucy her undivided attention.

"Good morning. How may I help you?"

Understandably, there was no accompanying smile this time.

"Lucy Foster?"

She waited for any spark of recognition, but when none was forthcoming she decided to add, "I came here recently to see the CEO. I saw the news this morning and thought there might be some people here who may wish to talk to me."

This time she received a brief, curt smile as the receptionist picked up one of the phones next to her computer screen and pressed a button.

"You're not a journalist, are you? Because they'll be an updated press release through the usual channels later...."

What?!

"No...."

Lucy was about to say 'I work here' but something stopped her.

"Very well. If you'd like to wait over there, I'll call up and...."

She indicated to an area set back from the main foyer. It had comfortable seats and tables filled with magazines and trade journals.

"....someone will be down to see you shortly."

Lucy thanked her before turning away, walking over to the visitors' area and taking a seat. She didn't feel like reading any of the magazines, so instead sat back and watched the main door as various people came and went. Outside, on the pavement in front of the building, she could just see someone being interviewed by a news presenter. The television crew were behind her with the camera and lights, and a few passers-by had stopped briefly to see what was going on.

Who would the receptionist have called to come and talk to her? Whoever it was, she couldn't assume they would have some, or any, knowledge of the work she had been doing for the CEO. But once certain events came to light then, Lucy knew, she would be walking through a minefield. Whether she could come out the other side unscathed she, at that moment, very much doubted.

"Miss Foster? I understand you wish to speak to someone? Of course, you'll understand that things are a little....difficult this morning, therefore if you could be brief I'd appreciate it."

The woman who had appeared beside her looked not much older than the receptionist but far more full of her own self-importance. A middle management trainee, straight out of university, Lucy guessed. Why hadn't they sent someone from the CEO's own team? They must have been expecting her to make contact, surely? Lucy stood up and held out a hand which was begrudgingly taken.

"Um, I'm not sure....I don't mean to be impolite but would it be possible see someone who was a little closer to the CEO himself?"

The woman regarded her with what could only be described as total and utter disdain as Lucy's confusion continued to grow. She had expected to be pounced on the moment her security pass showed up on the system. What had been the reason for all her meetings with the CEO over a long period of time? What exactly was their professional relationship? Might she know something which she could have used to blackmail him? Perhaps that last one was being overly pessimistic. But surely there would be questions to which they'd want answers?

"Miss Foster, I'm sure you'll understand that no one from his office is available this morning."

"But if you'll just contact them...."

"Miss Foster...."

She repeated her name with a mixture of pity and impatience.

"....it *was* the CEO's office that sent *me* down to see you."

What could she say to that?

"Right...."

Lucy was almost whispering.

"....then I'm sorry to have wasted your time. I expect you have my contact details when someone *does* want to talk to me."

"Yes, I'm sure we do."

She spoke the words with no conviction at all and, it seemed to Lucy, even less interest. Without any further pleasantries she turned away and disappeared back in the direction of the lifts. As she passed the reception desk, Lucy thought she saw her give a slight shake of the head to the receptionist.

Lucy walked back into the centre of the foyer. Should she simply leave? If she did then she knew she'd be forever looking over her shoulder, waiting for the phone call or the knock on the door. By returning she had hoped to, at least, begin the process of clarification and explanation. If she were to have a new life with Mattie, then she wanted there to be nothing waiting in the shadows to destroy it. But it appeared she wasn't going to get her wish.

Reluctantly, Lucy made her way towards the lift that would return her to the underground car park. It was as she was about to press the basement button that, out of the corner of her eye, she saw a familiar face. Tanya, the security guard, was standing a little way away, her attention fixed upon the main doors. As Lucy neared her she turned, but there was no immediate look of recognition in her expression.

"Good morning."

Lucy attempted her best smile and cheeriest voice.

"Morning."

She received a half-smile and an almost imperceptible nod in return.

"I'm sure you don't remember me. Lucy Foster?"

In fact, she *did* expect Tanya to show some spark of recognition, but there was still nothing. Fair enough. She probably saw hundreds of people each day. Why should she remember her? Lucy couldn't help feeling a little bit disappointed though, if she were honest. She had always thought of herself as supremely memorable.

It was then that she decided to offer Tanya her thanks and wish her a good day. But, just as she was about to speak, another possibility occurred to her. Her new-found anonymity might, after all, offer her an advantage if she played the situation in the right way. She had a very specialised skillset so why not try to use it now? And so Lucy set to work on Tanya. Slowly, carefully, she deployed some gentle, well-disguised, well-practiced persuasion, using all of her experience in eliciting information from an unsuspecting subject and, after a short while, it did seem that Tanya was in the mood for a chat.

"So what exactly did happen here? Is it true what I saw on the news earlier?"

Tanya took her by the arm and led her to a quieter part of the foyer.

"I haven't seen the news but, from what I've heard, he committed suicide...."

They hadn't said that on the news. It had merely been reported that he was found dead.

"....put a gun to his head apparently."

"How awful."

Lucy fought hard to remain impassive, knowing that this was her best chance to learn as much as possible before she left.

"And I overheard some really weird stuff that one of the management was telling the plainclothes guy earlier."

"Go on."

But Tanya now needed little encouragement and seemed almost desperate to talk about whatever it was she'd heard.

"They've got some people from the Fire Service up there right now...."

She moved a little closer.

"....it seems there were at least three places of intense, highly localised fire...."

As Tanya continued, Lucy began to feel a rising unease.

"....his laptop, safe contents and one of his mobile phones were all reduced to ashes. I don't think they've found any answers yet, judging by the whispered conversations and all the comings and goings."

She gave Lucy a conspiratorial smile.

"Are you sure that's what they said?"

"Absolutely. That's the beauty of being a humble security guard. You're invisible."

"Is there anything else you can tell me?"

Lucy asked, hoping to hear something that may shed more light into the ever growing darkness, but Tanya now had a question of her own.

"I don't believe you actually told me what your interest in this is, did you Lucy?"

It was clear that no further information was going to be forthcoming, at least until Lucy had provided a few answers in return.

"I work here."

Tanya regarded her for a moment, before slowly shaking her head.

"No. I don't think so. It's my job to know all the staff here, new and old."

Lucy looked around her, as if trying to find someone who might be able to inject some sanity into a situation she felt was rapidly spinning out of her control.

"But that's ridiculous! Try to remember, Tanya. You've seen me on several occasions. You took me to the CEO's lift."

Again, no spark of recollection, but then Lucy had a sudden thought.

"My security pass!"

She began to explore each of her pockets in turn. She recalled putting it in one of them after she'd used it to raise the car park barrier. Tanya looked on as Lucy finally completed an unsuccessful search.

"I don't seem to be able to find it."

Tanya regarded her with a combination of pity and impatience.

"Ok. Well, look, it really doesn't matter. I need to get back to my job now. Have to look like I'm doing something, don't I? It's been good to meet you...."

"CCTV!"

"I'm sorry?"

"Check the CCTV by the car park entrance. It'll show me using my pass to open the barrier. Or the computer records. They'll show my ID's use over the past few months."

Tanya gave an audible sigh.

"I really like you, Lucy Foster. I do. But I need you to ask yourself if you truly believe that, given the shockwave that's going to hit this company in the days ahead, anyone, including me, is going to have the time or the inclination to trawl through any records or CCTV for an, admittedly, attractive young woman who has delusions of being an employee here."

"But I...."

Before she could make any further plea, Tanya had turned and was heading back to resume her usual place by the reception desk. Lucy walked into the centre of the foyer and looked around her. Everywhere there was activity. One of the police vehicles that was parked outside the building drew away. Over by the reception, another police officer had appeared and was talking to an older man wearing a quintessential pin-stripe business suit. Young men and women were moving from here to there, phones pressed against their ears. Above her, she knew the offices would be buzzing with rumour and speculation. And, as she slowly turned full circle, surrounded by the blur and noise, Lucy realised that each and every one of those people were completely oblivious to her presence. This place no longer knew her. And she suddenly realised that she didn't want to be known here anymore. Despite all of her protestations with Tanya, anonymity was something to be welcomed and embraced. She hadn't found the escape route. It had found her.

She almost jogged back to the lift. The doors were open. Waiting for her. She pressed the basement button and seconds later was standing once more in the underground car park. It was deserted. Lucy took several deep breaths and felt her hands shaking as she fumbled for the Porsche's key. She closed her hand around it and walked towards the car. But it wasn't until she'd unlocked it and climbed behind the wheel that she remembered her missing security pass. Without it she wouldn't be able to raise the barriers.

Once more she tried to locate the pass, hoping that she might have missed it the first time but deep down knowing she hadn't. Reluctantly, she got out of the Porsche. Perhaps it was only right that she should have to give up the car. Whoever, or whatever, had conspired to release her from a world she knew she no longer wanted to inhabit, couldn't allow her to pick and choose what she wanted to keep and what she wanted to discard. All or nothing.

Lucy dropped the key onto the driver's seat and closed the door. She could duck under the barriers, walk out of the car park and get a black cab back to her apartment. As she neared the exit ramp she took one last glance over her shoulder at the Porsche and said a quiet 'goodbye'.

It was at that very same moment that Lucy heard a whirr and click. She spun around in time to see the red and white barriers slowly lifting. She looked around her, but she was still alone. There was no one, and nothing, in sight that could have caused the barriers to move. She stood for several seconds, transfixed as they reached the top of their travel and then stopped, fixed in the open position.

Without any further hesitation, Lucy ran as fast as she could back to the Porsche. In a moment the engine was alive and the tyres were screeching on the concrete floor of the car park. The vehicle hit the exit ramp and then was out into daylight and onto the side street behind the company building. She didn't look in her mirror until she was several blocks away and so didn't see, seconds after her exit, the red and white barriers slowly lower back down and quietly close together.

Chapter 37

Mattie's morning, although filled with continual thoughts of Lucy, had proved to be much brighter than she would ever have imagined. Vicky had been excellent company, providing conversation and silence in just the right proportion. They had talked like old friends, and Vicky had seemed to know exactly what to say and when to say it. Thinking back, Mattie considered that it was almost as if a perfect script was being relayed to her through some kind of hidden earpiece. At the time, of course, that hadn't mattered. What had mattered was that Vicky had succeeded in pulling Mattie out of a particularly vicious depression that had drawn all of its strength from Lucy's departure.

On leaving the tearoom Vicky had again suggested that she take Mattie to her shop and, after a little gentle coaxing, she had agreed. It had turned out to be a good decision because not only had she a number of online orders to deal with, but there had been a steady stream of customers throughout the rest of the morning, some willing to spend a not inconsiderable amount of money.

Mattie had been sitting in the backroom, just completing the last of the orders when she heard the bell ring announcing the arrival of yet another welcome customer. But before she had the chance to get up from her chair….

"I've come for the job interview. I heard there's a vacancy."
"Lucy!"
She ran into her arms and held her as if she'd never let her go.
"But how long can you stay?" Mattie asked when eventually she released her embrace.
"Depends…."
Lucy shrugged.
"….how long you want me to."
"You mean….?"

Lucy didn't get the opportunity to give any further explanation at that moment as Mattie, once more, threw her arms around her. But this time, as they stood together in the doorway, Lucy could feel her body gently shuddering as she began to quietly cry, overwhelmed by the thought that now, at last, she may no longer have to face losing her friend and lover to a life that had threatened to bring them both so much unhappiness.

For the remainder of the day it had been very much 'business as usual.' Lucy had immediately taken up her place in the shop itself, much to the delight of several customers who called in that afternoon. Several times, when they had been alone, Mattie had tried to elicit details about what had occurred in London but, on each occasion, Lucy had deflected her questions saying that she'd tell her all she wanted to know when they got back to Mattie's apartment that evening. It wasn't that she didn't want to tell her, but that she still wasn't sure herself quite what she could say. She could simply give the facts as she knew them, but as to any logical explanation, that was still eluding her.

So, nothing more was said on the matter until they sat together at Mattie's kitchen table some hours later. She was telling Lucy about Vicky's visit, and how their time together that morning had saved her from being overwhelmed by her shadows. It was then that Lucy felt able to voice a thought that she had been trying to deny ever since it had come to her on the journey back from London.

"Sarah's done all of this so that we can be together, hasn't she Matts?"

Lucy held Mattie's hands across the table.

"I believe she has. She wants me to have the life I never had with her."

Lucy was about to reply when the clatter of the letterbox cut across their conversation.

"Bit late for the post, isn't it?"

Mattie got up and went to retrieve whatever it was that had caused the interruption. She returned seconds later holding a small, folded piece of paper. As she sat back down she opened it up and placed it on the table in front of her. Lucy remained silent as she read it, waiting to be told what it said but, instead, Mattie turned it so that she was able to see the several sentences of shaky but legible handwriting.

She would like you to take her roses now

Underneath that one line there was written the name of a cemetery which Mattie knew to be a few miles out of town.

"She told me to bring her flowers. That's all she wanted, Lucy."

Lucy picked up the scrap of paper and examined it more closely. There was nothing on it other than that one sentence and the details of the cemetery.

"I knew she wouldn't be far away. She'd have made sure we weren't far apart."

Mattie managed a weak smile that prompted to Lucy to get up and go to her, putting a comforting arm around her shoulders.

"I wonder who delivered the note?"

Mattie shrugged.

"I did take a quick look out into the hallway but there was no one there. Maybe we'll never know, but that doesn't matter, does it?"

Lucy pulled her closer and rested her head on Mattie's.

"No Matts, I don't suppose it does."

A few moments of silence followed before she asked

"Can we go tomorrow, before we open the shop? The little florist a few doors down is always open early for deliveries. We could take her some beautiful roses."

"Yes...."

Lucy kissed her softly on the lips.

"....I think we could."

The alarm ensured they were both sitting and eating breakfast about an hour earlier than was usual on a 'shop' day. After a quiet evening in, helped by a bottle of good red wine and a film, chosen by Mattie on Lucy's insistence, they had gone to bed and made love, quietly and gently. The urgency and intensity of previous nights together had given way to something more, something that spoke of the beautiful truth of their relationship.

So, even though Lucy would have gladly had longer in bed, they were both outside the florist by the time the owner arrived, a friendly young woman who had started her business just a few months after Mattie arrived on the High Street. She helped them choose some perfectly formed roses of the most delicate pink and red, and tied them with a ribbon that complimented the colour of the blooms.

Mattie sat with the flowers resting on her lap as Lucy drove them to the cemetery, swinging the Porsche into a side road opposite. Together they made their way into the graveyard and looked around at the rows of headstones that stretched in all directions. As they stood wondering where they might begin, they were approached by a young clergyman, fresh-faced and, it occurred to Mattie, straight out of an Agatha Christie novel.

"May I help you, ladies? You seem a little lost."

It was Lucy who replied.

"Well, I'm not sure you can be of assistance, unless you know the details of the occupants of every single grave in this cemetery."

He gave a very delicate, refined laugh.

"I'm not sure I could make such a claim, but I shan't let that deter me from trying to help you."

Lucy turned to Mattie as if to say 'over to you'.

"I think we can narrow it down a bit" she said, eager for any help and not wanting to dent his enthusiasm at the outset.

"Do you know where the oldest part of the cemetery is? The grave we're looking for will most likely be there."

He thought for a moment before pointing over to the far side of the graveyard.

"There are more ancient graves there than anywhere else. I believe some date back to the seventeenth century. I would ask if you have a name but I doubt any headstone that old would be readable. Have you considered looking at the church's records for around the period you're interested in?"

Mattie shook her head.

"Sarah's burial won't be recorded in any official records."

He looked more than a little incredulous.

"Are you sure? I believe they kept quite detailed accounts even as far back...."

"Sarah won't be mentioned in any of them. I'm afraid you'll just have to take my word for it."

He glanced at Lucy, perhaps for some further explanation or reassurance, but only received one of her best non-committal smiles.

"Very well...."

To his credit, he immediately knew that any further argument would be pointless.

"....then I suppose all I can do is wish you luck in your search."

"Thank you for your help."

Mattie had already turned away and was heading in the direction he had indicated moments earlier. As Lucy walked past him she gave him another smile, this time much broader, and followed it up with a conspiratorial wink.

The young clergyman had been right. The graves in this part of the cemetery were clearly much more ancient, nearly all having headstones or tombs that had witnessed the passage of centuries.

"You can hardly read any of these. Pity whoever sent you that note wasn't a bit more specific."

But Mattie wasn't listening. She had walked off in the direction of a grave, although it was barely discernible as such. Its headstone was crumbling at the edges, and where there had been an inscription there were now just random indentations. It was covered with lichen and moss and was leaning at an angle, away from the grave.

There were no noticeable borders to the grave itself, and weeds grew in abundance although it looked as if there had been some minimal effort made, probably by the council, to tidy up the surrounding area so, Lucy assumed, it probably wasn't in as bad a condition as it may once have been.

"I've found her, Lucy. I've found Sarah."

Lucy joined her at the foot of the grave.

"Are you sure?"

Mattie knelt and carefully laid the roses near the headstone.

"I'm sure."

She reached out and rested a hand on the weathered stone. Lucy fought the urge to go to her because she sensed that, at that moment, she was being comforted by someone else. But, as she watched Mattie, her head now lowered and her eyes closed, Lucy couldn't help returning to the question that she had so readily dismissed. Who could have sent that note?

Chapter 38

It was a few weeks later when Mattie, once more, had to spend a short time alone. Lucy had returned to London the previous evening to remove the last of her belongings from the Mayfair apartment. It was the first night Mattie had spent on her own since Lucy had come back to her for good and, although she knew that she'd be returning the next afternoon, it still proved to be a night filled with the ghosts of past shadows. Even now she sensed that they were continuing to lie in wait for her.

That morning she had visited Sarah's grave, which was showing the results of her and Lucy's hours of work in tending it. In fact, it was now as well-kept as any in the cemetery. They had decided to leave the headstone, placed there shortly after her burial by the priest.

It was the first time she had been there without Lucy, but there was always the elderly man on the far side of the cemetery visiting the grave of a loved one. He was, at least, some kind of company. She had sometimes thought of going over to where he stood and talking to him, but had always decided against it. Mattie took one last look at the red roses, covered with raindrops from the previous night, before making her way back to her car. As she drove away she saw the elderly man walking towards the gate on the far side of the cemetery.

"Did you miss me?"

Lucy walked through to the lounge carrying a holdall, which she put down before dropping into the nearest chair.

"I might have."

Mattie appeared from the kitchen carrying a tray with two coffees and some assorted cakes and biscuits.

"Thought this might keep you going, and we'll get a takeaway on the way back."

Lucy was already attacking one of the chocolate muffins and so her reply was not immediately forthcoming.

"Mmm. Yes, ok. Sounds good" she finally managed to offer before a salted caramel biscuit followed the muffin.

"Your apartment empty now?"

Mattie took a sip of her coffee as she sat down opposite Lucy.

"I've got everything I want. I told the company what's left can go to charity shops."

"And there's still nothing come to light that marks you as an employee?"

Lucy shook her head.

"It seems as far as they're concerned I was just a tenant who's now ended her contract."

"And the car?"

"They didn't mention it and I certainly wasn't going to. Did you get the roses?"

Experience told Mattie that meant 'the Porsche is staying, end of discussion'.

"Yes. Thought I'd go for deep red again."

"Does she ever ask?"

"I'm sorry?"

"The florist. Does she ever ask why you buy roses virtually every other day?"

Mattie smiled.

"I told her they're for someone who loved me very much, and that I'm saying 'thank you' for all of that love."

"Loves, not loved."

Mattie nodded.

"Loves."

Lucy jumped up, grabbing another biscuit as she made her way to the door.

"Come on! It's still sunny. We can maybe have a walk afterwards if you like."

Lucy had seen a cloud pass over Mattie's expression as she thought about Sarah and, as they walked down to the Porsche, she took her hand and squeezed it. A simple gesture that said 'I'm here with you now and always, Matts, and you don't have to face anything on your own ever again'.

Lucy parked in a side road opposite the cemetery and together they made their way to Sarah's grave. It was as they approached that they saw there was someone already standing beside it and, within a few more steps, Mattie recognised the person as the elderly man she had only previously seen at a distance, visiting a grave on the further side of the cemetery. He turned as he heard their footsteps on the gravel path.

"Good evening."

He held out a hand which Mattie and Lucy took in turn.

"Evening. Nice to meet you, this is my friend Lucy and I'm…."

"I know who you are."

Lucy made no attempt to hide her suspicion.

"Really? May I ask how?"

He smiled but made no reply, instead returning his attention to Sarah's grave. After some seconds he spoke.

"I must congratulate you both on all of your hard work. This really does look splendid."

Lucy and Mattie exchanged bemused glances.

"Thank you…."

"Yes, really splendid. I've observed you on many occasions, Mattie. May I call you Mattie?"

"And what can we call you?"

Lucy stepped forward, putting herself between Mattie and the old man.

"I'm pleased to see you're still looking after your friend so well, Lucy. Sarah would be so proud of you."

This prompted Mattie to push past Lucy so that she stood just a few paces away from him.

"What do you know about Sarah? You can't read her name on the headstone, and there are no records. How do you know this is Sarah's grave?"

He reached out to Mattie, taking her gently by the arm. Lucy was about to intervene but Mattie looked at her and shook her head, allowing him to lead her aside.

"Mattie, why do you believe you have seen me so many times in this cemetery?"

She thought for a moment, slowly realising that the answer she was about to give was probably not going to be the correct one.

"You've always visited a grave over on the far side of the cemetery. I assumed you have a loved one there...."

It was his turn to shake his head.

"I have an association with only one person's grave in this place, and we are standing next to it."

"I'm not sure I understand. I mean, the grave I always saw you standing near, who....?"

He shrugged.

"I chose it at random, I have no knowledge of the person buried there, but it would have seemed strange to you if you'd seen me next to a different grave each time you visited, wouldn't it?"

Mattie looked back to Lucy, now utterly confused. It was then that a thought suddenly struck her.

"Was it you who put that note through my door?"

He gave a quiet laugh.

"I could attempt to deny it but I don't think you'd believe me, would you?"

This was too much for Lucy, who moved forward to stand next to Mattie.

"You know Mattie's name and where she lives. You've been here at the same time she's, we've, been here. You know about Sarah. I think it's time you started answering some questions. Let's start with the roses. How did you know Sarah wanted roses?"

He looked down at the grave.

"Because she told me."

"No...."

Mattie turned away, no longer able to deal with where she believed this to be going.

"It's true Mattie. I had to find a way of telling you where she was buried, and ensuring that you would carry out her wishes for you to bring her roses."

She stopped and looked back to him.

"How do you know where she was buried?" she asked in little more than a whisper.

He touched the headstone, allowing his hand to run along its rough edge. He then walked towards Mattie, pausing only to give his answer before continuing on, making his way along the path in the direction of the main gates.

"Because I found the plot for her body and I oversaw her burial."

Mattie and Lucy looked on, not taking their eyes off him until he had reached the gates and finally left the cemetery.

"The priest."

Mattie mouthed the words as she looked back to Sarah's grave.

"Come on, Matts, let's go. We'll come and see her again tomorrow."

Lucy took her arm and guided her away, following in the priest's footsteps. When they reached the gates Mattie stopped and looked back across the graveyard.

"We will come back, Lucy, and we'll bring her roses. But she's not in that grave anymore. I know she's not. She's back in that beautiful place, with the sun, and our horses, and the river. That's where she is. That's where you'll find her."

The End

Printed in Great Britain
by Amazon